Readers love *Fir*
by ANDREW

"All of Andrew Grey's books are good, but I think I just found a new favorite!"

—Love Bytes

"Once again, Grey delivers flawed but genuine characters that you can't help but love… I enjoyed every minute of this sweet and lovable comfort read."

—Prism Book Alliance

"Grey's writing in this story was phenomenal. It was such a beautiful story."

—It's About The Book

"This book had just the right mix of action, suspense, and sexual prowess… Definitely a sexy, steamy read and definitely a must read."

—MM Good Book Reviews

"This is a very good choice for lovers of M/M romance who enjoy Andrew Grey's work, those who enjoy a hurt/comfort story, and those who enjoy a sweet romance with a bit of mystery and adventure thrown in. Highly recommended."

—Hearts on Fire

"…this was a nice romantic little read with an edge of thriller thrown into the mix and I loved the ending. Very sweet."

—Bookpushers

By ANDREW GREY

Accompanied by a Waltz
Crossing Divides
Dominant Chord
Dutch Treat
Eastern Cowboy
A Heart Without Borders
In Search of a Story
North to the Future
One Good Deed
The Price
Shared Revelations
Stranded • Taken
Three Fates (Multiple Author Anthology)
To Have, Hold, and Let Go
Whipped Cream

HOLIDAY STORIES
Copping a Sweetest Day Feel • Cruise for Christmas
A Lion in Tails • Mariah the Christmas Moose
A Present in Swaddling Clothes • Simple Gifts
Snowbound in Nowhere • Stardust

ART
Legal Artistry • Artistic Appeal • Artistic Pursuits • Legal Tender

BOTTLED UP
The Best Revenge • Bottled Up • Uncorked • An Unexpected Vintage

BRONCO'S BOYS
Inside Out • Upside Down • Backward

THE BULLRIDERS
A Wild Ride • A Daring Ride • A Courageous Ride

BY FIRE
Redemption by Fire • Strengthened by Fire • Burnished by Fire • Heat Under Fire

CARLISLE COPS
Fire and Water
Fire and Ice

Published by DREAMSPINNER PRESS
http://www.dreamspinnerpress.com

By ANDREW GREY (continued)

CHEMISTRY
Organic Chemistry • Biochemistry • Electrochemistry

GOOD FIGHT
The Good Fight • The Fight Within • The Fight for Identity • Takoda and Horse

LOVE MEANS…
Love Means… No Shame • Love Means… Courage
Love Means… No Boundaries
Love Means… Freedom • Love Means … No Fear
Love Means… Healing
Love Means… Family • Love Means… Renewal • Love Means… No Limits
Love Means… Patience • Love Means… Endurance

SENSES
Love Comes Silently • Love Comes in Darkness
Love Comes Home • Love Comes Around

SEVEN DAYS
Seven Days • Unconditional Love

STORIES FROM THE RANGE
A Shared Range • A Troubled Range • An Unsettled Range
A Foreign Range • An Isolated Range • A Volatile Range • A Chaotic Range

TALES FROM KANSAS
Dumped in Oz • Stuck in Oz • Trapped in Oz

TASTE OF LOVE
A Taste of Love • A Serving of Love • A Helping of Love
A Slice of Love

WORK OUT
Spot Me • Pump Me Up • Core Training • Crunch Time
Positive Resistance • Personal Training • Cardio Conditioning
Work Me Out (Anthology)

Published by DREAMSPINNER PRESS
http://www.dreamspinnerpress.com

FIRE AND *Ice*

ANDREW GREY

DREAMSPINNER
PRESS

Published by
DREAMSPINNER PRESS

5032 Capital Circle SW, Suite 2, PMB# 279, Tallahassee, FL 32305-7886 USA
http://www.dreamspinnerpress.com/

Fire and Ice
© 2015 Andrew Grey.

Cover Art
© 2015 L.C. Chase.
http://www.lcchase.com
Cover content is for illustrative purposes only and any person depicted on the cover is a model.

ISBN: 978-1-63216-460-5
Digital ISBN: 978-1-63216-461-2
Library of Congress Control Number: 2015904002
First Edition May 2015

Printed in the United States of America
∞
This paper meets the requirements of
ANSI/NISO Z39.48-1992 (Permanence of Paper).

To Connie Bailey, for loaning me the name Ickle. Who'd have thought your dog would inspire a character? Love you!

CHAPTER
One

"So YOU finally convinced the captain to let you go out on patrol," Red said as he sat down across from Carter in the police department breakroom, which was in dire need of renovation. Carter accepted the cup he offered with a smile. "It took you long enough."

Carter Schunk grunted. "No kidding. As soon as everyone found out I had computer skills, they seemed determined to keep me locked away in the basement behind a terminal doing their investigative work while they got to go out in the world. I'm a trained police officer and I went to the academy just the same as they did." Carter sipped from his cup to cut off the diatribe that threatened to take over. He took a deep breath to calm down, but it wasn't working. Just this afternoon he'd gotten requests for simple Internet searches that he'd been told were so important his patrol duty had been delayed until the evening so he could get them done. It pissed him off—the officers could do those searches themselves—but he shouldn't be taking it out on Red. "I appreciate that you've been in my corner."

"Always will be, bud." Red flashed him a quick smile and then it was gone. Carter knew Red was still self-conscious about his teeth, so he rarely smiled for very long. His real smiles seemed to be reserved for Terry, his swimmer boyfriend, who was training for his chance at Olympic gold next year. "Everyone deserves a chance."

Carter snickered. "You know you've turned into a real sap over the past few months." He backed away, expecting Red to take a good-natured swipe at him. Red was huge—tall and wide—easily the biggest man on the force. He'd been in an accident as a kid, and while Terry

1

had worked with him in order to help Red feel better about his looks, Red still sported the visible scars from that accident. "Not that it wasn't well earned." Hell, Carter would turn into a lovesick sap like Red if it meant he had someone like Terry to come home to each night.

Red finished his coffee and tossed the paper cup in the trash. "Are you ready?"

Carter gulped the hot liquid and then tossed his cup as well before following Red out of the breakroom. He checked out a patrol car and got inside. Red stood outside his window as Carter excitedly went over everything in his mind. He'd done this before, but it had been a while and it felt damned good to be a "real" cop again instead of the computer geek in residence. "I'm all set."

"Good." Red patted the doorframe twice. "I'll be out there as well. You call if you need anything. Hell, call if you *think* you need anything. I'll be there."

Carter chuckled. "Thanks." Red had become a good friend over the past six months. Before, he'd always kept to himself, but since Terry had entered his life, Red had blossomed into a happy man. Truthfully, Carter was jealous of what they had, but not of Red. It couldn't have happened to a nicer guy. Carter just wished it would happen to him.

He started the engine and pulled out of the lot with Red following behind. Carter's area of patrol was the north end of Carlisle, so he turned in that direction and drove up Hanover Street before turning onto East Louther and slowly making his way through some of the rougher areas of the borough, making his presence known. Often just being out and about in some of these areas was enough to quell trouble. Tonight did not seem to be one of those nights. Almost immediately a report of a home invasion came over the radio. Carter's heart raced as he radioed that he was responding, flipped on his lights, and sped up. He'd been just a street away and arrived as two men were carrying a flat-screen television out a passageway between two row houses. As soon as they saw Carter, they dropped the television, took off, and got into their truck. Another patrol car came up the street from the other direction, boxing them in. Carter heard Red's voice boom over the street, and the men got out of the truck and lay down on the concrete facedown, as commanded. It was over almost as soon as it started.

2

He and Red cuffed the men and read them their rights as other units responded. Statements were taken from the homeowner, with Carter adding what he'd seen. Then the men were transported back to the station. "I'll handle the paperwork," Red volunteered. "Go keep the streets safe." Red winked, and Carter went back to his car and headed out.

The next few hours were quite normal and dull. Carter had forgotten how patrol could be: hours of waiting and watching around moments of excitement.

"Domestic dispute 100 block of East North," the dispatcher said over the radio.

Carter stifled a groan and responded. Domestic calls were the worst. Half the time it was nothing, like neighbors calling in because the people in the next unit were yelling too loudly. Most of the rest were people in need of help, but often they refused to press charges. Those were the most frustrating for everyone on the force. Carter pushed that from his mind, going as fast as he dared, reaching the house within minutes.

There was little doubt what had prompted the call. As soon as he opened his car door, high-pitched screaming rattled his spine. It seemed to be coming from inside the open-windowed row house. Carter called for backup and sprang into action. It sounded as though someone was being injured. Sirens blared in the distance and patrol cars arrived, blocking the street. Carter explained what he'd heard and the screaming began again, this time louder and more frantic. Officers spread out, and Carter headed to the front door. "Police," he yelled and tried the knob. The door opened, and he rushed inside, weapon at the ready.

Carter heard other officers enter from the back. He quickly cleared the front rooms and the others the back. The house was quiet now, and Carter motioned toward the stairs.

"Get out of my house!" a man yelled as he barreled down the stairs, red faced, eyes glazed over in rage.

"Down on the floor now!" Carter yelled forcefully and pointed his weapon at him, finger on the trigger. The man reached the bottom of the stairs, and Carter wasn't sure he was going to stop. His finger began to move against the trigger. His training kicked in. "Get down!" he yelled again, and the man stopped and dropped to his knees. Carter inhaled and released his finger from the trigger, but stayed alert. There was at least one more person in the house—this guy wasn't the person he'd heard screaming.

One of the other officers cuffed the man as Carter began climbing the stairs. He stayed close to the wall, gun in his hand, ready to defend himself. He reached the top of the stairs and heard crying. The officers behind him spread out, checking the other rooms while Carter moved toward the sound. He pushed open a partially closed door and gasped.

A woman lay on a bed twisted in dingy sheets, nearly naked, rocking her head back and forth as she cried, clutching the mattress. Carter took in the room quickly. Pills sat on the nightstand in a baggie. "Ma'am, are you all right?" Carter asked, but she just kept crying and rocking her head on the bed.

"Call an ambulance," Carter said over his shoulder.

"Already did."

Carter turned quickly, making sure he knew who was behind him. Aaron Cloud was an investigator on the force, and Carter instantly felt more comfortable knowing he was here. Aaron was an experienced officer and a man who believed in supporting his fellow officers, especially the newer ones.

"They're on their way." Aaron stepped around him to the woman. "Go ahead and check out the rest of the house. I'll stay with her."

Carter nodded and left the room.

"There's no one else here," Kip Rogers, another patrol officer, told him.

Carter nodded and began peering into the other rooms. They were mostly empty, but something in the corner of one of the bedrooms caught his eye. Carter stepped inside carefully. The house was a wreck, with torn carpet, damaged walls, and grimy paint that must have been applied decades earlier. He scrunched his nose at the urine smell from the carpet and bent to examine what he'd seen.

A small brown stuffed bunny lay in the corner of the room. Carter looked at Rogers and then pulled a glove out of his pocket. He put it on and picked up the toy. One of the ears flopped down while the other stood straight up, and the bunny smiled at him in complete contrast to this place.

"What are you thinking?" Rogers asked.

Carter set the stuffed toy back where he found it and pulled open the closet door. A pair of small shoes lay jumbled in the corner, and a pair of tiny jeans and a sock rested on the dirty carpet. "Is there a kid here?" Carter whispered to himself and then turned to Rogers. "We need to make sure there isn't a child somewhere in this mess."

Rogers looked in the closet and then at Carter. "That stuff could have been there for years."

"Maybe, but we need to make sure we've checked everywhere." Carter left the room and went back into the tiny hallway. "Could you make sure the basement has been searched? I'm going to see if there's an attic." He began opening doors but found no stairs.

The ambulance arrived and Carter got out of the way so the EMTs could pass. Then he went into the last bedroom. It had a bed with a bare mattress and nothing else. Carter opened the closet door, but it was empty. There couldn't be much attic space in the house, but he knew many of them had some. He then went back in the master bedroom and pulled open the closet. Pushing the clothes aside, he found what he was looking for: a set of stairs that went upward.

"What are you doing?" Aaron asked.

"Checking everything." He turned on his flashlight and carefully entered the space. The stairs curved and he had to bend so he didn't hit his head.

The smell was the first thing to assault him, and Carter had to stop himself from gagging repeatedly. It got hotter as he climbed, and the air, God—his eyes watered and he half expected to find something or someone dead. As he reached the top of the stairs and peered into the space, he nearly jumped back when someone looked back at him. Almost instantly he heard scrambling. Carter shone his light in that direction and gasped.

A small bed had been pushed against the far wall, if you could call it a wall. More accurately, it was the roofing studs. A small pile of clothes sat nearby.

"It's all right," Carter crooned. "I'm not going to hurt you, I promise."

Whimpering reached his ears, and Carter followed the sound. As he got closer to the bed, a tiny head popped up from behind it, and huge eyes filled with terror looked back at him.

Carter could hardly breathe as the realization of what he was seeing hit him. This was a child—a little boy, by the looks of it. "It's okay. I'm Carter and I'm here to help." Sweat ran down Carter's back, and he wondered just how long the boy had been up here. From the smell, long enough to have needed to go to the bathroom and not have a place to go. "I promise." Carter had seen plenty of shitty things in his life and heard even more at the police department, but this.... His throat went dry and fuck if he didn't want to cry at the sight. But he held it together and slowly extended his hand. "It's okay."

"They were yelling," the boy said without moving.

"Yes," Carter said. "But it's okay now. They aren't yelling anymore." Carter wanted to get a better look at the kid, but he didn't want to shine his flashlight light in his eyes. He glanced up to see if there was any light in the space other than the tiny window in front, but saw nothing at all. "Please come out. I promise it's okay."

The boy began to stand.

"What did you find?" one of the other officers called up the stairs, and the boy skittered back behind the bed. Carter swore under his breath.

"Just a minute," he said back without raising his voice. The last thing he wanted was half the police force up here scaring the kid even more than he already was. "It's okay. He's just a loudmouth."

"He yelled," came a muffled reply.

"It's okay. He was just talking loud. I promise."

The boy lifted his head and slowly stood up. He wasn't very tall. Carter waited for him to climb on the bed and then lifted him into his arms. "What's your name?"

"Piece of shit," he answered seriously. Carter needed like hell to get out of there, but was rooted in place by his answer.

"Is that all they ever called you?" Carter's eyes watered and his throat was starting to burn. And the heat—how could this little boy stand it up here?

"Mommy called me Alex sometimes."

"Then we'll call you Alex. That's a nice name." Carter held the boy closer, carrying him toward the stairs. He placed his hand on Alex's head and descended slowly out of the attic. Alex trembled in his arms the closer they got to the entrance to the attic. "It's all right. No one is going to hurt you."

"He said I was to stay there," Alex said and then began to cry. Carter thought he was going to cry right along with him. Jesus, maybe he wasn't cut out for this and should have stayed behind his computers.

"Well, I'm here now and I say you can leave." Carter bent nearly in half to get through the door and then squeezed into the closet and finally the bedroom. Various sets of eyes turned to him in near astonishment. Carter said nothing. He simply held Alex's head against his shoulder so he couldn't see his mother on the bed and got him out of the room and down the stairs to the main floor. Almost instantly Carter could breathe more easily, the oppression and smell from upstairs dissipating slightly.

"Oh my God," Rogers said when Carter walked into the living room. Carter put a finger to his lips, and Rogers lowered his voice. "Was he in the attic?"

"Yeah. You should send some people up there, but get masks for them. It's noxious." Carter shifted Alex in his arms, and the little boy gripped him even tighter.

Rogers nodded. "We should call…."

Carter put up his hand. He already knew what Rogers was going to say, but he didn't want Alex to hear it in case he reacted and got upset. He was calm in Carter's arms, and Carter wanted it to stay that way. "I know."

Rogers nodded his understanding and left the room. Carter moved farther into the room to sit on the sofa. Alex whined softly, and as Carter got ready to sit, he began to struggle and fight.

"No, no, no," Alex cried, releasing Carter and putting his hands over his little head.

"It's all right," Carter soothed and wondered what had been done to this poor child. He'd obviously been relegated to the attic. The emotional abuse was so evident it tugged at Carter's heart, but he had to push it aside. He had to do his job, and he knew he couldn't let it get to him or he'd be back in the basement with only his computers for company faster than they could say, "We knew you couldn't cut it."

Carter moved away from the furniture altogether and just stood off to the side, doing his best to soothe Alex.

"I not…," Alex said and then stopped. "I bad."

"No. You weren't bad." Carter took a deep breath.

7

Noise on the stairs caught Carter's attention, and he turned so Alex couldn't see what they were doing. The EMTs brought what was presumably Alex's mother down the stairs on a stretcher, and one of them broke away and joined him.

"How is he?"

"Can you get me some water and maybe a little food for him? He seems okay otherwise, but when you have a minute, I'd like you to check him out." Carter swallowed. "Phone calls are already being made."

"All right. I'll get some things from the truck and be right back. We're going to transport her. I'll stay behind and tend to him."

"Perfect," Carter breathed.

"I'm Chuck, by the way."

"Carter," he said and watched as Chuck hurried outside. He returned a few minutes later with a bottle of water and a small package of Oreos. Chuck opened the bottle and Carter held it for Alex, who drank and drank. Carter wasn't surprised; the little guy had to be thirsty. Carter sure was, and he had only been up there a few minutes.

"It's all right," Carter said as he moved the bottle away. "Take your time. You can have all you want." He spoke softly, and Alex lifted his head, his huge blue eyes filled with fear. "I promise. Just relax." Carter placed the bottle to Alex's lips, and he drank some more.

"Do you want a cookie?" He opened the package and handed Alex one of the Oreos. He looked at it and reached out to take it tentatively. Once it was in his hands, Alex shoved the entire thing in his mouth and chewed frantically. "It's okay. No one is going to take it from you, and I have some more. See? So chew and swallow and I'll give you another."

Carter pulled out another cookie. Alex snatched it from his hand and held it close to his body. As soon as he swallowed, the second cookie went in whole. Alex reached for another cookie, grabbing it as soon as he could and once again holding it to him. Carter noticed that Alex watched Chuck closely, hiding the food from him.

"I'm not going to take your cookies, little man," Chuck said. "I have more if you eat those. So don't worry."

Carter got Alex to stop eating long enough to drink some more water, and then more cookies were shoved in. Within minutes, all four cookies were gone and Alex settled down. Carter didn't want to make the comparison, but he reminded Carter of the dog he'd had as a child. Snickers had always attacked his food dish, eating like crazy, as if the food would suddenly disappear. What in the fuck had been done to this little boy?

Now that he'd eaten and had something to drink, Alex settled against him.

Chuck stepped closer. "Can I look you over?" he asked. Alex blinked at him, but didn't say anything or even move. He simply breathed. When Chuck moved closer, Alex parted his lips, baring his teeth.

"Hey. That isn't nice," Carter said gently. "He wants to make sure you aren't hurt, okay? He won't hurt you. I promise." Alex blinked up at him. "Will you pull up your shirt so he can see your tummy?" Alex continued looking at Carter, who nodded, and Alex pulled up his shirt.

He was covered in dirt. Carter wondered how long it had been since he'd had a bath. Chuck got out a stethoscope and listened to Alex's heart. Then he moved around to his back. "His heart and lungs sound good." Chuck took Alex's wrist and checked his pulse. "It's a little fast but probably because of what's happened. We can take him in if you want."

"I don't…." Carter wasn't sure what he wanted. "We have people coming. They can make decisions for him."

"Right now I think he needs food and water more than anything else." Chuck turned to Alex. "Thank you," Chuck said to Alex and then lowered his dirty shirt. Carter gave him more water.

"Do you need to use the bathroom?" Carter asked quietly. He wasn't sure how old Alex was—four was his initial guess—but he took a chance and guessed he was potty trained. Alex nodded, and Carter took him through the house to the bathroom.

"Are you done in here?" Carter asked one of the officers as he came out of the bathroom.

"Yeah. There wasn't anything of interest in there." He continued on, and Carter put Alex on his feet. He hurried to the toilet and lifted the lid, then lowered his pants and went.

Carter turned when he was tapped on the shoulder.

"Child services is here," Rogers said softly.

"Okay. We'll meet them in the living room in a few minutes." Carter waited while Alex flushed and then hurried to the sink. Carter lifted him up, and he turned on the water to wash his hands. The gesture seemed so foreign, given the surroundings. Carter set him down and found what appeared to be a clean towel. Alex dried his hands and then looked up at Carter. He lifted him once again, and then walked into the living room.

Carter suppressed the deep groan that threatened to erupt from his throat. Why the hell did it have to be him? "Hello, Donald," he said formally as he stepped into the room.

"Carter," Donald Ickle returned with his usually aloof demeanor. "Is this the boy I was called about?"

"Yes. We found him in the attic." Some of the other officers came into the room. They were finishing up in the house, and Carter saw them carrying things outside. "He has apparently been living there. I'm not sure for how long, but there's quite a mess in one corner, so I'd say for at least a few days. His things seemed to have been moved up there from one of the bedrooms on the second floor."

Donald turned to Alex. "Can you tell me your name?"

"Piece of shit," Alex answered just like he had before and in the exact same tone, like a parrot repeating what it had been told.

"You said your mommy called you Alex," Carter prompted. Alex squirmed to get down, and when Carter set him on his feet, Alex went over the arm of the soiled sofa, pulled down his pants and leaned over, his little bare butt in the air. Carter was floored and looked to Donald for guidance. When he looked back, Carter saw red lines striping Alex's skin. He let out a small gasp and then covered his mouth. *Jesus Christ.*

"No. It's okay. You didn't do anything wrong," Carter said as it dawned on him that Alex was expecting to be punished. Donald didn't say a word, and Carter wanted to punch the asshole's lights out right then. Yes, Donald Ickle was an asshole, at least in his opinion—a cold, arrogant, asshole. Carter went over and tugged Alex's pants back up. Then he lifted him into his arms and held him.

"You told me the truth. That's what good boys do." Carter glared over Alex's shoulder at Donald, who simply looked back at him as though this was completely normal.

"We gave him some water and a few cookies because we weren't sure how much he'd eaten or had to drink recently. I didn't see the marks on him until just now. There weren't any on his back or belly, or at least I didn't see any when the EMT looked him over. I figured you could decide if you wanted him taken to the hospital."

"I should, and then I'll call around and see if I can get him into foster care. Do you know anything other than the name Alex?"

"No," Carter said.

Donald pulled a notebook out of his case and began jotting down notes. "I'll get him to the hospital so he can be looked over thoroughly." Donald pulled out his phone and made a call. "I have a few emergency shelters that should be able to take him for a few days." Donald began making calls, but from what Carter heard Donald was striking out. "I have one more." Donald made the call while Carter continued to try to soothe Alex, who was getting jittery and fussy.

"Do you want me to stay?" Chuck said, putting his head back in the room.

"No. I'll take him in and make sure any injuries he has are documented," Donald told Chuck in the same disinterested voice Carter imagined Donald would use if he were ordering Chinese food. He told himself that no matter what Carter thought of Donald "Icicle" Ickle, he had Alex's best interests at heart, even if he didn't show it. At least that was his reputation.

"All right." Chuck nodded and turned to leave. Most of the other officers had gone as well. Red stood near the front door and closed it behind Chuck after he left.

"I'll make sure the scene is secured," Red told him. "You make sure the kid is okay."

"I will," Donald said and looked at Red, who ignored him and kept looking at Carter.

"Don't worry," Carter said and turned his attention to Donald, who had struck out once again and was making another call. It was dark outside and well after dinnertime. Carter's stomach told him he should have eaten a while ago, but he ignored it. There was someone more important to think about right now.

Donald finished his call. "I can place him with the county for now." He made more notes and then gathered his things. "I have a booster seat in my trunk. I'll get it installed in my car and take him to the hospital. From there, I'll take him to the county home for the night. They have a bed for him."

Carter seethed, but didn't want Alex to know it. Donald approached and tried to take Alex from him. Alex snarled and lashed out with his teeth. "Alex, don't do that. He's trying to help you, even if he is being a pain about it." Carter hardened his gaze, letting it bore into Icicle. "I'll get him to the hospital, and we'll meet you there."

Alex didn't settle down until Donald backed away. "All right. I'll meet you there."

Carter suppressed a smile at the slight amount of fear he saw in Donald's eyes. Carter moved away, and they went outside. Donald strapped the booster seat in the back of Carter's cruiser, and then once Alex was secured, Carter let Red know he was leaving and headed to the hospital.

Officially he was off duty, and he drove as carefully as he could to keep from jostling Alex. The kid looked white as a sheet as he rode, but he sat silently and still. By the time they reached the Emergency entrance at the hospital, he was breathing hard and shaking.

"It's okay," Carter soothed. He parked the car and hurried around, opened the door, and unhooked Alex from the seat belt. Then he pulled him out of the car and into his arms. He was shaking like a leaf. "There's nothing to be afraid of."

Alex looked up at the building and shook in Carter's arms. A car pulled in behind them, and Donald got out and strode over to where they were standing. "He's mean," Alex whispered as Donald stepped closer to them.

"No, he's not. He's just"—Carter smiled—"grumpy." He tickled Alex slightly, and Alex giggled and wrapped his arms around Carter's neck.

"I'm professional, not grumpy," Donald said and walked toward the front door of the hospital.

Carter followed along behind. "He is grumpy," he said to Alex and walked inside.

Donald was already at the desk, and after a few minutes, he returned and motioned them to the chairs. "We need to wait, but it shouldn't be long. I used your name as well."

12

Carter looked at the woman behind the desk, and she smiled brightly at him. He sighed and sat down. Alex stayed on his lap, and Donald sat next to him. They didn't talk, but every few minutes Donald shifted nervously. Carter kept his attention on Alex, but every few minutes he couldn't help taking a peek at Donald in his suit and tie, all buttoned up.

Carter knew the exquisite body that lay hidden under those clothes. He and Donald had… well, they'd had a fling, a one-night stand that had ended up stretching out over an entire weekend a year earlier. It had been hot, sweaty, and Carter had thought well worth repeating as many times as possible, but obviously Icicle hadn't. As soon as the weekend was over, Carter realized just why everyone referred to him as Ice, because Carter didn't just get the cold shoulder; he'd had his nuts frozen off completely.

"You can go on through," a nurse said when she came out to get them. Carter stood and followed her, still carrying Alex.

"I can take him. There's no need for you to spend your entire evening here with him," Donald said and carefully reached for Alex. He didn't try to bite him again, but he most definitely was not happy, and after a few moments, he simply began to cry. Not whimpers, but out-and-out wailing, with tears of desperation.

"It's all right. I'll stay with him. Maybe he'll calm down." Alex practically jumped away from Donald and back into Carter's arms. That seemed to settle things, and they walked together to an examining room.

Carter laid Alex on the bed and hoped he'd stay there. Thankfully it seemed comfortable enough, and Alex stayed still. Carter found the switch and dimmed the lights. Alex yawned, and Carter held his hand. Eventually the little guy fell asleep. "I have no idea how long he's been awake."

"How did you find him? You said he was in the attic," Donald said.

Carter nodded. "He was locked up there. It was hot as hell and all he had was his little bed and a pile of his clothes." He wished he could forget it. "How can anyone treat a kid that way? You were there. When you asked him his name, he told us what he'd been told, and then when I reminded him he had told me what his mom said, he expected to be punished. And someone has definitely hurt him. What the hell else have they done?" Carter cringed and swallowed hard. Sure, he'd been

13

trained as an officer, but he had to admit he was not emotionally prepared for a situation like this.

Donald glared stone-faced across the bed. "I have seen things you would not believe." He turned away and sat down in a chair, staring straight ahead.

"Are you really going to put him in the county home? He'll scream himself hoarse and…."

Donald didn't turn to look at him. "There's no other choice. Until we can find out who he is and if there is family who can care for him, I need to find a place for him, and that's all there is available."

"There has to be something other than *there*." Carter wanted to walk around the bed and smack Donald in the chest. "I know they call you Ice, but you can't be that fucking cold," he whispered threateningly. Carter knew he was hitting low, but if it got results, so be it. "This kid has been through hell, and you want to add to it."

Alex opened his eyes and began to fuss. "You yelled," Alex whimpered.

"No, I didn't," Carter soothed, stroking his little hand. "Just go back to sleep. Everything is going to be okay."

"What do you want me to do?" Donald kept his tone light. "If you're so concerned, then you take him for the night."

"All right," Carter said, crossing his arms over his chest.

Donald rolled his eyes. "Do you have a place for him?"

"He can take my bed and I'll sleep on the sofa." He'd done it before when his parents came to visit… once. He could do it again.

Donald exhaled dramatically. "Fine. I have an extra room. He can stay with me, and tomorrow I'll find him a more permanent place. Let's see if we can find out who he is. Then we may be able to get him into a permanent home."

"Fine," Carter said. Fuck, they sounded like a couple of schoolkids having an argument over who ate the last hot dog, rather than the care of a small boy. But he didn't want to upset Alex again, so he had to keep his voice low.

"You know we sound like something out of a stupid sitcom."

"Yeah, maybe, but I got you to do what's right. I'll take it."

Donald rolled his eyes once again. But before they could continue this argument, conversation, whatever the hell it was, the doctor came

14

in. Alex whimpered and moved closer to Carter. "What seems to be the trouble, young man?"

"Alex here was rescued from a potentially dangerous situation. He had apparently been locked in an attic for an undetermined amount of time. We have also seen evidence of possible physical abuse, so we wanted him examined to ensure he is truly okay, at least physically," Donald answered.

"All right," the doctor said.

"Be careful. He has a tendency to bite," Donald added quickly.

"Only you," Carter countered and turned to Alex. "Will you be good and do what the doctor says? He won't hurt you. It's going to be like the nice man at the house." Alex stared at him. "Will you lift your shirt for the doctor?"

Alex blinked a few times and then pulled up his shirt just like he'd done for the EMT. The doctor listened to his heart, and then Carter helped Alex sit forward, and the doctor pressed his stethoscope to his back. He checked Alex over everywhere, and the only marks on him seemed to be the ones they'd seen earlier. The doctor took Alex's temperature, and his blood pressure and pulse. Alex didn't mind the cuff too much, but after the doctor left and the nurse came in to draw a little blood, he screamed bloody murder as soon as he saw the needle. The nurse gave him a lollipop, which he ate in a matter of seconds. Then he handed the stick back to her. "Thank you."

"You're welcome," the nurse said and handed a few more lollipops to Carter. "Take these home for him. He needs them worse than the other kids." She left, and the doctor returned a while later.

"He seems fine. Maybe a little dehydrated, but otherwise okay. I've ordered some blood work and the initial tests are fine. I've asked that they run some others, as well as a DNA screening that might aid in identifying if he has any relatives who could take him right away. We'll send the rest to your office, Mr. Ickle, with a copy to the police as well as a report of what we observed. We'll just need you to sign some things on your way out."

Carter gathered Alex in his arms and lifted him off the bed. Alex folded against his chest, put his arms around Carter's neck, and rested his head on his shoulder. Donald signed what he needed, and then

Carter put Alex in the back of his squad car. "I have to stop at the station, and then I'll bring Alex to your place. I remember where it is."

"Fine. I'll see what I can do about rounding up what he'll need for the night." Donald turned and strode to his car. Carter got in and began the drive to the station.

CHAPTER
Two

"FUCK, FUCK, fuck!" Donald chanted once he was in his car on his way home. This was so not good. He blew out a deep breath and wondered what in the hell he was going to do. Somehow he'd let Carter goad him into taking Alex in. He'd always done his job and done it well, and had very little life of his own to prove it. But somehow he'd managed to keep his distance. Sure, people called him Ice. So fucking what. Like he really cared what most people thought. His job was to make sure that children who needed help got it. Pure and simple.

Donald pulled up in front of his small house on the south side of Carlisle and got out. He unlocked the door and went inside. The first thing he did was look around to make sure the place was reasonably clean. Hell, it was nearly empty. He'd bought the house a few years earlier. He'd had such grand plans for each room, but other than some paint and pictures on the walls, he hadn't gotten around to much. Every time he thought he was going to get time to start a project, something came up.

He gathered up the remnants of the meal he'd been about to eat when he'd received the call about Alex and threw it all away. He also made sure the paper he hadn't had time to read was tossed as well. The kitchen was clean and the living room looked fine, so he climbed the stairs and roughly made his bed before heading into his guest room.

The previous owners had painted this room a light yellow and he'd liked it, so with the white bed and its soft blue spread, the room looked cheery enough. Donald checked to make sure there were linens on the bed. Finally he went into the tiny extra room he used for emergency supplies—wipes, diapers, an assortment of clothes in various sizes, stuff like that. The county was such a pain and took so long to get what families needed that Donald had slowly laid in his own supplies and used them when necessary and then let the county replace them. It was easier, and the families got what they needed more quickly.

Donald glanced around until he found what he wanted: a pair of pajamas and some underwear that looked like they would fit Alex. He put those in the guest room as he heard a knock on the door downstairs. He hurried down the stairs and pulled open the door. Carter stood on his steps in all his geeky police officer glory, holding Alex in his arms while the kid shoved chicken nuggets into his mouth. "Sorry it took so long. I went through the drive-through for him." Carter bounced Alex lightly. "Take it easy. Those are all yours. No one is going to take them. I promise."

He stepped inside, and Donald closed the door and said, "Why don't you take him into the kitchen?"

Carter went through, and damn if Donald's eyes didn't gravitate to the way Carter's uniform pants hugged his ass. Donald wanted to slap himself for even going there. He was working, not ogling a guy he didn't plan to get any closer to than necessary. Carter put Alex in one of the chairs while Donald found a plastic cup and poured some milk. Alex grabbed it and drank it down. When he set the glass on the table, he smiled up at both of them with a huge milk mustache and sighed.

"I think he's full," Carter said with a goofy smile on his face.

"I hope so." Donald poured a little more milk, and Alex eyed the glass and then drank a little more before putting the glass back on the table.

"Did you have a chance to eat?" Donald asked Carter.

"Nope. This all happened and I've been too busy since."

Donald nodded and put a pan of water on to boil before getting out a box of macaroni and cheese. "I know it isn't much, but it's what I have right now. I was about to eat when I got the call. I figure we can share it with Alex here and then maybe get him in a bath and then to sleep." Donald realized the only way he was going to get Carter to go was to get Alex settled, so he might as well do it as soon as possible.

"I appreciate it," Carter said. "I probably should have gotten something when I got Alex the nuggets, but…."

"You were concentrating on him and not thinking about much else," Donald supplied when Carter seemed to falter.

"Yeah," Carter said meaningfully, cocking one of his eyebrows slightly.

Donald nodded and turned away, and when he saw that the water was boiling, he put the macaroni in to cook. He needed a little time to gather his thoughts and get himself back on an even footing. This whole situation was unsettling and brought up things he'd just as soon remained forgotten. He stirred the pasta for a few minutes so it wouldn't stick… and because it gave him something to do.

"I am not going back there," Donald mumbled to himself and took a deep cleansing breath. Then he turned and opened the refrigerator and pulled out a few slices of ham. He put them on a plate and stuck it in the microwave to heat. Then he set the table.

He managed to keep himself occupied until he set the food on the table. He made up a small bowl for Alex and handed him a spoon. Alex set right to eating.

"I think he's a bottomless pit," Carter commented as he began to eat as well.

"No," Donald said softly. "I think he's learned to eat all he can whenever it's available because he's not sure when he'll eat again." He'd seen this more times than he could count. "His little body has gotten so used to eating only on and off that he'll stuff himself, and if food is still available he'll eat more because his brain doesn't know when he'll eat again."

"Good God," Carter muttered and set down his fork as Alex banged his spoon on the table and let it go with half the macaroni and cheese still in his bowl. He stared up at Carter like he was asking what was next. "You're full?"

Alex nodded and his eyes started to droop.

"When Carter and I are done, we'll give you a bath and then you can go to bed," Donald explained gently so Alex would know what to expect.

Alex began to whine and slid off the chair. He raced into the living room and hid behind the sofa.

"Shit," Carter whispered without heat. "I bet he thinks we're going to take him back to that awful room in the attic." Carter pushed his chair back and bent down near the sofa. "Come on out. Hey! What did we say about biting?" Carter kept his voice remarkably calm, and eventually Alex came out. Carter lifted him into his arms. "It's okay. You aren't going back to that hot, smelly room anymore. Mr. Donald has a nice bed for you upstairs with clean sheets… and…."

"Bunny…," Alex said and wiped his tear-filled eyes. "Bunny… he took him away." He leaned against Carter's shoulder and began to cry. Donald looked at Carter to see if he had an explanation.

"I found a stuffed rabbit in one of the bedrooms. It was what got me thinking that there might be a kid in the house. I know it was a leap just from that, but I got this feeling, you know, and it wouldn't go away." Carter turned to Alex. "I need you to go to Mr. Donald for me so I can see if I can find your bunny. Okay?" Donald stood, and Carter slowly handed Alex to him. The kid was so light. Carter had thought he was three or four, but after holding him and getting a good look at him, he realized he could be older.

Carter pulled out his phone and made a call. "Red, it's Carter. Did you happen to see a stuffed rabbit at the house with the little boy?" Pause. "It was on the floor of the upstairs bedroom." Another pause. "You will? That's cool." Carter gave him Donald's address and then hung up. "A friend of mine is going to go get your bunny for you," he told Alex. "Now, will you let Mr. Donald and me finish eating? Then we'll take you upstairs and get you nice and clean before you go to sleep."

To Carter's surprise, Alex settled in Donald's arms, so he sat back down to finish his dinner. Maybe feeding him was the ticket into Alex's good graces, but he seemed content enough now, which was a relief, considering he was staying with Donald, at least for the night.

Alex tensed when a knock sounded on the door just as they were finishing up, the meal taking longer with Alex on his lap. "That's probably Red. I can get it for you," Carter offered and got up. He put his dishes in the sink and then walked through the house. Donald finished eating as best he could while Carter spoke softly in the other room. He heard footsteps approach and Carter came into the kitchen with another officer. "Donald, this is Red." The huge man held a stuffed rabbit and handed it to Alex, who grinned and cuddled it to his chest.

"It's good to meet you," Red said.

"Would you like anything? I can offer you a soda," Donald said.

"I'm good. Thanks."

"Red said he could stay a few minutes," Carter began, and Alex shifted, wanting Carter. Donald passed him over and Alex went right into Carter's arms. "I'll go up and see about giving this guy a bath."

"I put pajamas and things in the guest room at the top of the stairs. There are towels in the cabinet in the bathroom." Alex seemed more comfortable with Carter, so him doing the whole bath thing seemed like a good idea.

Carter went upstairs, and Donald offered Red a seat in the living room. "I'm just going to clean up." Donald took care of the dishes and then turned out the kitchen lights before joining Red. He didn't hear any cries from upstairs and eventually Carter came down with Alex dressed in clean pajamas.

"I'm going to see if I can get him to sleep, and then I'll be right down." Carter rubbed Alex's back, and Donald had to admit Carter seemed to have a way with Alex. The kid trusted him, at least up to a point.

"Do you usually take kids in?" Red asked once Carter had gone back upstairs.

"No. This is the first time." *And hopefully the last.* "All the other resources I have at hand were full, and it being a Friday night made it even tougher. I could have put him in the county home, but...." He left out the part about how Carter shamed him into taking Alex in.

"It's a good thing you're doing. His mother isn't faring well, and the man we arrested isn't talking about anything, so that's got us all wondering what was really going on."

"Do you know Alex's full name?"

"His mother is Karen Groves, so he'd be Alex Groves, but we need to confirm that she's actually his mother. This whole situation is turning into quite a mess, and we know almost nothing at this point." Red sighed.

"Will you let me know as soon as you have anything?" Donald asked. "I'm hoping we can place Alex with relatives. Otherwise it's foster care, and if his mother doesn't recover...."

Carter came down the stairs. "He's asleep. The poor kid was so tired. All he did was clutch that bunny to his chest, roll onto his side, and he was gone." Carter sat in the last chair. "Thanks, Red. I think that bunny really made the difference." Carter sighed. "Do we know anything about him?"

Red explained what he knew and then stood up. "I need to get home before Terry starts wondering. Donald, it was good to meet you, and it's a real nice thing you're doing for this kid. Carter, I'll see you on Monday."

"Let me know if you hear anything."

"I will. Enjoy your weekend." Red left, and Donald found himself alone with Carter.

"So…," Carter began, drawing out the word. "Do you usually give the guys you spend time with the brush-off or was that just me?"

Donald should have known that Carter had been waiting to ask something like that. Granted, it wasn't the first time he'd been asked a version of that question, so he had a ready answer. Too bad that wasn't what came out of his mouth. "Carter, we had a real nice time, but I don't do relationships. Hell, I rarely see the same guy for more than one night. Not that I see that many guys…." He'd veered off his usual script and now he was in uncharted territory. "This job requires odd hours and can be really unpredictable. So I don't get involved." There, that sounded pretty believable.

"Okay," Carter said softly. "I guess I can understand that." He leaned forward. "The explanation sounds very plausible, but I know bullshit when I smell it, and you, my friend, are up to your eyeballs in it. If you didn't like me, all you had to do was say so instead of not returning calls." He stood and walked to the door. "You have my number somewhere," Carter added and pulled out a card from his pocket. He wrote a number on the back and handed it to him. "But here it is again. Call me if you need anything… with Alex."

Carter walked toward the door and pulled it open. "I still have your number, so I'll call tomorrow, and I might stop by just to spend a few minutes with Alex." Carter stepped out and pulled the door closed.

Donald stared down at the card in his hand, wondering exactly what in the hell had just happened and why he felt very much alone. He sat back down and stared at nothing for a few minutes before turning on the television. He needed to relax a little before going up to bed. For some odd reason he figured this was going to be a long night.

FUCK IF he wasn't right.

Donald checked on Alex; he even watched him sleep for a few minutes with his bunny pressed so tightly to him it seemed nearly bent in half. Donald knew that was for protection; the fetal position an inbred defense mechanism. Still, Donald watched him for a while and then went to his own room. He got undressed and climbed into bed, then turned out the light and got comfortable.

He'd just dropped off to sleep when a bloodcurdling scream woke him. Donald bolted upright and then leaped out of the bed and raced to Alex's room. He was still lying down, but shaking like a leaf, screaming at the top of his little lungs. Donald lifted him out of the bed and into his arms, but Alex thrashed even more. "Hey, wake up. You're okay." He tried to mimic the tone Carter had used, but with little success judging by the screaming that continued loud enough Donald was afraid his ears would start bleeding at any moment. "Alex," he said more loudly. "Wake up. You're safe. No one is hurting you."

The screams lessened, followed by crying and nonstop tears. Donald tried his best to settle him, but he was having no luck. He retrieved Alex's bunny, handed it to Alex, and he took it, crushed it to his chest, and continued wailing. Donald carried him downstairs and found the card Carter had left. He got his phone and called the number.

"Yeah...."

"Carter—" he began but was cut off.

"Is that Alex? What are you doing to him?"

"I think he had a nightmare or something and he won't come out of it. I've tried soothing him, but it isn't helping."

"I'm on my way." The line went dead, and Donald dropped the phone on the chair and began pacing the floor, hoping regular movement would help calm Alex.

Nothing helped, and finally a knock sounded on the door. Donald yanked it open, and Carter charged inside, took Alex from his arms, and he settled right down. Tears continued to flow, along with nonsense words that Donald couldn't understand, but Carter certainly seemed to. "It's all right. The bad men aren't going to get you, I promise. No one is going to hurt you." Carter paced the same way Donald had. "Hold your bunny and calm down. It's okay."

"Bad men?" Donald asked.

"Yes. He's chanting about bad men. I don't know what's behind it, but he's afraid of bad men," Carter whispered in the same tone he might sing a lullaby. "It's all right. The bad men are gone."

Alex had finally settled down and rested his head on Carter's shoulder. Now that Alex was calm, Donald felt himself calm as well, and he realized a couple of things. One, he was standing with Carter and wearing only a pair of sleep pants, and two, Carter was wearing sweats and a loose T-shirt that had to be a size too small. At least it was too short, because every now and then it rode up, giving Donald a glimpse of pale skin. In Donald's opinion, Carter was a geek to the core. While he was better built than most geeky guys Donald had met—that had to be the cop in him—the glasses and the fact that he never seemed to have spent a minute in the sun gave him that "lives behind a computer" look. If Donald were honest, Carter was damned near his ideal, but that kind of honesty was a little more than he was willing to allow, even in his own thoughts.

"I should put something else on," Donald said and turned toward the stairs.

"You don't have to on my account," Carter said, and Donald turned just in time to see Carter look away and focus his gaze on Alex.

"I should smack that smirk off your face," Donald said lightly, trying to cover for the heat that coursed through him, the jolt of desire from Carter's attention that shot straight up his spine and settled at the base of his brain, sending a shudder through his shoulders. Not that it mattered, because he wasn't going to do a damned thing about it. He'd decided a while ago how he was going to live his life, and until today the program had been working. He intended to keep it that way.

"That would be assaulting a police officer, not to mention endangering the safety of a minor." Carter grinned and continued rocking Alex slowly. "Let's see if we can put him back to bed. He's asleep for now."

Donald nodded and headed toward the stairs, leading Carter upward. He pushed open the door to the room Alex had been using, and Carter gently laid Alex on the bed. He settled easily, gripping his bunny. Carter covered him up and then, to Donald's surprise, kissed him gently on the cheek. "Good night, little man. Sweet dreams—God knows you deserve them." Carter stood over Alex for a few seconds, just enough time for Donald to wipe his eyes.

Carter left the room with Donald following him back down the stairs.

"I can make up the sofa for you if you like," Donald offered. It was the least he could do given that Carter had come over in the middle of the night. "I have no idea if he's going to sleep through or if this is something that will happen multiple times."

"Thanks," Carter said.

"He really seems to respond to you." Donald wasn't sure if he should be insulted or not. After all, he had been trained as a social worker. It was his job to care for children, and it was Carter's job as a police officer to keep law and order. He'd always thought of police officers as big, tough guys, and he supposed Carter could be just that when he needed to.

"I was the one who found him and took him out of that place, and I gave him something to eat and got his bunny back. I was kind, and I think he's responding to that more than anything else. From the looks of him and his reactions, I'd say there hasn't been much kindness in his life. He only knows neglect, even abuse, and want." Carter sighed. "You didn't see that pathetic, dirty cesspool of a room that he was living in. No one could see that and not be affected, not even Icicle."

"Jesus," Donald countered. "So I didn't call you after we spent a weekend in bed. It was sex. That doesn't mean I'm the devil incarnate or whatever you seem to have built up in your mind. I'm a guy like you, and I wanted sex. We had it. You had a good time, and so did I. So I didn't call you afterward to see if… what? You wanted to go out to the drive-in and have a malted? Geez, maybe I could have seen if you could have borrowed your dad's Studebaker." Yeah, he was being absurd, but, God, what did Carter expect?

"You're right. I had no right to expect anything. We didn't make promises and we only exchanged phone numbers." Carter stepped closer, his normally intense blue eyes darkening to azure. "I guess I'm letting my judgment become clouded by my hurt feelings. What matters is Alex and what's best for that little boy, not whatever happened between us." Carter huffed softly under his breath. "If you'll get me a blanket, I'll stay down here on the sofa in case Alex wakes up again." Carter turned away and sat on the sofa. "Or if you want me to go, you can just call if you need anything."

"No. You're welcome to stay." Donald climbed the stairs and wondered why in the hell Carter could get to him so fucking easily. The way Donald did things worked for him and protected him. It made his life easier and definitely safer. He quieted his steps as he reached the top of the stairs and the linen closet, careful not to wake Alex. He retrieved a light blanket and a pillow, then carried them back down the stairs. He handed them to Carter, and after a quick good-night he went back up the stairs and into his room as quickly as he could.

He closed the door and breathed a sigh of relief. When he'd gone downstairs with the blanket, Carter had already pulled off his shirt and taken off his shoes. Donald had been about two seconds from throwing himself at him and had needed to get the hell away. He actually leaned against the back of the door and breathed like he'd just run a race. What was wrong with him? Carter was just another guy. He pushed away from the door and climbed into bed.

He could tell himself all he wanted that Carter was just another one of the random guys he'd slept with. But then why was he hyperaware that Carter was just downstairs, shirtless, sleeping on his sofa? Donald tossed and turned a few times and then got back up and opened his bedroom door, ostensibly so he could hear if Alex needed him. So why did he stand in the doorway listening as the sofa springs squeaked slightly? He imagined Carter rolling over, the blanket slipping off his shoulders.

Stopping the movie in his head, Donald went back to bed and closed his eyes, rolled onto his side, and did his best to fall asleep. Of course, the more he tried to sleep, the longer he lay in the dark, staring at nothing. Alex stayed quiet, and after a little while, no more squeaks drifted up from the living room. Donald figured the only one not asleep in the house was him.

Eventually exhaustion must have overtaken him, because the next thing he knew, light streamed in through his windows. He gasped and sat up, listening. When he heard nothing, he got up and walked into the guest room. The bed was empty. Donald's first thought was that Alex could be wandering around the house, or have left the house altogether. He barreled down the stairs to look for him and stopped dead in his tracks. Carter sat in the living room chair, head back, eyes closed, mouth hanging open, with Alex on his lap, his little head pressed to Carter's chest, holding his bunny close.

Donald stood completely still. He wished he had a camera so he could take the picture and give it to Carter. In his job, he saw some of the worst of society and how people treated the youngest, most vulnerable members. He took a deep breath, filling his lungs with oxygen as he filled with energy and hope. This image gave him hope. Yesterday, Alex had been living in unthinkable conditions, but there was none of that on his face right now. He seemed to feel safe and secure in Carter's arms. That was what Donald wanted for each and every one of the children in his care. So many times it didn't happen, and.... Donald pushed what he considered his failures away. He didn't want to think about them right now, not with this image of perfection in front of him.

Granted, it was only an image. Alex wasn't Carter's son, and he was still far from settled in a long-term home, but Donald was going to do his very best to make that happen. He stepped away and went back upstairs to put on a shirt. Then he brushed his teeth and ran a comb through his hair before going back downstairs to the kitchen. He got out some pans and began making breakfast.

After a few minutes, Carter came in carrying a still sleepy Alex, his head resting on Carter's shoulder. "Mommy," Alex whimpered and then grew quiet.

"It's okay, buddy," Carter soothed. "I know." Alex shook in Carter's arms, and Donald's heart thumped. He turned away and went back to his scrambled eggs, pouring them in the pan. He still listened to Carter as he calmed Alex. He wondered if he was capable of doing that—could he have done that if Carter hadn't been here? Yes, he could have said the right things, but was it what he would have felt? Carter seemed to have an instinct—he knew what would calm and soothe Alex. He didn't tell him what he wanted to hear, which is what Donald would have tried to figure out and then say as truthfully as possible. The words that came to his own mind sounded fake, while Carter's simplistic soothing was genuine.

There was little doubt that Carter cared about Alex. It came through in the way he held him and talked to him, even putting Alex over his own comfort by sleeping on Donald's lumpy old sofa. Donald wondered if he was capable of that at all. He'd gone into this line of work because he'd wanted to make things better for children like Alex, and he did his job well; he knew that. All his supervisors and the other social workers told him so. He worked each case as far as he could, going to bat and pushing for what the children needed. He did that every single day, but always from afar.

He realized he'd nearly burned the eggs and quickly switched off the heat. Then he looked down at the pan and realized that when he'd been lost in his thoughts, he'd forgotten to make anything else. He got some bread and began toasting it. After getting some plates and a bowl for Alex, he portioned out the eggs and set them on the table.

Alex slid off Carter's lap, climbed into the chair, and began eating right away, remaining quiet. Donald got some juice and poured glasses. Once the toast popped, he buttered it and placed one slice on Carter's plate before cutting the other slice for Alex, who was going at his eggs like a madman.

"You can have more if you want it," Donald told him and gently touched his hair.

Alex stopped for a few seconds, staring up at him with big blue eyes, and then he turned back to his food.

"I think he wants to believe you, but is having a hard time because of what's happened to him."

"I know," Donald said. "I'll have to make a point of explaining things very carefully to whoever I place him with."

Carter said nothing and took a bite of his eggs. Was it possible to chew angrily? If it was, then that was exactly how Carter ate. He didn't bite at his toast; he tore at it. Donald didn't understand Carter's sudden hostility, but he couldn't pursue it. Alex stopped eating, stared at Carter, and then jumped down out of his chair and ran into the living room, hiding behind the sofa like he had the day before.

"Shit," Carter whispered just loud enough for Donald to hear, and then he pushed back his chair. After a few minutes he returned with Alex. "Mr. Donald and I were talking, that's all."

Alex looked as though he wasn't buying it.

"Here," Donald said and handed Alex his bunny. "Does your bunny have a name?"

Alex shook his head as he snatched the bunny and pressed it to him.

"Do you want him to have a name?" Donald asked, and Alex blinked before turning away. After a few moments, Carter placed him back in his seat and Alex ate some more of his breakfast.

A knock on the door made Alex jump slightly. Donald stood and went to the door. Red, the police officer from the night before, stood outside his front door along with a smaller, slimmer man. "Donald, this is my partner, Terry. I hope we aren't interrupting, but Terry figured that the little boy wouldn't have much, so I went back to the house first thing this morning, and we got some of his clothes and washed them."

Terry lifted a clothes basket. "I hope these actually fit him."

Donald didn't know quite what to say. "Come on in. We're having a little breakfast, and then I need to see if I can find a more permanent place for him."

"Will you be able to do that on a Saturday?" Terry asked as he stepped inside the house.

"Child welfare isn't a Monday-through-Friday, nine-to-five job, but I wasn't able to find anything yesterday, so honestly I think he'll be here until Monday." Donald smiled, surprised that he liked that idea. Maybe the little guy was growing on him. "So I really appreciate your thoughtfulness." He took the offered basket and set it down beside the sofa. "Please come on into the kitchen. Can I get you some coffee?"

Red looked at Terry. "Some water would be nice," Terry said.

"He's already been swimming this morning. He got the club to let him use the laundry facilities so he could stay on schedule," Red said with obvious pride. They followed him into the kitchen. Alex was finishing off his last piece of toast.

"I told you we should have brought some toys too," Terry said to Red.

"The ones at the house were so dirty I didn't feel right bringing them over," Red explained. "Do you know how old he is?"

Donald snapped into professional mode. "When we went through the house, we found some papers and were able to locate Alexander's birth certificate. He just turned five. I would have guessed three or four, but if he hasn't been getting enough to eat, he could be behind in his growth and development. In some ways he seems a little older and in others…." Donald sighed. "His small stature and immaturity are probably the result of the way he's been treated."

Red nodded. "I would agree with you. He sure is a cute little guy now that he's cleaned up."

"You're such a softie," Terry commented, bumping Red's shoulder.

Carter joined them, and Alex walked around the living room and sat in one of the corners, playing with his bunny. They seemed to be having a one-sided conversation that Donald couldn't understand, but wished to hell he could.

"I came by because we need Carter's help," Red said softly. "The woman we tried to help didn't make it, and it seems that she was Alex's mother."

"She's dead?" Donald asked in a whisper.

"Yes. There were too many drugs in her system and her heart gave out."

"But you're certain she was Alex's mother?" Donald asked for confirmation.

"Yes, she was. He was born in Mifflintown. The birth certificate lists the father as unknown."

"Okay," Donald said and turned toward Alex, still in his pajamas, as he continued to play with his bunny, unaware of the complete change in his situation.

"So we need to explain to him what happened," Carter said with a sigh. "I'll do that."

Donald put his hand on his arm. "No," he whispered. "He likes you and trusts you." Donald took a deep breath. "I won't let you be the one who takes his mother away from him. I'll tell him. That way he can hate me if he wants." Donald looked at the others. "Besides, it's my job and what I'm supposed to do."

"What about the man we arrested?"

"Byron Harker," Red said. "He's a real piece of work. We'll never know how Alex's mother got involved with him, but he's one slimy piece of… crap." Red turned to Carter. "That's what we need your help with. Some of the things he was into are right up your alley as far as computers go. The chief said I was to bring your computer over and ask if you would see what you can dig up on Mr. Harker's activities." Red glanced at Alex and then back to them. "He's got a history of using children for… he was arrested on child pornography charges in Maryland, but the charges were dropped because of insufficient evidence."

Carter went white. Donald had seen this before and simply nodded. "How can you act that way?" Carter hissed. "What if he was…?"

"Carter," Red snapped in a whisper. "It isn't Donald's fault. But we need you to see what you can find because we don't want this piece of filth back out on the streets. All we can get him for right now is possession and maybe manslaughter. He's claiming he didn't even know the kid was in the attic. That his mother put him there, and who can refute that now? Him?" Red was fired up, though when Terry put his hand on his arm, he immediately calmed. "Sorry. It might be hard to get Alex to talk about it, so we need to find evidence that can do the talking for him."

"Okay. I should probably go in to the department and…."

"I brought your laptop from your desk and I have a network access token. They're in the car. I wasn't sure how long it would take you, and I figured it would be easier if you worked from where you were."

"Did you know I was here?" Carter asked.

Red smiled. "No. We were going to drop off the clothes and then go to your place, but you saved us a stop."

"Why don't you go get his equipment?" Terry suggested.

"I really think I should go in," Carter said, looking over at Alex, still playing with his bunny. "If I find anything, we'll need logs and traces."

"You can get everything you need here, but if you want to go in, that's up to you," Red offered.

Carter seemed torn. "I think I'm really going to need more than just my laptop for this." He looked over at Alex again, and Donald could see how torn he was. He obviously wanted to stay with him, and yet he also wanted to work to try to help him.

"We'll be fine," Donald said.

"I can stay too, if you like," Terry offered. "I know we don't know each other, but I like kids."

"It's all right," Donald said quietly. "Alex and I will be fine. You go ahead and see what you can find out about what Harker was up to. I won't say anything to Alex until you come back."

31

"All right," Carter said and got ready to leave. Terry and Red went with him. As soon as the door closed, Donald sat in one of the chairs and watched as Alex played. What felt strange was that he was in his own house, basically alone. Granted, Alex was there, but Donald was alone, like he always was. But now, after having Carter there, the house really felt empty. Donald steadied himself and took a deep breath. He was fine. He had spent much of his life alone, relying on himself, and that was what he was going to continue doing. That was the only way forward. He'd learned that long ago—a hard lesson he didn't plan to repeat.

CHAPTER
Three

CARTER LEFT Donald's house and walked to his car. He went home, where he showered and changed clothes before hurrying into the station and down into the basement to his desk and computers.

"All right," Red said as he plopped himself into the chair next to Carter's desk. "I e-mailed you Harker's pertinent information and I have his computer."

"Okay. What is it you're looking for?"

"Not sure. We need to know what he's been up to. Aaron hasn't let anyone look at the computer, and we're hoping there will be something incriminating on it that we can use."

"Okay. Let me get started."

"Is there anything I can do?" Red asked.

"Sure, get me some coffee while I remove the hard drive and get it attached to my machine. Then we can start taking a look around and see what we have."

Red left and Carter got to work. Removing the drive didn't take long, and he put it in a cradle that he attached to his computer. He also segregated the drive so nothing would contaminate his system. By the time Red returned, Carter was starting to have a look around. "I'm concentrating on video and picture files. Those are the most likely to be the ones we want." Carter began opening the ones he found, but there was nothing other than some that came with the computer and pictures of some nasty-looking dogs. No kids. Nothing. "I suppose that was too easy. There are no video files either. So we'll have to look deeper." Carter typed away and got his system examining the hard drive.

"Had stuff been deleted?" Red asked.

"Yeah. A lot of things," Carter mumbled as he continued working. "You know that when something is deleted it isn't necessarily gone, and I have been known to retrieve things, but this system has had things added and deleted so many times that it's all a jumble and I can't retrieve much of anything." He continued working, hoping for a miracle, but got nowhere. "Okay, this guy was smart. He didn't keep anything incriminating on his system, but that doesn't mean he isn't dirty. Just careful."

Carter went to Harker's browsing history. Of course, the cache had been cleared, and from the looks of things Harker always kept it cleared. So he dug deeper and got lucky. He found an old copy of the browsing history. "Yes."

"What?"

"It looks like there was a crash or the system detected an issue and it saved an emergency backup of some files." Carter smiled as he opened the file. "It's old, but it may give us a few clues as to what he was doing." Carter typed for a few seconds. "These are websites, and I know about some of them. They are questionable sites with very young men and women. They're legal, but just barely. That's a clue that we're on the right track, but it's not what we...." Carter paused, his fingers hovering over the keyboard.

"What's wrong?" Red asked, the chair squeaking as he shifted.

"I need to open a browser, but I want to do it so it looks like his computer is actually doing it instead of mine." Carter continued working. "Okay." He pointed to the screen. "I'm not going to go into details, but I'm faking things out so the web address thinks that we're on Harker's computer rather than ours." He activated the browser and a user ID and password screen came up. To Carter's astonishment, the user ID was filled in, as was the password. "Damn, this guy was so careful, but really stupid when it came to passwords. He actually had his computer save it for him."

The field filled in with asterisks. "Can you get it so it can be accessed by a different system, for evidence purposes?"

"Maybe if I have a lot of time, but...." Carter pressed enter and stared. On the screen was a web portal, a simple site for sharing files, and there were probably hundreds of them, maybe even thousands or more. "We need to call the FBI on this one," Carter said as he clicked on one of the picture files. He immediately closed it when he saw what it was.

"Can you find what was uploaded from this computer?" Red asked.

"I might." He looked around briefly and found a section of owner-exclusive files. They appeared to be the ones Byron had placed there himself. "Jesus Christ," Carter said softly as he saw the name on one of the files. He opened it and stared as a video started to play.

"Why did you pick this one?" Red asked as a sofa appeared.

"The title. It's called 'spanking a piece of shit.'"

"I don't get it," Red said and then gasped. Carter swallowed as he saw Alex being forced over the arm of the sofa, bottom bare, and then spanked with a cane. Carter closed the window before he got sick right there. The date on the file was four days ago. Carter moved away from the computer as though it were infested and his hands had contracted some contagious disease. "I'm serious. We need to speak to the captain and then call in the feds. This is bigger than just us."

"That's up to the captain. You know he's going to want to make sure our house is in order and he's going to be wary of calling in help. Last time we got shut out completely. That isn't going to happen again."

"Yeah, I know. I was the one who found the trail. But I nearly got my fingers metaphorically cut off because I'd actually been hacking… remember? Thankfully they were able to get in legally before the trail was gone." Carter did not want to go through that again. The whole situation had nearly cost him his badge. "We have access to this site right now, but I don't know how long we'll have it. These sites have to require regular password expiration and changes in order to ensure the continued privacy of their deviant little world."

"All right, but do we have enough to put our own deviant out of commission permanently?"

"Definitely. Let me get all this gathered and the evidence legally documented. Would you call the captain and get him to come down here so he can see this?"

"You want him to come here?" Red asked in disbelief.

35

"I can't very well take all this to him. He comes down here every once in a while, and this has the potential to be huge."

"Okay," Red said and got out of the chair. Carter got back to work, gathering the trail of the files from the computer he had to the website. He also downloaded the files that Byron had uploaded onto a secure partition. He made damn sure he didn't open a single one of them. The last thing he needed was to see any more of that filth. Just catching a glimpse of Alex being beaten had him fighting between rage and the urge to throw up. He let rage take over, figuring he could throw up later, when he was alone.

"Schunk, I take it you found something," the captain said as he strolled into Carter's little domain.

"Yes. I have the documentation we can use to charge Harker, but I also got access to a site with thousands of files. They link to people all over the country and possibly the world. I think it's out of our league." Carter explained everything he'd found and how he got there. He also showed him a sample of what was there, specifically what Harker had uploaded. He refused to open the file with Alex and even contemplated deleting it all together. Not that there weren't other copies, possibly, but....

"All right. You make sure we have everything we need and that our case is airtight. I want nothing to interfere with what we have here, and then I'll make a few phone calls."

Carter spent the next hour completing all the documentation and making detailed notes on where he'd found all of the files. Then he moved copies of everything Harker had uploaded onto a drive that he made sure was secured with a complete electronic trail on each file. When he was done, he sent his report to the captain, secured Harker's hard drive in the evidence locker, and left the station.

As soon as he stepped outside into the summer heat and sun, he took a deep breath, letting go of the stench from the job he'd just had to do. Carter then went to his car and drove home, then went straight to the shower to try to wash off the residue of what he'd had to see. He felt dirty, and even after scrubbing for ten minutes, it wouldn't go away. More than anything he wished he could get that image of little Alex being beaten out of his mind. He'd seen less than a minute, but it was more than he ever needed to see in his lifetime. He scrubbed harder and then gave up. The stain he felt wasn't on the outside but in his mind, and nothing could erase it. He turned off the water, dried off, and then left the bathroom.

His apartment was small and sat above one of the shops on the main street of Carlisle. He loved it. The people who owned the antique shop downstairs also owned the building, and they were good to him and kept the building in remarkable repair. He had a small living room, kitchen, bedroom, and bath. The whole place had been renovated just before he'd moved in, so it was clean and bright.

As soon as he was dressed and got his things together, he left and walked the two blocks to Donald's house. He paused at the front door, hand raised to knock. What was he doing here? Since leaving the station, he'd only thought about getting back to Donald's. Sure, he knew part of it was to see Alex. The little guy was something else, and he needed someone to help cushion the blow from the news they had to deliver. But part of him—the excited, frightened part that Carter didn't really want to acknowledge—wanted to see Donald. Why in the hell that was true, he had no idea. The man wasn't nicknamed Ice for no reason, and Carter had already gotten a taste of that iciness.

But he'd also felt the passion. Their weekend together had been mind-blowingly hot. They had spent most of it in bed. Hell, there had been times when Donald had Carter so out of it he'd barely been able to remember what day it was or his own fucking name. Yeah, they hadn't made promises, at least verbally, but after a round of sweaty sex that had left them both panting and gasping for breath, they'd stumbled into the kitchen, eaten whatever Donald had in his refrigerator, and then ended up in each other's arms again. Their lips had come together in a bruising kiss, and they embraced, only to fall to the kitchen floor, where Carter got Donald's and his sweats off, fumbled around in one of the pockets for a condom—thank the Lord it was lubed—and then he'd pressed fast and hard into Donald, both of them screaming—Donald for him not to stop and Carter simply from the pressure and heat that felt unlike anything anywhere.

Donald had sworn and cursed, mostly whenever Carter slowed down. Their coupling was nearly frantic, as though they'd already been apart too long and neither could bear it. Withdrawal was undeniably painful; thrusting was bliss. He had to have one with the other, but damn, he could thrust forever and never get deep enough, or make

Donald cry loudly enough or beg hard enough. Their climaxes rattled the windows, the two of them howling at the top of their lungs. Then they lay together in a heap on the cool floor, unable to move, until they needed to eat again, which they did, only to go back up the stairs, fall into bed, and nap until Donald woke him in the absolutely best way possible and they went at it again.

Carter glanced around, wondering just how long he'd been standing like this. He closed his eyes and willed his dick to stop trying to break out of his pants. Jesus Christ, he was standing on Donald's front porch, looking like some sort of demented stalker, with a hard-on. Anyone who passed would think he got off on brass doorknockers and oak doors. Not that those memories counted for anything now. Donald had made it perfectly clear just where Carter stood, and Carter wasn't about to let Donald batter his geek heart or his pride again. Yeah, he'd gotten over it and they had only been together a weekend, but Carter had let himself hope there was more to it. How could there not be after the connection they'd had? He'd gotten his answer pretty damned quickly, and Donald had proved his nickname fit. Carter had been frozen out once—never again!

He knocked and waited. Footsteps sounded and then Donald opened the door. Carter stepped inside, and Alex walked over to him. He could see Alex had been crying, and the little guy wrapped his arms around Carter's legs, hugging them, and began to cry again.

"He's been asking for his mother for the past hour and I can't get him to stop," Donald said. "I've tried taking his mind off it, and it works for a few minutes, but…."

"Okay." Carter lifted Alex into his arms.

"Mommy," he cried. "I want Mommy."

"I know," Carter soothed and walked over to the sofa to sit down. "We have to tell him." But how were they going to make him understand that his mother was gone and that the life he'd known, as bad as it was, was over, and things would never be the same? Carter tried to understand how that would feel but couldn't. He'd had two parents, and the thought of having grown up without them was unfathomable. They hadn't been perfect, far from it, but they'd been there as best they could. Alex was about to be told he would never have that.

"Alex, Mr. Carter and I have something to tell you and we need you to listen. Can you do that?" Donald asked.

Alex hugged him tighter, and Carter thought he was going to choke for a few seconds.

"Alex, please. We need to talk to you about your mommy," Donald said with incredible gentleness.

Alex lifted his head and turned toward Donald. "I want Mommy."

"I know, but your mommy died." Donald paused. "She's living in heaven with the angels, where she'll always be happy and no bad men will ever get to her again."

"But I want her. I want Mommy," Alex cried and put his head on Carter's shoulder, his little body shaking. Carter was a fucking police officer, trained to deal with just about anything, but hearing Donald tell Alex that his mother was dead rocked him deep to his soul. Life wasn't fair; it never had been, but telling a kid like Alex that his mother was dead seemed the epitome of unfair. Carter wanted to scream and cry right along with Alex, but he held it together even as his eyes filled with tears.

"Alex," Carter said a little more strongly. "We both wish we could bring her back to you, but we can't. She died and she's with the angels. Do you know what those are?"

Alex nodded against his shoulder. "In heaven," he said. "But when will she be back?"

"She won't come back. When you go live with the angels, you stay there forever."

"They should give her back. She's my mommy," Alex demanded and then curled into Carter's arms, breaking into deep sobs.

"It's okay to cry," Donald whispered. "And it's okay to miss your mommy." He took Carter's hand in his, and they sat together trying to comfort a grieving child. All Carter could do was hold him while Alex whimpered and cried for a mother who most likely hadn't been a real mother to him in quite some time.

Eventually Alex cried himself to sleep, and Carter took him up the stairs and into the room he was using. He laid him on the bed and covered him up after carefully removing his shoes. Then he went back down the stairs and joined Donald in the living room. "He's asleep for now."

Donald nodded. "Thank you."

"Were you able to find out anything while you were at the station?" Donald asked.

Carter closed his eyes, pushing back the images that sprang forward as quickly as he could. "Yeah. I found out plenty, and we're going to nail his ass good." Carter glanced toward the stairs.

"Was Alex…?"

Carter nodded. "He was on one of the videos I found. " He steadied his voice. "I know now how Alex got those marks on his backside. There was a video of him being spanked. It nearly made me sick to think of someone doing that to him… or anyone." Carter's hands clenched to fists.

"Did you actually watch it?" Donald asked.

"Less than a minute. By then I was so angry I wasn't sure whether to punch the screen or throw up." Carter stood and began pacing the room. "If they put me in the room with Harker, I swear I'd kick the life out of him without even thinking." The anger rose so fast it was a miracle he could think straight. Carter turned to Donald, who stared at him as level and calm as if Carter had just told him tomorrow's weather. "Doesn't that bother you? That Alex was abused that way? What if something worse was done to him?" He leaned closer to Donald, who simply blinked at him. "Fuck, you are one cold son of a bitch." He straightened up and pointed at the stairs. "How in the hell can that not affect you? Are you even human?"

"Yes, of course. But I've seen things that you can't possibly imagine." Donald stood and stepped closer to him. "How dare you judge me? You haven't seen any of what I have, then one kid comes across your path and you're up in arms." Donald moved even closer. "I get that what happened to Alex is upsetting. That sweet kid doesn't deserve what happened to him. But neither did the twelve-year-old I saw last month whose mother was in such need for her meth that she was whoring out her own daughter to get it. That's right. Or the kid two months ago—he was fourteen, and when he told his dad he was gay, his father tried to… cut him. Thank God the neighbors called the police and your officers arrived in time. But, hell, I had to find a safe place for him to live with people who would understand and help him." Donald's voice had a knife edge to it. "I see things like that all day, every day.

It's my job." Donald began breathing like he'd run a marathon. "I help every one of those kids as best I can. I give all I have to give when I'm at work. And fuck you if I'm not wearing my heart on my sleeve. I can't do that. I deal with hundreds of cases a year, and if I felt like you are now for each and every one of them, I would go off the deep end. Hell, look at you...." Donald motioned toward him. "You're already falling to pieces and—" Donald's breath caught and he stopped midthought. "Do you know how many children I have told that their mother or father is dead? Including today, thirty-six. Thirty-fucking-six! I got to tell them their life was over and that things would never be the same. Me, a complete stranger, letting thirty-six kids know their parent wasn't coming home ever again!"

Carter watched as Donald's face contorted in pain. He stepped back and collapsed on the sofa. "Fuck you, Carter. You don't know shit about me or what I do each and every day. So fucking what if people call me Ice. Do you really think I give a shit?"

Carter hesitated, then said, "Yeah, I think deep down you do."

"I care about every child I deal with, and I work miracles on a daily basis. But what do you think those thirty-six kids remember about me? That I found them a home and arranged for some of them to get out of foster care and into permanent adoptive homes? No. They remember me as the guy who told them that Mommy or Daddy wasn't coming home. So who in the hell are you to tell me how I deal with that?" Donald jumped to his feet. "I'll answer that for you. You're nobody. Until you've seen these kids' faces every day, you don't know crap." Donald poked Carter in the chest, and Carter grabbed Donald's hand. "No one knows the hell I go through, and if I have to be cold or a little distant to get through some of my days, I think I've fucking earned it."

Carter had no idea what to say. He had never given it any thought. Hell, he'd thought Donald was just some coldhearted bastard. But was it all a defense mechanism? "So why did you go into this line of work if it's so hard for you?"

Alex called from the top of the stairs, and Carter stood, glad for a distraction. Donald's glare followed him to the stairs; he felt it on his back like a beacon of heat. "Come on down, buddy. You don't have to stay in there if you aren't sleepy." Carter could tell by the way Alex rubbed his eyes and yawned that he was wiped out, but there was no sense pushing him. He took Alex's hand and led him into the living room, where he climbed on Carter's lap as soon as he sat down.

"I have some ice cream if you want some," Donald offered, but Alex didn't seem interested, which was a little shocking to Carter. But he just went with the flow, and soon Alex had fallen asleep in his arms. Carter gently carried him to the sofa, and Alex curled onto his side.

"I'll go get his bunny," Carter whispered to Donald and went upstairs. He found the bunny on the floor of the bedroom and carried it downstairs. Carter placed it in Alex's arms, and he pulled it to him. Carter stood back, watching Alex for a few minutes, and then he turned and joined Donald in the kitchen.

Donald handed him a bowl of chocolate ice cream and motioned toward the table.

"You didn't answer my question," Carter pressed. Maybe it was the cop in him, but he liked having answers, and he knew he could be a bulldog about getting them.

"I wanted to help kids and make a real difference," Donald answered, but Carter got the feeling that was a stock answer Donald gave everyone. But he figured it was all he was going to get. "Look, if you don't want to stay here, you don't have to. Alex is going to be okay now. On Monday I'll find a good foster family for him, and I'll continue as his case worker. I promise you he won't get lost in the system."

"Is that what you want?" Carter took a bite of ice cream.

"It's what has to happen. I know you've grown attached to him, and that's fine, but—"

"You act like that's a bad thing," Carter interrupted. "Maybe I'll foster him."

Donald stared at him openmouthed and shook his head. "You can't. There are rules, and to be a foster parent there has to be someone at home who can take care of Alex. What are you going to do when you're working? You can't take him with you. Put him in day care? He needs someone who will be there for him while he's grieving for his mother. I know you want that to be you—"

"And that you can't wait to get rid of him and dump him in the system somewhere," Carter countered. Yeah it was probably a low blow, but the words were out before he could stop them.

Donald's eyes hardened. "Alex is one child, and on Monday, there will be others who need to be cared for. He isn't the only one I have to deal with. He's just the one you goaded me into taking into my home and caring for through the weekend."

"So you did this just because of me? The guy you fucked for a weekend and then turned a cold shoulder to." Carter pushed his bowl away.

"What do you want from me?" Donald asked with a small crack in his voice.

"The truth," Carter prompted.

"The truth… okay. The truth is that I would love to be able to take in every kid who crosses my path. They all look like Alex in some way. They're kids who have the worst possible things happen to them. I'd love to be able to solve all their problems. Hell, I'd love to be able to bring their parents back from the dead or instantly take away the addiction that's ruining their mom or dad's life and make them see what they're doing to their kids. But I can't." Donald kept his voice low, but the pain in it surprised Carter. Then it was gone. "So I have to follow the rules and work within the system. You do too. If you break them, then criminals go free. If I break them, then the people who care for kids like Alex don't get the money they need to keep providing temporary or longer-term homes for children like him."

"So now it's about money…."

"You're impossible, you know that?" Donald snapped.

"Why don't you just admit that you care about Alex?"

"Of course I care about him," Donald snarled. He placed both hands on the table and pushed himself up, glaring at Carter with enough heat that sweat broke out on Carter's back and he shifted uncomfortably. Fuck, that was hot, and he swallowed hard and looked away before he blushed beet red. They were talking about children, but getting Donald's blood boiling was a definite turn-on. After all, he remembered what had happened the last time he'd gotten Donald revved up. "I care about him a lot, but there's only so much I can do for him. Don't you see that?"

Carter stood, meeting Donald's gaze. He leaned over the table, slipped his arm around the back of Donald's neck, and then paused. Donald didn't stop him, so he pulled him forward and crashed their lips together. He nearly lost his balance with the small table between them, but hell, it was worth it. Donald tasted of chocolate, musk, and rich male. Carter instantly remembered that taste and the exquisite hard press of those lips on his. He broke the kiss and stared into Donald's eyes.

Donald snarled at him, but didn't pull any farther away, so Carter cut him off by kissing him again.

Slowly, Carter took small steps around the table, and once he was free of it he drew Donald into his arms and then pressed him back until Donald was up against the kitchen wall. Damn, he was hot, and the quivers that ran through Donald sent small shakes through him as well.

"I don't see guys more than once," Donald whispered when they came up for air.

"Do you want me to stop?" Carter asked, prepared to back away, even as he thrust his hips slightly, grinding against the hard ridge in Donald's pants.

"No," Donald whispered. "But we have to...." He put his hands on Carter's shoulders, holding him in place without pushing away. "Otherwise we'll be on the floor and... my back wasn't the same for a week after that." Donald colored. "Neither was my ass."

"Fine." Carter put more distance between them, even though that was the last thing he wanted. "But later...," he said in his deepest, richest voice, and Donald quivered. Fuck, that was glorious to see and did his geek heart good, especially when Donald nodded his agreement, his eyes big as saucers and as deep and dark as the ocean during a storm.`

Carter returned to the table and began eating the now melting ice cream. He watched Donald prowl around the kitchen, apparently unable to settle anywhere. Carter had obviously upset a little of Donald's emotional applecart. He was still trying to figure out if that was a good thing or not when Donald sat back down. Carter finished eating and took his bowl to the sink. He was about to return to the table when his phone rang. He answered it quickly, peering through the kitchen doorway to where Alex still slept on the sofa.

"Hi, Mom," Carter said.

"You know you can call me more than once every few weeks. Sometimes I wonder if you're lying dead in a ditch somewhere."

"I'm sorry." What the hell else was he to say? He turned to Donald and rolled his eyes but got the strangest look in return.

"Carter," his mother snapped slightly, "are you still there? There are times I think I'm talking to a brick wall."

"Sorry." He turned away from Donald. "I'm a little preoccupied. I'm helping a friend take care of a kid. He was abused and lost his mother, and there were no shelters available other than the county home, so he's staying with my friend."

There was a long pause. "So you aren't coming up for dinner?"

"Shit," Carter said. "I mean, crap. I forgot all about it. I'm here with Donald, and Alex is sleeping right now."

"Bring them along," she offered.

"Mom, I don't think that's a good idea. Alex's mother died and we had to tell him today. He's just turned five, but he acts younger because he hasn't been treated or raised very well. So while we told him, I don't think he understands, and...."

"Sweetheart, I raised four children and I know all about loss and heartache. Remember when your nana died? All of you were inconsolable for days. Bring them both down for lunch tomorrow. Your father and I never get to see you." He got the feeling his mother was hedging a little.

"Okay. I'll ask and get back to you today."

"Don't forget," his mother said.

"You know I rarely do," he countered. Carter couldn't remember the last time he'd forgotten one of his mother's dinners. He understood why it had completely slipped his mind, but he still felt bad about it. "I'll call you in a little while and let you know what's happening." He hung up and turned to Donald. "As you can guess, that was my mother. I was supposed to go to dinner tonight and forgot all about it."

"Was she angry? Because you can go if you need to."

"Mom's pretty cool. She raised four kids and I don't think anything fazes her. She did say that she'd like us all to come for lunch tomorrow. You and Alex."

Donald swallowed. "You want me to meet your mother?"

Carter couldn't help chuckling. "It isn't like we're dating, and this isn't some huge relationship commitment. Think about it. You don't have to work tomorrow, and it might be good for Alex to be out among people." The image of him hiding behind the bed in that filthy attic room flooded Carter's mind. "Who knows if he's ever been around

45

other kids, and I bet my brother, his wife, and their two boys will still be there if my mother gets her way."

"Where do they live?"

"Chambersburg. Not far." Carter peered into the other room and saw Alex stirring. "It could be good for him… and it would mean a home-cooked meal." Carter wasn't above playing the full-stomach card to get what he wanted. Guys were simple creatures in his view. They generally wanted three things: food, football, and sex. Hell, he did. If he could have sex while watching football and eating a chicken leg, that would be perfection. Well, maybe that was an exaggeration, but the food part was very important.

"That does sound nice," Donald said.

"When was the last time you had a home-cooked meal? Other than by your mother?" Carter asked. Instead of an answer, he initially got a blank stare. "I take it it's been a while."

"Yeah. A long time," Donald said softly. Carter wondered if he heard regret coloring his voice.

"Then you'll think about it?"

"Let me call my boss and see what she says. Since Alex is a ward of the state, I can't just take him anywhere. Granted, we're not leaving Pennsylvania, but this situation is already different enough that I want someone else to know what's going on."

"Does she know he's here?"

"Yeah. I told her. I'm qualified as a foster parent, so there was no issue there. But I don't officially have custody, so things are kind of in limbo."

"Mommy," Alex called from the other room.

"You go in to him," Donald said, but Carter shook his head and took Donald by the hand.

"I know you're used to being the bad guy and doing what has to be done. But not today. You get to comfort him and be the one who takes away whatever is scaring him, because I need to run out for about half an hour." Carter didn't give him a choice. He got Donald settled with Alex in his arms before hurrying out the door.

CHAPTER
Four

DONALD SAT with Alex on his lap, sniffling against his shoulder. Once Alex calmed down, he called his supervisor, Karla, to ask about taking Alex to Carter's parents' house the next day.

After he finished the call, Alex looked up at him and said, "But when is Mommy gonna come back from the angels?"

"She isn't," Donald said as gently as he could. "Your mommy is gone and she can't come back." He stood and slowly walked around the room. Alex was starting to get heavy, but Donald still walked and held him. "But there will be wonderful people to take care of you. I promise." He hoped the police would be able to find some of Alex's family. He knew Mifflintown—it was small and everyone knew everyone and many of them were related in one way or another. It was just a matter of tracing Alex's family until they found the closest relative. Hopefully someone Alex already knew was out there waiting for him.

Donald stopped pacing at a knock on the door and hurried to it, expecting it to be Carter. When he pulled open the door, a uniformed police officer he recognized stood on the steps.

"Mr. Ickle."

He nodded. "Officer Smith. Please call me Donald, and come in." Donald stepped back to let him enter and closed the door after him.

"Everyone just calls me Smith," he said with a smile. "Is the little guy doing all right?"

"Yes. We told him about his mother a little while ago, and he's been having a hard time." Alex lifted his head so he could see what was going on, but he clung tight to Donald, and Donald found it comforting in a strange way.

"Well, we've been looking into his family. His mother was an only child, and she apparently ran away right after high school." Donald motioned for him to sit, but Smith shook his head. "His grandparents passed away a few years ago. There are likely some distant relatives, and the police in Mifflintown have said they'll try to help...."

"But the closest relatives, the ones who could step in, aren't there." Donald knew the drill well. "What about her remains?"

"They'll be turned over to the county and she'll likely be cremated," Smith said. Thankfully Alex seemed to be paying little attention and simply rested in Donald's arms with his head on Donald's shoulder.

"So, basically, at least for now...."

"It would be best if he remained in your care," Smith said.

"Damn," Donald said softly. "I was really hoping for something better." He knew Carter would be upset about this bit of news as well.

"I need to get back, but I wanted to stop by and let you know what we have so far as far as this little guy is concerned."

"What about Harker?"

"No," Alex whined and began to cry. "No spankings. I not bad. I being good." Then he began to cry again and rubbed his bottom as though it hurt.

"I heard about the videos." Smith shook his head. "We have enough to charge him and put him away for a long time. The more information we get from the videos, the more charges the DA seems to add."

There was another knock on the door and then Carter opened it and came inside. The idea that Carter felt comfortable enough to just come in made him happy. Lord knew why he felt that way, but he did. Carter closed the door with his elbow, carrying a plastic bag in each hand. He set them on the sofa and turned to the other officer.

"What brings you by?" Carter asked after shaking hands with his colleague. Smith brought him up to speed on Alex's family situation. "I'll see what I can find as well."

"There's a detective on that. But we do need your expertise. There are deposits into Harker's bank account, regular ones from someone, and we need to trace them. He isn't talking at all and has lawyered up tight. But we think he was being paid for his video productions and we'd like to figure out who's behind it. We're still gathering information but hope you can lend a hand. The chief asked for you to get on it first thing Monday. In the meantime, we'll continue to pursue other areas of inquiry."

"I could do it now," Carter volunteered.

"The chief has been in touch with child services, and they agree that helping the kid the way you are is for the best right now." Smith motioned for Carter to step away, and the two of them talked quietly. "I need to be going," Smith said when they were finished. Donald said good-bye, and Carter opened the door for him and then closed it after he left.

"Is there a big secret?" Donald asked as he put Alex down on the sofa.

"Not from you," Carter said and sat next to Alex on the sofa. "I brought you a few things." Carter pulled toys out of the bags and began opening the packages. He started with a wooden train pull toy and then opened a truck and some blocks. A small pile grew around Alex, and he stared at them. "Those are for you." Carter put the packaging in the bags, and Donald took them.

"That was very nice of you," Donald said as Alex slipped off the sofa and began to play with the blocks, making very little sound as he did. Donald noted that he'd already learned to try to be invisible. He watched him for a few minutes, playing by himself as quiet as a mouse. "What I don't understand is why the research they want you to do can wait until Monday. It seems to me that the information you could provide might be valuable." He turned to Carter.

"My particular skills are only valued when other avenues have been exhausted," Carter answered. "The chief is a traditional police officer. He believes in getting answers by pounding the pavement, speaking to witnesses, and even intuition, but the computer digging I do... he only comes to me as a last resort. It's his normal way of doing things." Carter shrugged. "My work life is very different from what you see on television. I've solved cases and helped identify new lines of inquiry in cases, but my work isn't particularly valued. That's why I wanted a chance at some actual time on the street."

Donald turned away from Alex. "I don't understand."

"I'm the department geek. Don't get me wrong—I love what I do and I love being a police officer. There's nothing better than digging into a case and finding that piece of information no one else has because I can take different pieces of seemingly unrelated data and find the connection." Carter's expression brightened and his eyes lit from within. It made him incredibly attractive.

"You've never looked like a geek other than your glasses."

"I've always looked like a geek. In school I was a super nerd: math club, good at my studies, the kid most likely to be folded into a locker. But as long as I can remember I wanted to be a policeman. So I went to the academy, got through the physical requirements with hard work and determination, and got the job on the force here. Only to be branded the geek once again and relegated with my computers to the basement, where they put all the other things they aren't quite sure what to do with. When my request for a shift in duty was approved, I hoped they might come to see me as an officer like everyone else, but I guess not. They were just humoring me, and aside from a few exceptions, I'm still just the department computer guy."

Donald was at a loss for words. He'd never seen Carter that way. He was a good-looking man with incredible eyes and—Donald had come to realize—a huge heart. "I'm sorry." He glanced to Alex and then back at Carter. "I spoke with my boss, and she saw nothing wrong with Alex and me going to your mother's for lunch tomorrow, so if the invitation is still good, I think we'd both like to go." Donald swallowed and turned away once again. He hated feeling vulnerable, and fuck if that wasn't what came over him in a huge wave. Carter was such a nice guy. Sure, during their weekend together they'd had a hot time, but that had just been sex… at least it had been at the time.

He could feel his heart engaging, a soft warmth running through him. He sighed softly and turned away from both Alex and Carter. He slowly walked to the kitchen and turned on the cold water. He filled a glass, added ice, and then waited for the water to chill before gulping it the way a drunk would hard alcohol.

The cold went down his throat and settled in his stomach. That was a feeling he understood. He wasn't going to let Alex or Carter get around his carefully built defenses. He had relied on himself for a long time, and he'd learned that was all he could rely on. That lesson had been drilled into him by life time and time again, and he sure as hell wasn't going to forget that now.

Laughter drifted into the kitchen, high-pitched giggles that built, died away, and built again. Donald turned from the sink, following the laughter like it was a siren song. Alex lay on the floor with Carter tickling him. The giggles filled the house with mirth, and Donald smiled. He tried to remember the last time there had been laughter of any kind in the house. His life was not one that included a great deal of laughter. His work certainly didn't inspire mirth of any kind.

But his life was safe, and that was the most important thing. Laughter, he could live without, and its absence was a small price to pay to keep turmoil, worry, disappointment, and despair away from him. They had been companions for such a long time that once he'd put them behind him, he'd vowed never to let them become a permanent part of his life again. Donald couldn't allow it under any circumstances.

"Come on in and see what Alex built," Carter called, and Donald rejoined them in the living room. A tower of blocks as tall as Alex sat on the wooden floor. He grinned widely. The thing looked ready to topple at any second, but Alex seemed so proud of it. "Okay," Carter said, and Alex swooped down with his arm, pushing the tower over. The blocks clattered to the floor, making all kinds of racket. Alex laughed and immediately began gathering the blocks and building another tower.

This one toppled over on its own. "Watch, Alex. If you put the blocks just like this," Donald said as he carefully placed the blocks so they lined up with each other, "they won't fall over as easily." Alex immediately mimicked him and lined the blocks up very closely. "That's it."

"I build it high." He scurried to get the blocks that had traveled the farthest and added them to the tower.

"I thought I'd order a pizza for dinner if that's okay," Carter said. "I've been eating your food and...."

"That would be nice," Donald said.

"You play too," Alex commanded, pointing up at him. He sat on the floor and watched as Alex toppled the tower once again and then scrambled to pick up the far-flung blocks.

"He doesn't want to be alone," Carter said as he reached for a block. "I know it seems strange for us… but it will hit him eventually."

"What?" Alex asked as he began stacking the blocks.

"Nothing, buddy," Carter said and handed him a block. "I'm going to order the pizza. Why don't you two keep playing?" Carter got up and went into the kitchen. Donald heard him on the phone placing the order.

"Look," Alex said, calling his attention to the now rebuilt tower. Donald hadn't even realized he'd been watching the way Carter's jeans hugged his narrow hips until Alex called his attention back.

"Are you ready to knock it down?" Donald made earthquake noises and shook Alex lightly. He giggled and kicked the tower over. Then Donald scooped him into his arms, holding him close while they both laughed.

"The pizza will be here in half an hour." Carter sat down with them, and they built many towers—with all of them meeting their end at the hand of Godzilla Alex—until the pizza arrived.

Alex didn't seem to know what pizza was when they first sat him at the table. He poked at it and smelled it, initially turning up his nose. But when he saw Carter taking a bite, he gave it a try, and after that he ate until he seemed ready to burst.

"Why don't you go play for a few minutes?" Carter said as he wiped Alex's hands and face after he was done. Alex slipped off the chair and raced back into the other room. "It kills me to see him eat like he doesn't believe he's going to eat again."

Donald nodded. "That will go away, but it can take time. His mind and body need to build up the trust that food will be there when he needs it." Donald peered into the other room. Alex ran the small truck Carter had bought for him around the floor. Most kids would have made engine noises, but Alex was silent.

"He's so quiet."

"It's all a result of the way he was treated. I imagine he was punished for being loud, and God knows what else was done to him."

"Maybe we can ask him," Carter suggested. "He's talked about being afraid of bad men. Remember? I'd like to ask him what the bad men did. It might help him give voice to what he's carrying around in that little head of his. It could also help us figure out who's behind this whole thing."

"Do you think he saw the other man at some point?" Donald asked, thinking that was a stretch. If what he'd been told was correct, then tracing the money seemed the likely way to find him.

"People don't pay attention to children when they're in the room. They think they don't hear or remember what they're told. And adults are especially likely to discount someone as small as Alex. So maybe he did see this guy, or maybe he heard Harker on the telephone, I don't know. But I was hoping you could give me some pointers as to how I should talk to him."

Donald snapped his gaze back from where he'd been watching Alex. "You want my help? The cops I know... hell, the last time I had one of my kids questioned by the police, I became the bad guy because I wouldn't allow a lot of his questions." Donald kept expecting the übercop he sometimes saw in Carter to come out. In Donald's view, Carter was an interesting mix. He was a cop, and Donald saw those traits in him—the decision making, the power, the ability to get what he wanted. But he also saw the geek, the guy willing to ask for help. Sometimes he had a difficult time putting it all together.

"Of course I want your help. I need to be able to do this without scaring Alex half to death. He woke up screaming last night because he was afraid of the bad men."

"And he'll probably do it again tonight. His little mind will play all the things he's afraid of." Donald glanced into the other room for what felt like the millionth time. "It's natural for him, and even though he's had a pretty decent day, all things considered, he'll probably have a rough night. The grief over his mother is going to catch up with him eventually."

"So when do you think I should talk to him?" Carter asked.

Donald thought about it. "You'll know when the time is right. It'll just happen, and you'll ask the questions and he'll answer. Just don't think of it as an interrogation." Donald paused a second. "When you ask him, think of yourself as a parent. Be gentle, keep your voice soft, and coax his answers from him. Also, don't be surprised if talking about it scares the hell out of him. He's likely been told over and over that he's never to talk about these things. That he was bad and that what was done to him was all his fault. Abusers are very good at making kids think the abuse is because of something they did. That's how they maintain power, and without that the abuse can't happen."

"Okay. Should you be there?"

"When you talk to him, I'll be close, but two on one isn't going to be productive. If you want him to answer your questions, you need to be gentle and caring… just be yourself. But you should make sure I can hear, for his protection."

"You know I'd never hurt Alex," Carter said a little more loudly than necessary.

"I know. But it's for your protection too. You're trying to get information that you'll use in a police investigation, so we need to follow the rules, and a child is never questioned without an advocate. Right now his advocate is me. You know that—you're just a little too close to the situation."

"Yeah," Carter sighed. "We should make sure he gets his bath and then into his pajamas. Last night was rough, and I agree, tonight is likely to be a repeat."

"Come on, Alex," Donald said. "It's bath and pajama time."

Alex ignored him and continued playing with the blocks. He built the tower and knocked it over. Then he stood there, shyly looking up at Donald, before taking off and heading toward the back of the sofa once again. Donald stopped Carter from going to get him. "Alex. You aren't in trouble and you haven't done anything wrong. So come out from behind the sofa and pick up your blocks. Then we'll go upstairs and you can have a bath and put your pajamas on. You can come down and play a little more afterward."

"Promise?" Alex asked without coming out.

"Yes. Mr. Carter and I will never hurt you." Donald stood and waited. Eventually Alex poked his head out and then stepped away from the sofa. Donald held out his hand and waited for Alex to take it. Then, after they picked up the blocks together, he led Alex up the stairs.

TWO HOURS later, after bath, a snack, and more towers that crashed to the floor, Carter put Alex to bed. Carter had bought him a book along with the toys and now sat with Alex in his arms, reading *Curious*

George to him. The sight brought tears to Donald's eyes as he wondered when Alex had last been read a bedtime story, if ever. Now Alex was asleep in his bed, holding his bunny.

"That was wonderful how you handled him when he was hiding," Carter whispered from behind him. Donald tensed a little as Carter slid his arms around his waist and then he relaxed, leaning back against him.

"Carter...," Donald began. He wanted to remind him that things hadn't changed between them. But danged if Carter didn't slip a hand under his shirt, rubbing small circles on his belly. Donald's excitement level went from zero to stratospheric in a matter of seconds, and he let Carter tug him closer and away from Alex's room.

"You'll make a great father," Carter whispered and then sucked on his right ear. Donald closed his eyes, inhaling deeply, filling his nostrils with Carter's deep, almost woodsy scent. He remembered it from the last time they were together and it instantly took him back.

"Let's not talk about that now." Donald slowly turned around. Carter had made him a promise earlier. At the time Donald had been overwhelmed, and he wasn't sure if this was a good idea, but Carter continued pressing him back, ramping up the energy in his kisses with each and every step until they were in Donald's bedroom with the door closed and locked.

"What do you want to talk about?" Carter asked, and Donald groaned when Carter tugged off his shirt and tossed it away. Then he ran warm, strong, confident hands down his back and cupped his ass hard. "We can talk about how firm you are." Carter slid a hand into the back of his jeans, as bold and forward as anything. Donald quivered as Carter slipped a finger between his cheeks, lightly tapping his opening. "How much you like this." Carter sucked on his ear again. "I can feel you twitching for me. You want this so bad you can't stand it."

Carter's hot breath on Donald's wet ear drove him insane. "Carter.... Jesus...."

He pulled back and Carter tugged open his belt and pulled the buttons on his fly. "Damn, I love the muffled pop of your buttons giving it up for me."

Donald's legs vibrated and then downright shook when Carter pushed the waistband of his boxers aside and took his cock in hand, gripping it hard, stroking with purpose. Donald thrust his hips, driving his dick through Carter's fingers, and when he pushed back, Carter pressed a finger to his opening.

Carter seemed to know exactly how much to give and when to pull back. Donald had been revved up to come when Carter eased back. He didn't pull away, but kept Donald from falling over the edge. Then, before he knew it, Donald tumbled onto the bed, bouncing as Carter prowled after him. God, the man was an animal—fierce, wild, and yet controlled enough to give Donald what he wanted.

Carter tugged off his jeans and underwear, strewing them on the floor. "God, I love you like this," Carter nearly growled as he slowly crawled between Donald's legs and dipped his head to swipe his tongue up Donald's aching cock. He groaned and his cock leaped toward Carter, wanting him; he needed more. But Carter took it slow, moving up Donald's body until he could lick and suck on a nipple as he raised Donald's arms over his head. "Naked, laid out, wanting me." Carter stopped, gaze boring into him. "There is nothing and no one hotter in the entire world than you are right now."

"Jesus," Donald groaned.

"I never lie, and you are amazing. I want to roll you over and slide into you forever."

Donald quivered as those words rumbled through his brain. Hell, he'd turned halfway over before Carter stopped him. Locking their gazes, Carter tugged off his shirt, and Donald reached forward, running his hands over the planes on Carter's chest. Fuck, he loved that strength. "There's no geek here," he said. He ran his thumbs over Carter's nipples and reveled in the way Carter's muscles rippled under his hand. He was doing that to Carter, making his pecs shake and dance.

He wanted Carter naked, just as he was, but Carter seemed to want to take his time, and Donald wasn't going to argue or fight. So many of his encounters were fast and unsatisfying, but Carter had been anything but that the last time they were together.

Carter kissed him, taking possession of Donald's mouth. He closed his arms around Carter, and soon they had rolled on the bed with Donald looking down into Carter's eyes. How in the hell could he have missed those? His eyes were a warm brown, and right now they shone up at him. Carter placed his hands behind his head. "You have me all to yourself. What do you plan to do with me?" Donald wanted to smack that wry smile off Carter's face, but he chose to kiss it away instead.

"You're very sure of yourself."

Carter stroked Donald's cheek, a gentle gesture combined with the slight rough of Carter's hands. "I know you, Donald. I see the way you look at me."

Donald turned his head, but Carter touched his chin, bringing his gaze back to Carter's.

"Don't you know that I look at you the same way?" With the lightest touch, Carter brought their lips together. Donald's essence screamed out for more, but Carter kept the touch gentle, allowing him to taste and savor. His lips were perfect, and God did Carter know how to kiss, with firm moist lips that took and gave in equal measure. Donald wanted him, ached for him. But he kept a mental distance. He had to.

It would be easy to let himself get completely caught up in the moment, and when that happened he'd forget himself, his defenses would crumble, and that would be all. He'd be bare, laid open for Carter, and then, as so many times before, when it counted the most, what he wanted would be taken away and he'd have nothing.

"Hey," Carter whispered. "Don't pull away. I can feel you doing it. Right now it's just you and me. That's all I want. Just you." Carter kissed him again, taking possession of Donald's mouth with his tongue, and Donald was a total goner. He tried to hold on, but it was too much and Carter overwhelmed him. All he could do was hold on for dear life. "That's it." Carter kissed him again and then licked down his neck, the tip of his tongue blazing a trail. Donald stretched and lifted his chin, giving Carter access, wanting whatever he was willing to give. He'd pick up the pieces later.

Donald groaned as Carter sucked his chest, worrying a nipple with his tongue and lips until Donald rolled his head back and forth on the pillow and finally stilled Carter's head to make the sensation stop. Each touch built on the other like small ripples in a pond. Except in this case they built and grew into rolling waves that threatened to overwhelm him.

"Carter, for God's sake!" Donald gasped.

Carter chuckled and took pity on him. He moved lower, then licked up Donald's shaft and blew on his wet skin, sending waves of lust through him. Donald swallowed hard, gasping and whining as he tried not to scream his delicious frustration at the top of his lungs. Finally Carter parted his lips, and after confirming he had Donald's rapt attention, he slowly sucked him inside.

Donald lolled his head back, arms splayed to the side as he gave himself over to the heated sensation around him. This was what he remembered from the last time they were together. No one had ever made him wish for something so badly and withheld it to the point where he'd nearly come apart, and then given it to him at the moment of highest need the way Carter seemed to. Carter knew Donald's limits and pushed up against them before giving him a reward that damned near melted his brain.

Carter sucked him deep, taking all of Donald and holding him there in a nearly unparalleled demonstration of control. When he slid his lips back up the shaft and released him, Donald blew out the breath he'd been holding only to have Carter suck him deep again and take his breath completely away.

"Fuck, you're like fine food. I can't get enough," Carter whispered between breaths before taking him once again.

"Carter...." Donald tried to warn him as pressure built and his head began the tingly, floaty sensation that portended release. Carter continued sucking him, driving Donald higher and higher. He pressed his eyes closed, legs and arms quivering as he held on as long as he could and then tumbled into blissful release.

Donald's mouth hung open as he came with Carter swallowing around him, taking everything he had to give. When the high of orgasm passed, Donald lay unmoving on the bed. Breathing was all his sweat-covered body could manage.

"Did I kill you?" Carter asked playfully.

"No, but dang near." Donald smiled as the bed moved and Carter lay down next to him, skin to skin, pants now gone. "But I have to say, what a way to go." He continued breathing heavily as Carter pulled him to him, stroking his back slowly until Donald could see straight once again. "I swear you were going to suck my brains out."

"Mission accomplished." Carter kissed him and he tasted his own salty sweetness on Carter's tongue as Carter turned Donald onto his back, pressing him into the mattress, Carter's thick, long cock sliding along Donald's hip.

"I don't have anything in the house," Donald whispered. "At least I don't think so." He turned toward the nightstand, and Carter pulled open the drawer. He rummaged and then turned to him with a grin, holding up a rainbow-colored foil packet. "Thank goodness for pride."

"Amen," Carter whispered as he dropped the packet on the sheets. He shifted between Donald's legs and spread his legs before leaning forward. That simple movement brought their lips in contact and lifted Donald's legs in one smooth movement. As Carter kissed him, he ran his hands down Donald's flanks and over his butt, teasing him.

Donald wrapped his arms around Carter's neck, groaning softly as Carter teased the sensitive skin around his opening. When Carter broke their kiss, he ran his hands up his legs to his knees and pressed upward, sliding down his body. "What are you...?" Donald gasped when Carter licked near his opening. It felt so damn good he had to put a hand in his mouth to stop the cry that threatened to erupt.

When Carter stopped his exquisite torture, Donald gasped and held his breath, waiting to see what he had in mind next. Carter knelt in front of him, his lips close enough to Donald's for him to feel his warm breath. "I want you more than I've wanted anything or anyone." Carter tore open the condom and rolled it on. Donald waited, unable to move in case Carter changed his mind. Then slowly, Carter pressed to his opening.

He resisted at first, and then like a sunrise, his body opened and lights flashed behind his eyes as Carter slid deeper and deeper inside of him. The man was big, and Donald breathed through his mouth to keep his body from going nuts. Carter paused, and Donald concentrated on relaxing his muscles. Then Carter proceeded, filling him with exquisite heat.

When he started to move, Donald gasped and moaned. He felt so damn good. Carter leaned over him, their kisses sloppy but perfect as they moved together. Damn, he loved how Carter filled him over and over again.

"Do you have any idea how good you feel?" Carter whispered when he stilled completely, cock throbbing inside Donald's body. Carter lightly stroked Donald's chest. "You're heaven and Shangri-La all rolled into one."

"No. I'm just me," Donald protested. He was so out of control he needed to ground himself somehow.

Carter withdrew and slowly drove back into him. Donald gasped, and the small amount of control he'd been able to muster flew right out the window. Carter shifted slightly, and when he moved, Donald gasped and thrust his hand into his mouth to keep from yelling in heart-stopping, breath-stealing, overwhelming pleasure. Whatever Carter did, he played Donald like a fine instrument, melody, harmony, and percussion all rolled into one.

Donald pulled his palm from his mouth and reached down to stroke his cock. He needed more, and with each stroke, the intensity built. "How do you do that?" Donald asked.

"What?"

"Make me forget who I am?" Donald swallowed as Carter snapped his hips. "I don't care about anything but you." The entire world seemed to have narrowed to this bed, him, and Carter. Nothing else mattered, and it was frightening as hell and as liberating and incredible as anything he had ever experienced. Carter leaned close, thrusting hard and driving Donald to heaven. He held on for dear life and gave his pleasure over. It was in good hands. And those brown eyes shone with each and every movement, telling him that at least for now Donald was the very center of the universe. He liked knowing that, for the moment, he was the center of something.

"I want you to come with me," Carter whispered. "I'm getting so close I can taste it, and I want to feel you come around me."

"I'm almost there," Donald whimpered.

"I know. I can feel it. You're driving me wild with those little sounds you make and the way you shake whenever I touch you just right." Carter thrust slow and deep, pushing Donald toward ecstasy and tearing at the remnants of his control. "I love the way your eyes shine and the way your breath hitches." He did it again and Donald held his breath. "See?" Carter whispered into his ear. "I know you're so close you're thrumming with energy. I can read you like a book, and it's one hell of a best seller."

"Carter... I...." He stroked faster and harder, desperate for that last bit of sensation.

"Yeah. I'm right there with you, so let it go. Just give it up for me."

Energy coursed through him, and Donald stroked himself, gripping tight as his climax ripped from him. He felt Carter still and then throb inside him. Donald didn't move, and Carter didn't either. They stayed just like that, their gazes locked as though they were under a spell. Maybe he was. Maybe Carter had him under some sort of spell, because he could remain with Carter pressed to him, their breath mingling, sweat pouring off both of them, for the rest of his life.

Their bodies separating sent a shudder through Donald and seemed to act as a signal for both of them. Carter lay down next to him and took care of the condom, throwing it away and then leaving the bed to head to the bathroom. Water ran, and then Carter returned, washing him up as gently as if he were made of precious china. It felt good to be cared for. But Donald refused to let himself get used to it. Carter was being nice and he liked it, but it was just for the night. Things would be different in the morning. Everything was always different in the cold light of day.

Carter took the cloth and towel back to the bathroom and then got into bed. He turned off the light, and Donald waited to see what would happen. Carter rolled onto his side, extended his arm, and pulled Donald to him. "You need to stop thinking so much."

"I do?"

"Oh yeah. That's when you start wondering about everything instead of just being happy." Carter yawned and didn't release him. Donald fell asleep before he found out if Carter ever did.

CHAPTER
Five

CARTER WOKE in the middle of the night. Donald had moved away from him slightly, so he was able to get out of bed without waking him. The man was exhausted. Carter smiled to himself as he remembered the glazed look in Donald's eyes as he came for the second time, like he'd been having an out-of-body experience. The thought that he'd brought Donald to that place was amazing to him. Carter turned and watched Donald sleep for a few seconds, relaxed and peaceful, before pulling on his underwear and pants and leaving the room.

He wasn't exactly sure what had awakened him, but he peeked into Alex's room and found he'd kicked off all his covers. Carter walked in and pulled them up, but Alex's little legs began to move as though he were running in his sleep. Carter placed his hand on Alex's back and rubbed small circles. Alex settled quickly and grew quiet, his legs stilling. Carter pulled the covers back up and turned to leave the room.

"Mommy!" Alex yelled. By the time Carter turned around, Alex had sat up in bed. "I want Mommy!"

Carter lifted him into his arms and held him, quieting him as best he could. Alex's yells dissolved into tears. "I know, buddy. I'm here," Carter crooned as a lump built in his throat. He wasn't always going to be there. In a day or two, Alex would go to a proper foster home. When that happened, who would comfort Alex in the middle of the night? All he knew was it wouldn't be him. He'd thought about trying to find out if he could take Alex, but there were obstacles. Big ones. He was a single man, which wasn't an issue in itself. But he was also a police officer and sometimes worked very odd hours. It would be different if he had a partner, someone who could help take care of Alex while he was at work. Given his age, Alex should be entering school soon, but Carter knew he wasn't ready for that. He was so immature that the other kids would make fun of him.

"Carter," Donald whispered from the doorway.

"He was having a bad dream," Carter said, turning toward Donald.

"The bad men were chasing me," Alex whispered once his tears abated. "I runned and runned, but they still found me." He rubbed his bottom and then hugged Carter around the neck.

Carter lifted his gaze, looking to Donald over Alex's shoulder. He knew he had to have that talk with Alex pretty soon. He had to try to find out what Alex knew. "It's okay. The bad men aren't here. Just me and Mr. Donald, and we aren't going to let the bad men get you. I promise." The words were out of his mouth before he could stop them. He shouldn't be making promises to Alex because he might not always be there to keep them. He meant that he and Donald would keep the bad men away for now, but what about tomorrow, or the next week?

"I runned and they found me," Alex muttered through drying tears. He was so tired Carter could already feel him relaxing into his embrace.

"You're safe now." Carter cradled him and pressed his eyes closed. Alex was very quickly winding his way into his heart. He could feel it, and come Monday morning, it was going to hurt when Alex went into foster care. "I'm going to put you back in bed. You hold Bunny." Carter picked up the stuffed toy and handed it to Alex. It damn near killed him the way Alex clutched the bunny to him as if it was the only friend he had in the world.

Carefully, he helped Alex back into bed and covered him up. "Good night, buddy. Sleep tight, and I'll see you in the morning."

Alex went right back to sleep, and Carter quietly stepped to the door. He watched Alex sleep until Donald placed his hand on his shoulder.

"Come back to bed," Donald said. He took Carter's hand, leading him back into his bedroom.

Carter crawled under the covers, and Donald joined him, moving up against him almost immediately. Carter encircled Donald in his arms, wondering just what he had in mind. Donald's slow, deep, soul-touching kiss told him everything he needed to know, and they made quiet, deep, gentle love under the covers. When their passion was spent, Carter listened to Donald's soft breathing in the lingering warmth and wondered just how long this would last. He'd spent an equally passionate and caring weekend with Donald before, only to have it end with a cold shoulder and an appearance from Donald's icy alter ego. He hoped that wouldn't happen again, but he needed to be prepared for it, just in case.

After a little while, Donald rolled over, and Carter pulled him close. He could worry about what would be or he could enjoy what he had right now. He tugged Donald to him, kissed him lightly on the shoulder, and fell asleep.

"WHAT ARE you doing?" Donald asked when he wandered into the kitchen in his barely fastened bathrobe. Dang, he was gorgeous, with that strip of chest and belly that showed to his navel.

"I thought I'd make breakfast. But you do realize you don't have a thing in this house. Pancakes are out, as are waffles." Carter opened the refrigerator and pulled out a carton of orange juice.

"So what are we having? Did you wave your magic wand?"

"Smartass," Carter retorted.

"I'm here so seldom that I don't keep a lot in the house. Usually I grab something in the morning on my way to my first appointment."

"Well, I found some bacon in the freezer, and there's some bread left, so I'm making eggs again. I hope that's okay."

"It's great. I somehow doubt Alex will mind. He wolfed them down yesterday."

Alex ate everything put in front of him with equal gusto, and Carter didn't think that would change soon. Water ran upstairs, and Donald left the kitchen while Carter finished making breakfast. Donald returned with Alex a few minutes later. Alex immediately climbed into the chair and looked expectantly at him, licking his lips but not saying a word.

Once Carter had everything ready, he made up a plate for Alex and placed it in front of him. "Take your time. There's more if you want it, so you don't need to rush."

"Okay, Mr. Carter," Alex said and then tore into the food the way he always had. Not a crumb left his plate as he shoveled the food into his mouth. Carter sat next to him and touched his arm.

"I mean it. Stop a second. You can have all you want. I promise." He kept his voice light, but it was important to him that Alex understand that his food wasn't going to be taken away and that he was going to eat again at lunch.

Donald touched his arm and shook his head. "It's all right, Alex, just eat." Donald got a plate, and Carter joined him by the stove. "He'll learn eventually. But right now it's too soon for his instincts to stop. It's only been a few days, and he's still in survival mode. It could take months or longer for him to feel safe, but it needs to come in his own time."

Carter nodded and watched as Alex finished up the food on his plate. The kid was a vacuum cleaner. Carter gave him a little more, and this time Alex paused to say, "Thank you." Of course then he went back to stuffing his mouth and only stopped to drink some juice.

"I just wish he hadn't had to go through all that," Carter whispered.

"I know. But you can't take that away simply by making him eat slower. He's been deprived, and that deprivation will take time to heal." To Carter's surprise, Donald slipped an arm around his waist. "We've done a good job helping him take those first steps, but months of hurt are not going to be smoothed over and forgotten in a few days. It takes a lot longer than we have with him. But it will happen, with care and understanding." Donald squeezed slightly and then released him.

Carter began making up plates for the two of them. He handed Donald one and then walked to the table. Alex had slowed down and was staring at a nearly empty plate with eyes as big as saucers. He put down his fork, picked up a piece of bacon, and began chewing it.

"I think he's getting full," Donald said. "You can go in the living room and play if you're done." Alex looked at both of them and then slipped off his chair. "Don't forget to use the potty if you have to, and wash your hands after." Alex bounded toward the powder room, and Carter listened for the flush and then the water running in the sink. Then Alex hurried out, and soon the blocks hit the floor in a cacophony of wood on wood.

"What do I need to do to become a foster parent?" Carter asked.

Donald nodded. "I've been waiting for you to ask me that. You need a bedroom for him and you need to arrange for child care. Given that you're a police officer, the background checks will not be an issue. But it's a big responsibility, and I hate to say it, but with the hours you work…. If you weren't alone, it would be a lot easier."

"There aren't single foster parents?" Carter asked.

"Yes, there are. A lot of them work from home or run small group homes, and the state helps with the care of the kids. It takes a pretty special person to be a foster parent. But you know that isn't what you want, not in the long term. I can give you an application to fill out if you like, and I'm sure I can get you approved right away. That wouldn't be an issue."

"But you don't think I'd be a good foster parent?" Carter asked.

"I think you'd be wonderful. But I'm also afraid that you would find it difficult to meet the demands caring for Alex would put on you. Are you still living in the same place?" Donald asked, and Carter nodded. "Then it isn't really big enough. You have one bedroom, and Alex can't stay in the same room as you. He could share a room with other children, but not with you. So you'd have to move."

"So I'll move. I can afford a larger place." He was starting to get excited about the prospect.

"Okay," Donald said, his voice tinged with disbelief. "What sort of child care are you picturing? I could help some, but I get calls at odd hours too. Day care isn't too difficult to arrange. But you work nights and weekends sometimes." Carter nodded. He could see where Donald was going with this. "Your hours aren't predictable, so you'd almost need a nanny, and that can get very expensive." Donald touched his hand. "I understand how you feel. Alex is a great kid, and I know you've opened your heart to him."

"A lot of good that is going to do either of us." Carter set down his fork with a clang and pushed his plate away. He knew he was acting petulant, but he hated getting bad news or being told he couldn't have something. It grated on him.

Carter's dad had told him he was a fool for wanting to become a police officer. "You could make a lot of money designing your own applications," his father had said. "Besides, how are you going to pass the physical requirements?" Carter had proved his father wrong, and everyone who had ever shoved him around or stuffed him in a locker as well. He was a geek, but now he was a strong one, and it was his determination not to be told no that had carried him through.

"Hey. When he's placed you can go visit him. So many kids end up alone when they enter the foster care system." Donald paused and turned away, but not before Carter saw momentary hurt flash across his face. A crash in the other room, signaling the demise of one of Alex's towers, made them jump a little, and then the expression he'd seen was gone. It had been just for a fleeting moment, a flash so quick that if not for his police training, Carter would have wondered if he'd seen it at all.

"I suppose," Carter said.

"If you really want to help Alex, then when you get back to work tomorrow, trace Alex's family and try to find a relative. It's best if he's with family, and who knows, he could have a ton of aunts, uncles, and cousins who will adore him and be able to tell him stories about his mother."

"But what if there aren't any? Could I adopt him?"

"You could apply to adopt him, yes. But the same requirements would apply as far as child care, living space, and everything else." Donald sighed. "These are not decisions that should be made lightly, but if you truly want to try to do either of them, I'll help any way I can."

"Thanks," Carter said.

"If you're not hungry, then go on in and play with him. Since you cooked I'll clean up."

Carter's appetite was long gone, so he took his plate to the sink. "I need to go to my place before we head to my mother's. We can walk over, and then I can drive."

"Sounds perfect." Donald checked his watch. "When do we need to leave?" He chewed slightly on his lower lip.

"By eleven, so in a couple hours." He walked back to the table. "There's no need to be nervous. My mom can be pushy, but she's going to like both you and Alex, I know it."

"What about your father?" Donald asked.

Carter shrugged. "Dad is Dad. He had his expectations for all of us, and if we somehow veer from them, then he takes it as some sort of failure on his part... and ours. He and I don't talk very much, even when we're in the same room." Carter lightly squeezed Donald's shoulder and then went into the living room, where blocks were strewn all over the floor and Alex almost silently weaved his car around them in a preschool obstacle course. Carter sat on the sofa and watched Alex play. At one point, Alex stopped, put his bunny in the back of the truck, and gave him a ride around the room. Once Donald was finished with the dishes, he took Alex upstairs to get him dressed. As soon as he was done, Alex bounded back down the stairs and went right back to giving Bunny truck rides.

CARTER AND Donald spent the next couple of hours playing with Alex. They had a good time, and every time Alex's laughter filled the room, Carter counted it as a victory. Hearing him laugh was the most amazing sound ever. "We need to get ready to go," Carter prompted. "So put your toys away and get Bunny."

Alex came to a stop and stared at him, holding his bunny in front of him like a shield. "No bad men," Alex cried and looked around, probably for a hiding place. "I be good."

"Alex," Donald said. "We're going to see Carter's mom and dad for lunch. That's all."

Alex stared at him with watery eyes. "Your mommy?"

"Yes. We're going to see my mother," Carter said.

"I wanna see my mommy," Alex said, head lowering and his little arms falling to his side. "I don't want her with the angels no more."

Carter scooped him up and held him, silently cursing himself. He should have known that would set Alex off.

"It's all right. He's going to be dealing with this for a while," Donald said. "Come on. Let's make sure we have everything we need, and then we can walk over to your place." Donald gathered the blocks into a bag and hurried upstairs. When he came back down, the bag was stuffed nearly to the brim. "Is there anything else we need?"

"It looks like you packed everything."

"It pays to be prepared," Donald countered. "I'll get my keys." He hurried away and returned a few minutes later with a booster seat as well, and they left the house.

Once they were outside, Carter put Alex down, and after putting Bunny in the bag, they each held a hand as they walked the few blocks to Carter's. He let them in the building and led them up the stairs.

The apartment overlooked the main street of town. "I need to clean up quick and change clothes. It shouldn't take long and then we can go." Carter didn't have many guests at his place, and he was thankful he led a simple and relatively clean life. He hurried to his bedroom and closed the door. He stripped out of his clothes and dumped them in the nearly full hamper. Then he went into the bathroom and started the water. He took one of the fastest showers in history and dried off in record time before dressing and joining Donald and Alex in the living room.

He stopped in the doorway and stared. Donald had Alex on his shoulders as he walked around the apartment, and Alex was laughing at the top of his lungs. The amazing thing was the grin on Donald's face—like he'd just won the lottery. Alex had his fingers curled in Donald's jet black hair, and damn if the man didn't take his breath away.

Carter remembered the first time he'd ever seen him. He and Donald had first met at a fundraiser for the police department the year before. Carter had been in his dress uniform, and Donald had been wearing a simple tuxedo with a black bowtie. He had been breathtaking. Other men in the room had been wearing the same basic outfit, but for them, the clothes seemed to be wearing them, while Donald wore the clothes to stunning effect. Carter had wanted to meet him, but he'd been unsure, so he'd stayed back until Red introduced them. Donald had flashed a smile, and Carter had been at a loss for words. He stammered something and figured he must have sounded like an idiot, but Donald had continued smiling and asked him if he'd like a drink.

When Donald returned with two glasses of champagne, they talked for the rest of the evening, and when Donald invited him to dinner the following weekend, which turned into breakfast, then Saturday and Sunday in bed, Carter figured he'd hit the jackpot.

"Are you mad?" Alex asked as Donald lowered him from his shoulders.

Carter realized he'd been scowling at the memory of what had happened. "No. I was just remembering the first time I met Mr. Donald."

"Was he nice?"

"Mr. Donald was really handsome." Carter pulled out his phone and searched back through the photographs. He thought Smith or someone had taken a picture at some point during the evening. He might have deleted it, but then he saw it and brought it up and showed it to Alex.

"Wow," Alex said and turned to Donald. "You're pretty."

Donald blushed, and Carter chuckled. "Yes, he is," Carter said.

"Shouldn't we get going?" Donald prompted.

Carter put his phone away. Out of habit, he made sure the apartment was secure, and then they left. Carter locked the door and followed Alex and Donald down the stairs. He led them through to the back of the building and unlocked his Ford Escape.

"I pictured you driving a Corvette or something," Donald said.

"Nope." Carter laughed as he unlocked the doors. They got Alex's booster seat installed and buckled and settled in with his bunny. Then he and Donald climbed in, and Carter started the engine. This whole process seemed so domestic. To anyone walking past they could be a couple buckling in their son. Carter had to remember that he and Donald weren't a couple, and despite what had happened last night, they most likely weren't going to be.

"What was so funny out there?" Donald whispered before Carter put the SUV in gear.

"We've been together more than once. Do you think I have anything to compensate for?" Carter asked just above a whisper.

"Compensate…?" Donald's mouth formed a silent "oh."

"Yeah. Corvettes are the ultimate compensation car." He winked, and Donald rolled his eyes.

"You know, you're such an a-s-s sometimes," Donald quipped, with a definite upturn to his lips.

"If you say so. But the important thing is, am I lying?" Carter told him and got a smile in return. They stopped at one of the traffic lights in town, and Carter checked on Alex, who seemed content to look out the windows. After the light changed, Carter continued through and got on the freeway heading south. Once they were up to speed, he got comfortable and drove the familiar route.

"Does your dad have a thing with you because you're gay? You said you don't talk much, and I was wondering if that was the reason." Donald turned toward him.

"Heck if I know. Sometimes I think if he yelled and screamed, I could do something with it. I mean, if whatever I did to disappoint him was out in the open, I could deal with it. But all I get are small pieces of information. Like I said, he wanted me to be some hotshot computer guy, make a lot of money. Become my own version of Bill Gates. But instead I went to the academy and became a cop."

"Is that a theme?"

"No. Nothing but his silence is a theme. My mother always tells me all these things my dad says, and I used to believe it, but now I think it's just her covering for him. She's been doing it so long I doubt she even realizes it." He slowed down when he glanced at the speedometer and realized he was going eighty. It wasn't likely another officer would give him a ticket, but still…. "It's not like he's different with any of the others, except William, my older brother. He did exactly what Dad wanted. He went to law school, has a successful practice in town, gave my parents two grandsons, and has the perfect wife who's always helping everyone. Sometimes it's enough to make me want to puke."

"Is William a prick?"

"That's just it. He's a great big brother, always has been." Carter flashed a half smile. "When I said I wanted to go to the police academy, William took me out and helped me train so I could pass the physical tests. He didn't say a word to Dad about it and then crowed about how well I did when I passed. Hell, I did graduation-level results on the entrance trials in all but push-ups, and then I just missed it by a few. No, the problem isn't William—it's my dad. I just don't know what makes him tick or how I can live up to his expectations."

"What does he do?"

"Dad owns an auto repair garage and still works on cars every day. He's going to have to pack it in soon, though, because most cars require computer diagnostics that he can't do. But it will be time soon, and the business is in a prime location, so he could sell the land for enough to fund his retirement."

"Could it be that he just wants you to have a better life than he does?" Donald asked.

Carter shrugged. "I don't know what he's thinking." Only that sometimes the way he acted hurt like hell. "I mean, how would you like a father you can sit in the same room with for two hours and have him say three words to you: 'Pass the remote.' Mom likes to gloss over it, probably because she doesn't know what to do either. And maybe there's nothing to do." Carter stopped. No need to drag Donald into this. Out of the corner of his eye, he saw Donald sitting still, looking straight out the window. "What is it?"

"Maybe some of us would like to have had a father at all," Donald said, turning toward him briefly and then staring out the window once again.

"Are we there?" Alex asked from the backseat.

"We'll be there soon." Carter had hoped that Alex would fall asleep in the car, but no such luck. He looked out the window constantly.

"No bad men," Alex whispered to Bunny and crushed the stuffed toy to him.

"Not ever again," Carter told him. Not if he could possibly help it. No way, no how. Alex continued holding his bunny and looking out the windows, but he said nothing more. Carter could almost feel the tension in the car. Donald still stared out the window, and Alex looked half scared out of his wits with his eyes wide, clutching his rabbit. "Donald, could you try to see what's got Alex upset?"

"Sure." He seemed to snap out of what had been occupying his thoughts, turned around, and spoke softly to Alex. Carter thought about what Donald had said. He'd been rambling on about his family and their problems, but it hadn't occurred to him that while Donald had asked questions, he'd never volunteered any information about his own family.

"Can you pull over?" Donald asked, and Carter switched on his hazard lights and pulled to the side of the freeway. Donald unsnapped his seat belt and got out. He went around to the driver's side and got in the backseat. "It's okay," Donald said. "He's having an attack of nerves."

"Why?" Carter asked.

"I'm not sure," Donald said. "I don't think he can put it into words, and I doubt it's where we're going so much as riding in the car." Carter peered into the rearview mirror and saw Donald sitting next to Alex, holding his hand. He was whispering to him quietly. "Let's just get there."

Carter pulled back onto the highway and sped up. They were fifteen miles away, and he was determined to make them go as quickly as he could. He kept checking the rearview mirror as he drove. Alex sat still, holding his bunny in one hand while Donald held the other.

They pulled into the nearly full driveway and Carter turned off the engine.

"How many people are here?" Donald asked.

"It looks like the entire family," Carter said. He took off his seat belt and got out, hurrying around to Alex's side of the car. He was wondering if this was such a good idea. Carter hadn't been expecting the entire family, and now that Alex was having such a hard time with the drive, he wondered how he would do in a house full of strangers. He lifted Alex out of the booster seat and into his arms. "Hold your bunny," he whispered and closed the door.

What really surprised him was that Donald had the same rather dazed and overwhelmed look as Alex. "It's okay. They're just my family. They can be nuts, I suppose, but they're going to like you." Carter smiled and took Donald's hand. He didn't know why—it just seemed like the right thing to do. "I promise it'll be fine." He squeezed Donald's hand.

Donald carried the bag of stuff while Carter carried Alex, and they walked hand in hand into the breach. It felt akin to going to war in a way, like they were about to be outnumbered. As soon as Carter opened the door, a cry went up from the kitchenful of people. Alex buried his face in Carter's shoulder, and Donald squeezed his hand so hard it hurt.

"Pipe down," his mother called, and everyone quieted for a few seconds. "Sweetheart, we're glad you're here."

"Mom, this is Donald Ickle. And this big guy is Alex."

"Is something wrong?" his mom asked when Alex burrowed so close that Carter swore he was trying to crawl inside him.

"No bad men," Alex kept chanting.

"I think it's the noise." Carter soothed Alex as best he could and felt him relax a little. "It's okay. All these people are my family. They're noisy, but no one is going to hurt you. Remember what I promised."

"No bad men," Alex whispered as he lifted his head away from Carter's neck.

73

"That's right. So look around." Carter waited for Alex to turn toward the table. "Everyone, this is Alex. He's had a pretty rough time of it and he gets scared of new people sometimes. So quiet, unlike the way we usually are, would be a big help. And this is Donald."

"Hello," Donald said.

"Okay, let's start. My mom you met. This is my brother, William, his wife, Liz, and their two boys, Blaine and Robert, my sister Karen and her boyfriend, Steven." Karen held up her hand with a rock big enough to be seen from space and grinned. "Sorry, now fiancé." He leaned over to give her a kiss on the cheek. "And this is my youngest sister Margie."

"Dad's in the living room," Karen explained.

Yeah, where else would he be?

"Is Donald your boyfriend?" Margie asked.

Carter glanced at Donald to gauge his reaction, but his expression told him nothing. "No. Donald is a friend. I've been helping him with Alex this weekend." He really didn't want to get into things too deeply in front of Alex.

Blaine walked over and looked up. "Do you want to play cars? We have lots of them."

"Alex, do you want to play?" Carter asked and waited for an answer. He didn't receive anything other than a few blinks, but he put Alex down, and Blaine handed Alex a blue Matchbox truck. It had probably been Carter's when he was a kid. "There are lots of cars. Blaine and Robert will share, and they're really nice. I promise." He'd done a lot of promising lately. "Robert is five and Blaine is four. They'll be your friends if you let them."

Blaine had never been a shy child, and he took Alex's hand. "We have lots of cars and you can bring your bunny. I have my teddy, and they can be friends too." Blaine led Alex away. Carter was concerned, but Donald smiled.

"Let them play. It will be good for him."

"Where are they going?" Carter asked his mother.

"Your father set up a race course in the corner of the living room, and the boys have been playing there," she explained. "Go ahead and sit at the table. There are snacks and things, so help yourself," she told

Donald with a grin. William and Steven had already left for the sanctuary of sports and testosterone in the other room.

He and Donald took two of the empty seats at the table. Donald munched on a few chips while Carter gave warning looks to his sisters and sister-in-law. He knew they were waiting for their chance at their version of the inquisition. "Be nice to him," Carter warned.

"We're always nice," Karen said right away. But damn if she didn't look like a barracuda about to go on a feeding frenzy. "So I get to start. He didn't call you his boyfriend, but you must be special." Karen's steely gaze shifted to Carter. "This one has never brought a boyfriend home before."

Donald glanced at him. "He and I are friends."

"Oh," Margie said. "Girls, they're at the 'we're not quite sure what to call it' stage." The others nodded knowingly. "I bet they're bumping like minks but aren't ready to talk about it yet." She sighed as though she had all the answers and was taking pity on them by imparting her wisdom.

"Actually, we're at the 'screw till we scream' stage, and that's just fine," Donald countered. All the girls looked shocked for a split second and then burst into laughter. "We all need some hotness, you know what I mean?" Donald leaned closer in a surprisingly close, intimate move. Carter liked that he was feeling comfortable enough to let this playful side out. It was really nice to see. Donald was usually so serious. The only time he'd really let go was when they'd been in bed and Carter had pulled that joy out of him.

"That's a great stage," Karen quipped.

"Puh-lease. What would you know?"

Karen flashed her ring again, and the other two laughed. Donald looked to him for clarification. "Karen was voted most wholesome in high school as well as 'Miss Most Likely to Save Herself for Marriage.'" Carter knew he was picking on her, but she deserved it.

"There was no such thing," Karen countered.

"Apparently our Karen is an animal," Margie said with a giggle.

"That's enough," Mom said, putting an end to that particular conversation.

"Fine," Margie said. "So is Alex your son?"

"No," Donald began. "I'm a social worker, and Alex...."

"Alex was mistreated by the adults in his life," Carter said. "I found him locked in the attic. His mother didn't make it, and the man in her life was a real lowlife pile of crap." Carter ground his teeth when he thought about it. "Alex is staying with Donald for the weekend until he can find him a really good foster home." He actually allowed himself to say it. It was the way things had to be, even if he hated the very thought of it.

"Oh," Liz said breathily.

"Yeah. He's had a hard time of it," Donald said.

All four women stared at him, and Carter's mother came over and lightly placed her hands on his shoulders. "It's a nice thing you're both doing."

"Hey," Donald whispered. "He's going to be all right. You know I'll see to that."

Carter nodded as the realization hit him that after tomorrow he would go back to work, and Donald would place Alex in permanent care. "I know."

"Jesus," Liz said under her breath. "Damn." She began to shake. "The poor thing."

"He's a strong little boy who's been through a lot and somehow came out reasonably whole on the other side. He has nightmares and his worst fear is bad men." Carter looked at Donald, who nodded. "We don't know who they are but we're hoping he can tell us."

"Well, I agree with Liz," Karen said. "It is a great thing you're doing." She got up and left the room. Margie followed her.

"Karen has always been the sensitive one," Carter explained to Donald.

"Is that why you didn't tell them anything more?"

"Yeah. Karen would have broken into tears and taken Margie right along with her. They're both strong girls but they have a soft spot for children. Karen starts her first teaching job this fall. Second grade. I think she's going to be amazing because she cares so much."

"I think so too," Liz agreed, glancing between them. "So what about the two of you? Is this the start of something more?"

Carter wished he knew the answer to that. "We'll have to see." That was the best answer he could give.

"Well, I think you make a hot couple." She winked at them before leaving the table. Carter grabbed a few chips to have something to do.

"I'm going to check on Alex," Carter said, excusing himself. Karen and Margie returned, and as he left the room, Carter heard them talking to Donald. He figured that was good and that they wouldn't be too hard on him. All the women in his family certainly were interested in Donald.

Carter entered the living room and shook his head. William and Steven sat on the sofa, and his father reclined in the chair where he spent most of his time when he was home. Over the years the chair had so conformed to his father that when anyone else sat in it, it was so uncomfortable they never stayed for long. The three boys played trucks in the corner. Well, his nephews played. Alex sat back, watching them, holding his bunny. Blaine handed him a car, and Alex ran it around the floor for a few seconds, but didn't seem to really join in.

His nephews were typical boys, full of energy and making a lot of car sounds as they played. The television was on loud so the men could hear the program. Carter wondered if all of that was just too much noise. Alex was quiet, even when he was playing. As Carter watched, Blaine turned to him and appeared to ask a question. He held out two cars. Then Blaine reached forward and took Alex's bunny. Carter's stomach clenched and he was about to get involved, but Alex released the stuffed toy and Blaine placed it on a nearby child's wooden chair, right next to a stuffed bear that Carter remembered Blaine always carrying. Then Alex bent down and started to play.

"I see you made it," his father said, pulling Carter's attention from Alex.

"How are you, Dad?" Carter felt Donald come up behind him. He knew just from his amazing, earthy scent. "This is Donald."

"The one with the quiet kid," his dad said. "You have a very well-behaved young man there. A little quiet, but with this bunch, it's a nice change." Carter briefly explained who Alex was. "I see." His dad sat up. "You're going to turn him in tomorrow?"

"He isn't a used car," Carter explained. "Donald is going to find him a more permanent foster home, though he'll remain his case worker so he can make sure he's doing okay."

His father turned to him, gaze searching. "What about you?"

"I figure I can visit Alex after work." He turned away and watched Alex play. The worry he'd had earlier had slipped away. Alex seemed to be happy and was playing fairly normally with the boys. He was quiet, but active. "I don't intend to turn my back on him."

"Hmmm," his father said and then turned away and began watching the television once again. Carter shook his head and turned to Donald, shrugging before leaving the room. He wasn't particularly interested in the game, and it was obvious he'd been dismissed by his dad.

"Your sisters are a hoot," Donald declared in the hallway, halfway between the women in the kitchen and the men in the living room.

"How so?"

"Well, apparently, according to them, you're in love with me, and if I break your heart, they'll make sure that certain parts of my anatomy are fed to me for lunch." Donald grinned. "We seem to have had the 'don't you dare hurt my brother' speech. What I want to know is are there any other speeches and or talks I need to be aware of?"

"I hope not. They seem to have pulled out all the stops for you today. They must really like you."

"Like me?" Donald whispered. "I was lucky to get out of that kitchen with my nuts, and I'm surprised my ears aren't bleeding from all the talking they do. Are they ever quiet?"

"Not that I can remember. Why do you think the men are in the living room? They'll sit in there without saying a word except to yell at the television until lunch is ready. Then afterward they'll do that the rest of the afternoon. Well, that and sleep off the food."

William joined them and shook Donald's hand. "Sorry about earlier, but I had to get out. When my wife and sisters get together there's no stopping them. I suppose that's what I get for marrying the girl down the street. Liz and my sisters used to play together as girls."

"So you've always known her?" Donald asked.

"Yeah, but I didn't notice her, at least not like that, until I was home on one of my breaks from law school. Then I wondered how I had missed seeing her all these years and…. Sorry, the thing is that when she, Karen, and Margie get together, it's like they're back in high school again, and the men just need to run for the hills. So I watch the boys, see the game, and let my ears have a rest." William looked them both over with the same gaze Carter imagined he'd use with a hostile witness. "So are you two together?"

"We're friends," Carter said.

"It's time you found someone, little brother." Carter rolled his eyes, and William glared at him in return. "I know you don't want to hear this, but being alone sucks. And it's not like you have the easiest job in the world. I'm prosecuting a guy who shot a cop in town right now. Scares the crap out of me."

"I'm fine. Mostly they keep me behind my computers. You know… the department geek."

Donald turned to him, hands on his hips. "I don't know why you keep saying that. Other than the fact that you work with computers and wear glasses… I can tell you there's nothing at all geeky about you." Donald didn't smile. Carter kept expecting him to, but he simply stared with heat banked in his gaze. "I swear."

William cleared his throat. "Jesus, you two need to go somewhere and talk this shit out." He shuddered. "I don't know what going on with you guys, and I don't really want to because, well… what you guys do is something I don't want to know about… ever." William opened his mouth to say something more, but no words came out.

"What is it?"

"Look, you told me you were gay a long time ago, even before you said something to Mom and Dad, and I appreciate that you trusted me enough to say something, but…." He looked at Donald. "Just talk shit out." After that he turned and walked back into the living room.

"What the hell was that?" Donald asked.

"I have no idea. But something just turned my brilliant brother, who is never at a loss for words, into a gibbering idiot." Carter watched him join the others. "I wish I understood any of them."

"I don't know if there's really anything to understand," Donald told him. "They all seem to care about you. Some more eloquently than others, but they care."

The loneliness in Donald's voice tore at his heart. He wondered what was behind it, but he figured Donald wouldn't tell him if he asked.

Carter's mother walked through the hall, past them, and into the living room. The television went silent. "It's time for lunch," she pronounced. "Boys, go on into the kitchen. Your mother has plates for you."

Carter went in. Alex sat on the floor, staring up at Carter's mother, lower lip trembling. Carter rushed over, scooped Alex into his arms, and grabbed his bunny for him.

"What's wrong?" Blaine asked.

"It's okay. Alex is a little upset," Carter explained. "But not at you." He looked at his mother with a raised eyebrow.

"Mommy," Alex crooned between gasping sobs. The other times were nothing compared to this. He only stopped crying when he inhaled and then sobbed even louder. Carter took Alex down the hall and into the bedroom he'd had as a kid. It was now a guest room. He closed the door and sat on the side of the bed, comforting Alex as he let him cry it out. He'd been such a trouper, coping with all the sudden changes in his life. But now it all came out in a wave of wails and tears. "Angels are bad men," he said at one point and began crying again. "You said no more bad men." Alex hit him on the shoulder and kept crying. "You promised."

"I know. I know you want her back. So do I." What he really wished was that they'd found her sooner so they could have been able to help her. But he couldn't say that to Alex. All Alex knew was that his mother was gone and not coming back. Someday Carter would tell him everything he knew, but not until Alex was much older. "It's okay."

The door cracked open and Donald came in. "What happened?"

"Nothing really. My mom set him off without knowing it and the meltdown started." He held Alex close and rocked him. It was all he could think of to do.

"I've been waiting for it. I think it took a while for him to take it all in."

Carter nodded. "What are we going to do?" he asked. He wasn't really expecting an answer, and Donald didn't provide one. He shrugged and looked as lost as Carter felt. There was no sign of the Icicle in his expression now, only deep concern. Carter patted the bed next to him, and Donald sat down. Together they calmed Alex until he finally went quiet.

"Are you hungry?" Carter asked Alex after a few minutes. He nodded and wiped his eyes. "Do you want to eat in here or go out with your friends? I'm sure Robert and Blaine are waiting for you."

Alex blinked up at him, and Carter put him down. Then he stood and took Alex's hand. They waited for Donald and then left the room and headed toward the eat-in area of the kitchen. Blaine slipped off his chair and met Alex. "I saved a place for you next to me." He took Alex by the hand and led him over.

"I'll make him a plate," Donald said, and Carter made sure Alex got settled. Carter's mother got up and helped Donald.

"You sit here, okay? I'll be right over there." Carter pointed, and Alex nodded. Donald came over and set a plate in front of him along with a spoon and a glass of milk. "Just eat what you want." Carter held his slender shoulder for a second and then released it when Alex started to eat.

Carter turned, and he and Donald took seats at the table. The family conversation stopped, and all eyes turned to him. "What?" he snapped with more force than he intended. He looked up and down the table and then at his brother for some sort of clarification. He got none, and the conversation started up again.

"Dang, Carter, that boy can eat," his dad said from the other end of the table.

"I wish all you kids had appetites like him," his mother added with a smile.

"No, you don't," Carter said, and the conversation grew quiet once again. "Alex is five."

"I thought he was younger than Blaine," Liz commented. "He's so small."

"That's what happens with malnutrition." Carter lowered his voice. "What you're seeing is him eating like it's his last meal because he thinks each one is." He took a deep breath and swallowed hard.

"It can't be that bad," his father said dismissively from his seat.

Carter leaned forward. "He was found locked in an attic, scared to death, with no bathroom. So you get part of the picture." Carter kept his voice low, but he let the menace shine through. "He hid from me behind a bed that probably hadn't been cleaned in any way in weeks. He was dirty, hungry, thirsty, and alone." Carter's anger that his father would dismiss Alex's hardship had him clenching his fists under the table. "When I asked him his name, he told me it was 'Piece of shit,' because that's what his abuser said his name was. So, Dad, that little boy has already been through more hell than you can imagine. And if you don't believe me, I'll show you the videos."

His father went white and the women all gasped, but Carter held his father's gaze. "You can think whatever you want of me, but you will not call me a liar and you will not belittle what he's been through."

"This is my home, and…."

"No, it's Mom's home. You happen to live here and take up space." He turned to his mother. "If you want us to leave, just ask and we'll go." He refused to look at his dad. He'd had enough. Whatever his problems were with him, Carter was going to stand up for Alex.

"Mr. Carter," Alex said, and Carter turned toward him. Alex held up his clean plate, and Carter got up to get him some more.

"My God," his mother said quietly. When Carter turned around he could see his father getting up a good head of steam. "Don't you dare," his mother hissed, and the air went out of his father like a popped balloon. "That boy is doing good, so…." Carter had to think back to when his mother had verbally stood up to his father. Carter had no doubt that she ran the house, but she usually did so quietly. "Eat your food before it gets cold." It was like a pronouncement from on high, and everyone went back to eating.

Carter put the plate in front of Alex, and he went back to eating.

"Will he stop?" Margie asked as she watched him. "Does he get sick?"

"He eats until he's full and doesn't stop until then. He's actually slowed down a little. You should have seen him that first night. I swear he watched both of us and ate faster whenever we came close." Carter turned around and said softly to Alex, "Remember what we talked about at breakfast."

Alex stopped and turned around. "I slowed down," he said with his mouth half full. It was like eating was a sport and he was determined to win.

"There is dessert, so save some room." Carter knew Donald had been right and that Alex would slow down and become less desperate at meals once he grew sure that he would eat regularly. Carter went back to his lunch, feeling like shit that he'd ruined everyone's meal. But he'd be damned if he was going to apologize to anyone.

"Can we go play?" Robert asked.

"Of course, sweetheart," Carter's mother said, and the boys, including Alex, hurried into the other room. Carter turned and saw that

Alex had left some beans and potatoes on his plate. He turned and finished his lunch.

"Mom, this is delicious."

"It certainly is, Mrs. Schunk," Donald agreed.

"Call me Shirley, and I'm glad both of you like it. Alex sure did." She grinned at them a little nervously.

"I have yet to find anything he won't eat. You know how you always said we were picky eaters? Alex isn't. He shovels in everything we've put in front of him without a single word."

"After what you said, I don't doubt it. The poor baby is just trying to figure things out." She turned to Donald. "Will you be able to get him help?"

"Yes. I'll get him anything he needs," Donald whispered. Carter was getting the idea that Alex had wormed his way into Donald's heart the same as he'd touched Carter's.

"What that boy needs is a family," his father said in his usual accusatory tone.

"That's my next task," Carter said without directly addressing his father. "Tomorrow I'll be researching Alex's mother's family to see if I can find any relatives. We're hoping that we can find family for him." Carter sighed. "There is also someone who was paying for—" He swallowed. "—the videos, and we need to follow the trail to him as well."

"Sounds like you'll be busy," William said.

"I will be, I'm sure." Of course there would be other work for him to do as well. It was likely he'd be swamped for a few days. He'd been hoping for another patrol shift, but that was becoming more and more unlikely, at least right away.

"I hope you find someone who will love him," his mother said, looking at him without blinking. His mother's implication wasn't lost on him, but as Donald had explained, Carter's hands were tied, at least in the short term. The best way for him to help Alex was to do his job as best he possibly could. He knew that. But it still hurt. Donald slipped his hand into Carter's under the table and quickly shared a smile with him.

"It will be all right. I'll make sure it is." Donald squeezed Carter's fingers slightly, and he sat back in the chair, full and a little happy, especially when Donald looked at him that way.

"Dessert will be in a little while," Carter's mother said.

"I'll help you clean up," Liz volunteered. Everyone got up from the table and scattered through the house, with the men heading back to the living room. Carter shared a look with Donald because he wasn't quite sure where he fit in any longer. Before he'd have gone in the living room and watched the game. But that didn't really interest him now.

"Why don't we see if the boys want to play outside?" Donald suggested. "It's a nice day."

"The county turned that lot that's been empty forever into a small park," his mother supplied. "Take the boys there. They have swings and a big wooden castle that they can climb on."

"See if William wants to go too, that is, if you can tear him away from the television." Liz rolled her eyes, and Carter figured she was right.

In the end, the television was too much of a lure, so he, Donald, and the three boys walked down the sidewalk toward the playground. As they got close, the screams and laughter of children playing signaled that they were almost there. When they entered the park, Carter found a place to sit, and the boys raced off, with Blaine holding Alex's hand.

"It's so cute the way he seems to watch out for Alex."

"He's the youngest and he's used to Robert being there for him, so I suspect he's just returning the favor." Carter set the bag of stuff they'd brought along on the bench. Donald moved the bag and sat down next to him. "Do you think Alex will carry that bunny with him on his first day of high school?"

Donald laughed. "It represents security for him right now. He hasn't had any, and the only thing that's been there for him is that bunny. When Harker took it away, it must have been devastating for him."

"Do you think he was holding it ransom? Using the bunny to get what he wanted from Alex?" The thought made him even angrier than he'd been with his father.

"Take it easy." Donald patted his hand. "You've been fired up for a while now." Donald turned toward him. "I knew you were a passionate kind of guy, but I didn't know you had a temper. I don't think your dad knew what hit him."

"I wasn't going to let him make light of what Alex has been through." Carter turned back to watch Alex playing. He held his breath as Alex climbed to the top of the play castle, still holding his bunny.

Carter stood and walked over, climbing to where Alex was. "Do you want me to hold Bunny for you? Mr. Donald and I will watch him."

Alex looked at Bunny and then at the other kids playing before handing him the toy.

"Don't worry. He'll be with us, and you can have him when you're through playing." Carter backed out of the castle and walked back to Donald, placing the toy on top of the bag. "He seems to be having a great time."

"Normal activities are good for him. He probably hasn't had much of that." Donald touched his arm. "I think your nephews are wonderful. Watch how neither of them leaves him behind. I think they get that thoughtfulness from their uncle." Donald bumped his shoulder.

"I take it I'm starting to grow on you."

"Carter...."

"Well, what do you expect of me?" Carter turned toward Donald. "Sometimes you're hot, other times you're cold. I don't know quite what to make of it, and I don't know why you act this way." Carter locked his gaze onto Donald's, trying to get him to open up, even a little. He refused to let him off the hook. Eventually Donald turned toward where Alex was playing without saying anything.

Carter sighed and followed Donald's gaze. "How long did you want to stay?" He could already feel Donald pulling away. His voice held an icy edge that hadn't been present in a while, but there it was. Carter knew what that meant, and he had to make a decision. "How long before Icicle shows up?" He figured it was best to call Donald on it and see what happened. This felt a little like an interrogation.

"I don't like to talk about my past," Donald told him without shifting his gaze to Carter. "That isn't who I am anymore."

"Then why not come clean about it?"

"I'm not a criminal," Donald countered. "And I'm not in an interrogation room."

"No, you aren't, and I wasn't interrogating you. I simply asked a question, and you're the one making a huge deal out of it, which makes me wonder what you're so afraid of. The whole icy thing is a cover-up, some kind of defense mechanism that you use to push people away."

"Don't try to analyze me," Donald said with little heat.

"Why not?" Carter pressed. "You analyze me and everyone around you. Don't think I don't see it. You listen to what everyone says and your eyes shift and either go blank or come alive depending on whether you think they have some ulterior motive. Despite the circumstances, we've had a good time this weekend. It's been nice taking care of Alex, and I won't lie and say that I don't have feelings for him... I do. But I've liked being with you more."

Donald turned and focused on him. "You've been paying attention to Alex the whole weekend. Don't tell me the only reason you've even been around isn't because of him."

"Was I paying attention to Alex last night?" Carter countered. "No. It was only you."

"That was just sex."

Carter reached to Donald's chin, lifting it to meet his eyes. "It may have been just sex for you. But I don't do that. For me nothing about last night qualified as just sex. I haven't done the quick and easy thing in a long time. I'm over that crap. When I'm with someone, it's a hell of a lot more than just sex." Carter kept his voice low, but intense, and he saw Donald quiver. "You're the one who needs to decide if last night was just sex or not." Carter stood and walked away. If he stayed any longer, his anger would surface again, and he didn't want that. He'd been running at high speed ever since his outburst with his father, and he didn't want to go there with Donald.

There was little he could do to help Donald make up his mind about what he wanted. Last night, in his arms, Donald had gone to pieces. It couldn't be an act, and Donald needed to see that as clearly as Carter could.

"Mr. Carter, watch me!" Alex called and then hung upside down from one of the bars. It was such a simple move and yet so cute to see him playing like any other kid.

"That's great!" Carter told him and walked closer.

Alex righted himself and hurried over. "Will you play with us?"

Carter chuckled. "I don't think it's built for people my size. But you go have fun and play. We have plenty of time."

"Can I do that?" Alex asked, pointing to the swings. Carter nodded and held out his hand. He led Alex to the swings and got him situated before pushing him. Blaine rushed over and took the swing next to Alex.

"Push me too, Uncle Carter." He ran to get himself started and plopped his butt on the seat. Carter gently pushed both boys until they were swinging happily. Robert joined them as well. Thankfully, Donald came over, and the two of them shared the pushing duty.

"I think it's good they waited a while, otherwise there would be a mess and some upset tummies," Donald said. "I've never been able to swing without feeling sick. Even as a kid I stayed away from them."

"I used to love them. I'd beg my mom to take me to the park and I'd swing for hours, or play on the monkey bars. They don't even have those anymore."

"Too dangerous. Most playgrounds have taken them out." Donald continued pushing Robert. "I used to love those too. I'd hang upside down, or imagine it was a space ship that would take me anywhere I wanted to go. There was a playground near one of the places I used to live, and I'd go there whenever I could." Carter knew Donald was opening up a little and he smiled. "The playground is a happy memory."

Carter stepped back and let the boys swing, watching Donald. If something as simple as going to the playground was a happy memory, then what kind of other memories did Donald have? He'd wondered about Donald's family, but that comment opened his eyes. Maybe Donald didn't want to talk about his past because it was too painful.

"What are you so fascinated with?" Donald asked, glaring back at him.

"You," Carter answered honestly. Donald was gorgeous, with his black hair a little messed up and his shirt open just enough to show a glimpse of his chest with its sprinkling of dark hair. Sometimes Donald's eyes could be huge and as expressive as hell, but then he could close them off so his eyes were deep, like a void, with no bottom, showing nothing at all. Carter loved the depth of emotion Donald could express, but hated it when he closed himself off. It made Carter feel disconnected, on the outside looking in, which totally sucked. He really wished Donald would open up and let him in, trust him. "I'm serious."

"I know you are," Donald said.

"Uncle Carter," Blaine said, pulling his attention back to the swing that had slowed. He gave both Blaine and then Alex a push, both boys laughing and calling to go higher.

He wanted to ask what Donald meant, but this wasn't the place. After a while the boys tired of the swings and went back to the play castle. "Ten more minutes and then we need to go back to Grandma's for dessert," Carter said. Once that was over, they could go home without his mother making a federal case out of it. Heck, the family was probably ready for him to go.

"I know you're serious, but I don't know if I can believe it," Donald whispered when the two of them were back on the bench watching the kids.

"Why not?"

His question was met with another of those silences—that wall Donald was not willing to climb over or build a gate through.

After a couple of minutes, Donald said, "It's just hard for me to think that you won't change your mind later. I know you're being honest with me, I don't doubt that, but in a week, a month, or a year? What then?"

"I don't have an answer for you. I can't predict the future, but I'm not a fickle person who changes his mind on a whim, and my heart doesn't wander from guy to guy like a bee to flowers. No one can give guarantees… but caring for someone isn't about that. At least it shouldn't be. It's about taking a leap of faith."

"I don't have any faith. It's all been used up." Donald checked his watch. "Five minutes, boys."

"That's not true," Carter said, ignoring the interruption. "I can understand if you just say you aren't interested and don't want me around. I can deal with that. But the cold shoulder and this whole ice-man act is wearing a little thin, even for you."

"How would you know?" Donald challenged.

"I was there last night, remember? I saw the way you leaned into each touch like you craved it as much as air or water. I'm trained to watch for the smallest indication that a suspect is lying. That training extends to other kinds of observations. So you can say whatever you want, but I'm not really buying it." Carter stood and walked over to the boys.

"Just a few more minutes," Robert pleaded.

"You know it's time to go. Grandma will not be happy if you miss cake."

All three boys looked at each other. Blaine and Robert's grins spread and Alex even joined in. He might not know about Carter's mother's desserts, but he definitely wanted some cake. They raced over to the bench. After gathering everything together, they began the walk back to his parents'. The boys talked, but he and Donald remained stubbornly quiet.

When they arrived at the house, his mother immediately fussed around the boys, getting them to wash their hands and then settling them at the table with plates. Of course Alex dug right in. By the time he was done, the cake was gone and he had frosting all over his face. But the smile was well worth any mess. His mother gave Carter and Donald slices as well. "I'll cut some for you to take home," she told him.

"Alex will love that."

The boys left the table, and Donald took Alex to wash up.

"You were hard on your father," his mother began as she pulled out the chair next to him and sat down. "Not that he didn't deserve it." She set her glass of water on the table. "I love him to death, but sometimes he can be the world's biggest ass. But he wants only the best for his children."

"Maybe what's best for his kids is for him to let them make their own decisions and not have to live up to whatever he wants." Carter wasn't going to back down, not even with his mother.

"Okay, I'll give you that."

"I'm not going to apologize to him. If he wants to be that way, he can. But Alex has been through hell, and for him to make light of it...."

"You took care of that quickly enough," his mother said. "Along with the appetite of everyone around the table. But that isn't what I wanted to talk to you about." She leaned back, peering down the hall. "Alex isn't the only one here today who's been through hell. I see the touch of the devil himself on your friend. He's been there and somehow come back."

"Donald helps people all day. He's a good guy...."

"I didn't mean that I think he's evil. I mean I believe that he's seen things and done things that would make the rest of us shudder. He's seen hell and survived. Lord knows how, but he has. And it's written in those eyes of his." She patted his hand. "I know you're interested in helping Alex, and that's commendable." She leaned close and kissed him on the cheek. "That little boy is so adorably special. But I think Donald needs you too. Even if he doesn't realize it." She stood up and left the table as Donald and Alex came back in the room. "I'll get a plate and cut some cake for you to take."

"Thanks, Mom."

"Did you have fun at the park?" she asked Alex. Carter wasn't sure if he would answer.

"Uh-huh. I swinged and played on the castle thing. Mr. Carter pushed me and he held Bunny too." Alex had the stuffed rabbit in his arms once again.

"That's good. I put an extra piece on the plate for Bunny. But if he's not hungry, then maybe you can eat it for him." She reached forward and lightly tickled Alex's belly. He giggled and backed away, still smiling but a little wary, holding his bunny like a shield.

"Can you say thank you?" Carter prompted.

"Thank you," Alex said, and Carter took his hand.

"I'll call you in a few days." Carter poked his head in the living room and said good-bye. Then he led Alex toward the back door. Donald said his good-byes as well, with Carter's mother telling him he was welcome anytime.

By the time they got Alex belted in his seat and then onto the road, Carter was exhausted. Alex fell to sleep within minutes of them entering the freeway, and Donald sat back in the passenger seat.

"Is your family always like that?" Donald asked. "They seemed really nice."

"They are, for the most part. They can also be tiring. No one is ever quiet, and they talk over each other all the time, but they're a good family, I suppose. I wish Dad were different, but he is who he is, and I guess if I want him to accept me, then I need to accept him, flaws and all."

"I think that's what it means to be part of a family." Donald turned away and stared out the window. The afternoon sun cast a warm glow on the trees around them. Carter drove and didn't try to push Donald to talk. It wouldn't do any good anyway.

"I thought we'd order Chinese for dinner," Carter offered. "Unless you want me to just go home. I'm sure you can take care of Alex." Given how withdrawn Donald seemed to be getting, he wouldn't force himself where he wasn't wanted.

"Sweet and sour sounds nice, and you can do whatever you'd like. If you'd rather sleep at home, then Alex and I will be fine. I can soothe away any of his nightmares." Donald didn't turn from where he watched the landscape pass by. "It makes no difference to me."

Carter gripped the wheel tighter. "Is that how you really feel? I was trying to ask what you wanted." Carter glanced over as the frost grew thicker inside the car. He could feel it starting from Donald and spreading out. Donald shrugged but didn't answer. "You need to tell me what you want, not what you think I want to hear."

"I hoped you'd stay," Donald finally said, and Carter reached over and placed his hand on his leg.

"Was that so hard?" Carter asked gently. "Just open up a little and tell me what you want. I can't read your mind. I'll need to stop by my apartment so I can get some clothes for the morning, but after that, we can order pizza, maybe watch a movie, and recover from family overload."

"Okay." Donald turned away from the window. Carter thought he might have won a small victory, but only time would tell if it was significant or not.

CHAPTER
Six

THE HOUSE was quiet. Almost too quiet. Alex was upstairs asleep, and Donald came down the stairs after checking in on him. Carter was still in the kitchen. He had offered to clean up, so Donald sat on the sofa, put his feet up, and closed his eyes. It had been a long time since he'd been this tired. Once they'd gotten home, Alex had awakened from his short nap with way too much energy. He'd barely stopped to eat, which was out of character, before going back to his toys, running his cars and trucks around the room. He still did it silently, no car sounds or noises the way Carter's nephews had, but it had been good to see him display normal childish energy.

Dishes clinked in the kitchen, and Donald was about to get back up to help when the sounds quieted and the soft click of a light switch reached his ears. Footsteps approached and strong arms wrapped around his legs. Carter sat and put Donald's legs across his lap. He nearly sat up anyway when Carter took off his shoes, letting them clunk onto the floor. Then his socks followed, and Carter began lightly massaging his feet. Damn, that felt good, and tension that had built up over the past few hours melted away.

Donald knew he probably should have just told Carter what he wanted to know. But he hadn't spoken about anything like that in so long that he wasn't sure he was capable of providing an explanation… to anyone. Those memories and experiences were locked away in their own neat box, and opening it was likely to unleash horrors best left where they were.

"Damn," Donald moaned. "That's amazing."

Carter stroked his feet and over his ankle and up his calf with just enough pressure to keep him interested and his desire lightly simmering. Carter pushed the leg of his pants upward, exposing more skin, his hands continuing their magic up and down Donald's leg and foot before switching to the other one.

The room was quiet, and Donald only heard Carter's occasional light breathing over the ever increasing pounding of his heart in his ears. Carter didn't make any additional advances or even anything overtly sexual; he didn't need to. Each touch was caring and intimate. Special. The guys he'd been with had always been about getting to the main event. That was what Donald preferred, because once that was over, they would generally go home, and Donald's walls remained intact. But this was so under the radar, Donald didn't even realize what had happened until it was too late. He opened his eyes, saw Carter looking at him like he hung the moon, and gasped. Carter was in love with him. He saw it in those few seconds before Carter turned away. Worse, he felt the same way. How that could have happened, Donald had no idea.

He'd been so careful. Sure, Carter had been nice. He'd helped him with Alex the whole weekend. Sure, they'd had sex. It was what he did when there was a hot guy who wanted to spend time in his bed. But it was only sex. That's what he'd told Carter and what he'd told himself, over and over again. It had to have sunk in. It had to. Donald closed his eyes once again so Carter wouldn't see his surprise or discern what he was feeling. He knew Carter saw a lot more than Donald meant for him to see, and he couldn't let him see this. If he did, there would be no turning back. But after tomorrow, Carter would go back to his life, Donald would place Alex in a proper foster home, and they would have no reason to see each other again. Somehow Donald would pick up the pieces and go on. He'd done it before and he'd do it again. It was best for him and for Carter.

Donald was afraid to open his eyes now. Carter's magnificent hands hadn't faltered for a second while he'd run through his ruminations. A small moan escaped his throat, and as soon as Donald heard himself make the sound, he couldn't stop the one that followed for the life of him. His leg began to shake, and after a few moments, Carter stopped, his hands resting on Donald's feet, then the touch faded away. Before he realized it, Carter was kissing him, lips touching lightly but with an intensity that sent him flying.

Carter deepened the kiss, shifting on the sofa and slipping his hand around the back of Donald's neck. He lifted him slightly, cradling his head as he plundered Donald's mouth, taking everything and giving all in return. "We need to take this upstairs," Carter whispered and pulled Donald to him.

Donald knew this was the now-or-never moment. He should pull away. Alex was in bed, and if Donald asked, Carter would go home. Asking him to leave would be the ultimate act of his Iceman persona, the one he'd built and cultivated to keep situations like this from happening. But fuck if he could bring himself to do it. Carter slipped out from beneath his legs and took his hand. Donald gripped it and let Carter tug him to his feet. He followed Carter up the stairs, through the largely dark house.

Donald expected Carter to lead him toward his bedroom, but they stopped in the hallway, and Carter peered into Alex's room. Donald followed and saw Alex curled on the bed, sound asleep, his face free of tension, pain, and confusion, Bunny held in his arms. "That's the most precious sight I've ever seen in my life." Carter sighed and pulled Alex's door until it was nearly closed. Then he took Donald's hand once more and led him down the hall.

His own bedroom door clicked closed behind them and then Carter wound his arms around Donald's waist and his warmth surrounded Donald. "Is this okay?" Carter asked. Donald hummed his approval as Carter guided him to the bed. He expected to fall back on it, but Carter held him upright and tugged off his shirt. "Damn, you smell good," Carter whispered and inhaled deeply from near the base of his neck before licking and sucking on his skin.

"Carter, I don't want to have to explain marks on my neck tomorrow," Donald whispered but he already knew it was too late. He could feel Carter's ardor already marking him.

"So you'll remember," Carter whispered, and Donald arched his back as Carter licked down his chest, before sucking hard and sure on his nipple, then scraping lightly over his sensitive skin with his teeth. Donald moaned loudly as little jolts of excitement raced through him. When Carter stopped, Donald breathed deeply, only to have his breath stolen when Carter performed the same exquisite torture on the other nipple. The line between pleasure and pain was so close, and Carter seemed to know exactly when to stop, which he did only when Donald was breathless.

Carter propelled him back, and Donald collapsed on the mattress, bouncing slightly once, but paying little attention as Carter pulled his own shirt over his head. Donald reached out, sliding his hands over Carter's smooth skin, letting his knuckles bump slightly over his abs. Carter was near the perfection of manhood as far as Donald was concerned—strong without being hugely bulky, with carved lines of muscle that led from his abs down into his pants, pointing the way to the good stuff. When Carter inhaled and pulled his muscles in, they became more pronounced. Donald traced them with his fingers, lingering over the top of the waist of his soft, thin jeans.

Donald worked Carter's belt open and then popped open the button at the top. He was about to open the rest of the package when Carter leaned forward, capturing his lips, the kisses reaching to his heart. Donald held Carter tight, stroking down his strong back to the curve of his ass. With Carter's pants undone, Donald was able to slip his hands inside, pushing past the denim to cup Carter's cheeks.

"Damn," he breathed just loud enough to be heard. "You must do squats until you're dead." Carter's ass was rock hard, and when he flexed those muscles, they were like granite.

"You know what I can do," Carter whispered in his ear before sucking on it lightly. "Is that what you want?" Carter opened Donald's jeans, popping the buttons and pushing them roughly down his hips. Donald thrust his hips forward.

Carter pulled Donald's jeans and underwear off, letting them fall. Then he knelt next to Donald, looking down at him as he ran his hand down his belly and along his hip, past his cock and balls, between his legs and under his ass. He pressed his arm against Donald's cock and balls and teased at his opening with his finger. Fuck that felt amazing, and Donald lifted his butt off the bed, thrusting upward for a little more friction. Carter leaned forward, sucking the head of Donald's cock between his lips.

Donald thought he was going to die. He felt so awesome, it had to be too good to be true. Every part of him felt on fire, and when Carter sucked him deeper and tapped on his opening at the same time, he gasped, clamped his eyes closed, and shuddered from near sensory overload. Carter had pressed all his buttons at the same fucking time, and he was going over the edge. He nearly lost control as Carter took all of him. When he relaxed, Carter slipped a finger inside him to the first knuckle, and he whined. He sounded needy as hell to his own ears, but he really didn't care, not right now. He had to have more of everything.

"You taste fantastic," Carter whispered before licking the base of his crown and then sliding Donald's cock past his lips again, slowly but with enough friction that Donald could feel as he slid down him inch by inch. Fuck, he loved that, and it took all his willpower to hold still. It felt too good and he wanted it to last.

"Carter, what are you doing to me?" Donald gasped.

Carter pulled off just long enough to say, "Sucking your brains out through your dick," and then he pressed his finger deeper inside of him. Hell, Donald was beside himself. Each and every movement Carter made brought more sensation and pleasure. Wherever Carter touched him, he came alive and burned with volcanic heat. When Carter bent his finger, brushing over his gland, Donald nearly went to pieces. He clutched Carter's hair, pressed his head down on his cock, snapped his hips a few times, and exploded. At least that's what it felt like as he pumped his release down Carter's throat.

He wasn't aware of himself for a few seconds. When he came to, he realized he was still clutching Carter's hair and bucking like a wild man. He slowed and then stopped his hips, heaving for breath, and let go of Carter's hair. God, he felt like an idiot. He'd never lost complete control of himself like that and….

Carter backed away and then kissed him, hard. "Fuck, that was hot," he whispered against Donald's lips. "You were flying with the birds for a few seconds there."

"Yeah," he admitted. "Sorry if I…."

Carter kissed away his words. "I'm not fragile and I'm not going to break. You were gone, out of your mind, and I took you there. Do you know how hot that is?" Carter flashed him a smile and then tugged him into a kiss. "Now I'm going to do it again."

"Jesus…," Donald groaned. He wasn't sure he would live through that. Carter slipped off the bed. Donald watched, riveted, as Carter stripped off the rest of his clothes. Damn, he was gorgeous. Donald's mouth watered. Carter's cock bobbed slightly as he approached the bed. Donald rolled onto his belly and moved to the edge of the bed. When Carter got close enough, he guided Carter's cock between his lips, sucking him hard, the head of Carter's cock sliding along his tongue. Carter was thick, so Donald had to open wide to take him, and he loved every second of it.

Carter slowly rocked back and forth, sliding his cock along Donald's tongue. Salty sweetness filled his mouth, and Donald gave it everything he had. It didn't take long before Donald realized from the small quivers and the way Carter's movements got ragged that Carter was getting close. Carter pulled away and tugged Donald into his arms, pressing him back on the bed. "I want you, Donald." Carter fumbled in the nightstand, coming up with another of those rainbow condoms. It had to be the last one, but all Donald could think about was Carter as he slicked his fingers and then pressed them to his opening.

He gasped and closed his eyes as Carter prepared him and then climbed between his legs.

Carter lightly touched his chin. "I want to see you," Carter whispered, and Donald opened his eyes. Carter was right there, looking deep into his eyes. Donald wasn't sure just how much Carter could see and he wanted to close his eyes once again. Things were getting too close to the edge for him, and if he reached it, Donald would tumble over and there would be no returning.

Carter pressed into him and Donald's body bloomed. The stretch, the fill, the closeness, and the way Carter continued looking deep inside him took his breath away. When Carter started to move, he came closer and seemed to be listening. There were no words, but when Donald's breath hitched, Carter slowed, and when he gasped, Carter sped up.

"What are you doing?"

"Listening to your breathing," Carter whispered. He snapped his hips, and Donald gasped. Then he did it again and again, until Donald's gasps tumbled out of him one after the other. Carter held him, his movements slowing and becoming shallower. Donald loved that feeling and the closeness. He'd had sex with a number of guys. Some had been good, others not so good, but none had been great. This, with Carter, felt mind-blowing—so much so, he had to remember to breathe. Even more, all he kept thinking was that he hadn't known what he'd been missing until Carter, and once this was over—and it would be over, because for him relationships ended—he would miss him, probably for the rest of his life.

"Carter...." Donald groaned as they rocked together, Carter driving them both to heaven, and Donald held on for the erotic ride of his life. Since he'd come once, it took a while for his ardor to return. Not that Carter was any less exciting, but things took more time, and Donald loved that there didn't seem to be a rush. Even Carter was taking his time, using small touches and intense looks to add to the intimacy.

"Donald... have you ever had a nickname?" Carter asked as he paused, holding still inside him. "When we're like this, Donald seems so formal, and I don't want to be that with you. I want to be close. I want you to open up and let me in."

Donald chuckled. "I'd say you are."

Carter thrust slightly and then held still once again. "No." He placed his hand on Donald's chest. "I want you to let me in here. I know it's hard for you and you aren't willing to tell me why. But I wish you'd trust me." Carter kept his hand right in the center of Donald's chest as he increased his pace. The bed shook, Carter's deep thrusts sending ripples of aching need through him. The energy all seemed to settle into Carter's hand, and it got hotter and hotter the longer it lay there.

The funny thing was, it was just a hand touching him, nothing more. Yet Donald's attention rested there he couldn't think about anything else.

"I care about you, Donald Ickle. I have since our first meeting." Carter thrust faster and harder. Donald gasped for breath. Finally, Carter slid his hand down Donald's belly and wrapped his fingers around Donald's cock, stroking hard and fast, just the way he liked it.

Donald's desire was now firing on all cylinders, and he moved in time with Carter. He was so ready to reach the pinnacle with him. Carter thrust deep and hard, pulled completely away from his body, and then thrust inside in one smooth, swift movement. Donald hadn't been expecting it and he gasped, then moaned, when Carter did it again.

"See, your body craves me when I'm gone doesn't it?" Carter's breath was hot on his ear.

Donald didn't answer. All he wanted was for Carter to move and bring him back to the heights like he'd done before.

"You need to tell me."

"Yes. All right, I missed you too," Donald admitted with frustration. "Why do you have to do this?"

"Because I need to hear it and you need to say it." Carter withdrew and pushed back inside.

"So full."

"I know. I can see how you're feeling in your eyes. You don't know whether to kiss me or hit me. Everything is roiling inside you. Let it all go. Don't hold on to any of it—just release it." Donald blinked and stared back at Carter. "You're going to come in a minute. You're so close to the edge you don't know which way to turn. When you do, just let go. Give me everything—your pleasure, your pain, hurt, frustration, whatever it is you hold on to so tightly. Let it all go."

Donald tried to ignore what Carter was saying to him, but his body and instincts betrayed him. He wasn't sure if he could let go of those things. His pain and worry had long ago been used to build the walls that kept his heart safe from assault. "Carter...." Donald trembled.

"That's it. Let go of all of it...." Carter thrust deep, stroking him hard and sure.

Donald tingled from head to toe. He tried to hold off, but as soon as he felt Carter reach the top, thrust deep, and then still, Donald tumbled into the abyss of release.

He was falling, but he never reached bottom. Eventually his descent slowed and stopped. He knew Carter was with him, holding him as he floated on wings of rapture. Eventually Donald opened his eyes. Carter was right there, lightly caressing his cheek, looking at him with shining eyes. "You're breathtaking like that," Carter whispered, his raspy voice filled with... awe? Donald had never heard that tone from anyone... not that he could remember, anyway.

"No, I'm not," Donald countered.

"Yes, you are." Carter continued lightly stroking his cheek and then down his shoulder to his chest. "You certainly are." Carter leaned forward, lightly licking a nipple. "You are beautiful all over."

"Beauty is only skin deep," Donald commented.

"No. Beauty is as deep as you'll allow it to go. That's up to you." Carter slowly withdrew from him, and Donald shuddered at the sensation and loss. Carter held his gaze for a few seconds and then got off the bed. Donald didn't watch him as he took care of the condom, but he was aware of each move Carter made.

He was sticky and covered in sweat. Donald thought about getting up to wash, but soon Carter took his hand and gently tugged him up and off the bed. They went toward the bathroom. Carter started the shower, and once it had warmed he guided Donald under the spray.

The hot water felt good, but Carter's soapy hands felt even better. He worked Donald's shoulders, digging deep until Donald could barely lift his arms. The tension he usually carried around with him was gone. Donald hadn't even known how much until he was limp and wrung out like an old rag doll. He might have collapsed to the tub floor if Carter hadn't been holding him up. "You know I won't let you fall."

"I guess I do," Donald whispered, and Carter turned them, positioning Donald under the spray.

"I really like you this way," Carter whispered.

"What, wet?"

"And quiet. You sometimes think too much. Just allow yourself to feel. Thinking is good, but it can't take the place of your heart."

Donald humphed and held on to Carter. He didn't have the energy to argue with him. His heart… there was very little left of it. He had walled it off, starved it until he thought it was gone. Then along came Carter and Alex, who proved to him that it was still strong, just silent. Carter was right, he wasn't sure whether to hit him or kiss him. Hell, all he'd ever wanted was to feel safe. For most of his life that had been sorely absent, and he'd only felt safe when he cut himself off and lived only for him. He'd given up worrying about others or letting them in. They weren't needed, or so he thought. Now Donald wasn't sure he could forgive Carter for proving him wrong.

Carter turned off the water, pulling him out of his thoughts. They stepped out of the tub, and Carter wrapped him in a towel. Donald dried off and combed his hair while Carter did the same behind him.

"I can feel you pulling away. You need to stop doing that."

Donald turned around. "I…."

Carter pulled away Donald's towel and dropped his own. "We're both just us." Carter placed his hands on his hips. "I'm standing in front of you with no shield at all. I have no armor or clothes, just me, as I am, and I'm telling you, Donald Ickle, that I care about you. I see you for who you are, flaws and all." Carter ran his finger along the scar on his hip. "No one is perfect. I'm not and neither are you. But the amazing thing is that sometimes we find someone who doesn't care." Carter took a tiny step closer, and Donald nearly stepped back, but stood still. "Occasionally, in this world full of hurt and pain, we find the one person who will see us and love us for who we are, nothing more and nothing less. The smart people open their eyes and realize what a blessing that is."

"How can you be so sure?"

"I've seen it. For all their faults and as huge a pain as they can be, my mom and dad love each other. They always have. My brother was able to find it, and months ago I thought I might have found it too. But you turned your back on me, and I let you. This time I'm not leaving without a fight. So if you want to walk away, you can and I can't stop you. But I'm telling you I can be sure standing bare and open in front of you."

Donald gasped. "What if I'm not good enough for you?"

Carter stopped. "Is that what you really think?"

"Of course. I've never been good enough for anyone in my entire life, so why would I be good enough for you?" Donald covered his face with his hands. Carter touched his hand, but Donald kept it where it was until he could somehow regain control.

"Whatever happened to you to make you think that, you need to let it go," Carter said gently. "If you were one of the kids in your care and he came to talk to you, what would you tell him?"

That was so not fair. Donald inhaled deeply and slowly let his hands fall away from his face. "I'd probably tell him to live his life to the fullest regardless. Bad things happen, and it isn't possible to change them—you can only learn to live with them. Which I was doing just fine with until you came along with your glasses and your hotness, and the fucking fact that you're such a damn nice guy."

"You were?" Carter asked, and Donald scoffed in dismissal, not that Carter seemed to be buying it. "You seemed miserable to me.

That whole Icicle act was just that, wasn't it? It was your defense mechanism. You pushed people away so you wouldn't be in danger of letting them in and getting hurt." Carter paused and glared at him. "Fuck, I thought it was something I'd done wrong, and here it was you all the time." Carter stepped closer, resting his hands lightly on Donald's shoulders. "Do you know what you end up with when you do that?"

"An unbroken heart," Donald answered flatly, as though it didn't matter at all.

Carter nodded. "And a very lonely one," he said before he stepped back and finished drying himself. Donald reached for his towel and began drying his arms, but stopped as he watched Carter bend down, running the towel up and down his thick thighs. Donald's hands seemed to have a mind of their own. They stopped moving and he let go of the towel. It fell to the floor, and Donald continued staring.

"What?" Carter asked softly, turning toward him.

Donald swallowed hard. He'd been caught staring in a huge way. "I was watching you."

"I know, and you're allowed." Carter straightened up in almost slow motion. "You're allowed to look all you want." Carter came closer once again. "What I don't understand is why you're content to just look."

"If you remember, we were doing a lot more than just looking a few minutes ago." Donald glanced toward the bedroom.

"I'm not talking about that. I mean your life. You spend all your time looking in from the outside as other people live theirs. You watch without getting involved." Carter tugged him closer and into his arms. "Don't you want to live? Because I sure as hell do. I want to be as happy as I can."

"If that's the case, why are you here? Lord knows I'm not Mr. Happy… not by a long shot."

"I know," Carter breathed. "But you could be if you let yourself."

Donald held him tighter and didn't say anything more. He wasn't sure he was capable of that. He'd been hiding his heart away for so long. The protective walls had been built over a long period of time and he wasn't sure he had tools to tear them down without destroying everything around him. "We should go back to bed," he said. He had to have time to think about all this, and he couldn't do that with Carter's heat so close to him. Hell, with Carter naked, pressed right against him, he couldn't think about anything else.

"I know what's going through that head of yours." Carter held him closer, sliding a knee between his. "Sometimes thinking is way overrated." Carter smiled then kissed him. Before Donald realized it, Carter had the bathroom door open and then lifted him off his feet.

"What are you doing?" Donald gasped, holding on to Carter so he didn't fall.

"Taking you back to bed. I know one sure-fire way to get you to stop thinking, and it involves me, you, lips, hands, and as many orgasms as I can pull out of you."

"We just cleaned up," Donald said weakly.

"That's the nice thing. The bathroom isn't going anywhere, and I like you all nice and wet." Carter laid him on the bed, and Donald stared up at him until Carter turned off the light and climbed in next to him. "Hold on, sweetheart, I intend to give you the ride of your life."

Damn if that wasn't exactly what he did. Carter might have intended for them to take another shower, but neither of them made it that far. They wore each other out and fell asleep a few hours later.

Donald woke at some point in the night to an empty bed. He knew Carter was still in the house, so he got up, put on his robe, and left the room. Donald found Carter outside Alex's room. "Was something wrong?"

"He had a nightmare," Carter answered. "I didn't want to wake you."

"You didn't. I was dead to the world until the bed felt a little cold. Is he okay?"

"Yes. He said that bad men were after him and he couldn't get away." Carter turned to him. "I didn't get a chance to talk to him like I wanted." He sighed. "Is there any way you can keep him out of foster care for another few days? I know it's hard, but I think he feels comfortable here. I'll call you tomorrow and arrange to meet with him so he and I can talk."

Donald huffed a little. "I'll speak with my supervisor." The truth was, he wasn't in a hurry to have Alex leave. The little boy had wormed his way into Donald's once-frozen heart the same way Carter had. Both of them scared him to death, while at the same time other fears kicked in and he didn't want either of them to leave. "It's really up to her. This is a little unorthodox, but under the circumstances…."

"Thank you. Do you have someone who can watch him while you're at work?"

"Yes. We have day care in the office. He can spend the day there. He'll be able to be around other children. That will be good for him." He didn't say it would also help Alex get ready for when he and Carter weren't with him, which was going to happen soon enough. Donald peered into the room. Alex was asleep once again, his bunny next to him on the covers. As they watched, Alex rolled over and pulled his bunny to him.

Carter turned away and walked toward the bedroom without another word.

Donald pulled the door to Alex's room almost closed and then followed him. "You know I'll do my best for him."

"I know," Carter said. "I just wish…."

Carter got into bed and Donald climbed in right behind him. "I know what you want for him, and you can help with that."

"I know," Carter said. "Tomorrow I'll turn over every rock I can find to see if he has any family. But if not…."

"Alex is young, and I don't think there will be any problems with finding a family to adopt him. I already have a few families that have expressed interest in taking in young children. The easiest to place are babies, with children like Alex not too far behind. As they get older, it gets harder, and teenagers…." Donald couldn't go into what happened to some teenagers in the foster care system. Not right now.

"I know," Carter whispered into the darkness, then said no more. Donald rolled onto his side and gently stroked Carter's chest. He really didn't know what to say to help Carter feel better. Maybe there was nothing for him to say. Donald would speak to his supervisor, and he didn't expect her to have a problem with Alex staying with him for a few more days. But that would be all they would allow—little more than a temporary reprieve.

Eventually Alex would need to move on, and Donald thought it would be best if that happened relatively soon. Alex was already bonding with them, and it was going to be harder on everyone once he was placed. Donald closed his eyes and used the back of his hand to wipe them as an image of Alex standing in the doorway of some nondescript foster home flashed in his mind. In Donald's vision, silent tears ran down Alex's cheeks as he stood there holding his bunny in front of him.

A lump formed in Donald's throat as the image faded and his own memories took over. Suddenly he was the one standing on the steps watching as he was left alone once again. Donald rolled away from Carter and buried his face in the pillow as the grief welled inside. He only hoped Carter didn't realize what was happening.

CHAPTER
Seven

CARTER WALKED into the station on Monday morning and went right down to the basement to his computer. He checked his e-mail and messages before getting to work. The information the department had been able to gather on Alex's family, what little there was, Carter found in his inbox, and he began searching the records. Thankfully, the county had digitized a lot of the records a few years back. He was able to find out that Alex's mother had a sister and a brother, which gave him hope.

"Shit," Carter swore as he looked through the information he'd been provided more closely. Alex's uncle was deceased, killed in Afghanistan a few years earlier. The grandparents were both dead.

"What's the problem?" a voice said from the doorway.

Carter looked up from where he was working. "I'm looking for someone who might be able to help raise Alex."

"That's not going to be easy," Smith said as he came in Carter's office and leaned over the desk. "We couldn't find any close family."

"What about his aunt?" Carter pointed to the screen. "His mother's brother is dead, but I can't find anything about his mother's sister."

"We don't know. If she's alive, she's outside the area. We were hoping you could cast a wider net for us." Pennsylvania was notorious for not sharing information with other states, so they didn't share information in return. "We have a name and a date of birth, but not much else."

"I can try, but unless she has a police record or bought property, I probably won't find her."

"I agree," Smith said. "This may not be a fruitful search. Sometimes we get lucky, but in this case it doesn't look like we will."

"No," Carter said, already feeling defeated. Not that he'd really held out hope, but sometimes, particularly with people on the fringes of society, they found estranged relatives. It didn't appear to be so in this case. "I did get Alex's DNA profile from the lab, but I doubt that's going to help us either."

"Probably not. If some relative were to come forward, we could verify their claim, but it's not going to really help us otherwise."

Carter set the information aside and stared at his screen. "This seems like one unhappy family. Plenty of tragedy." He absently went through other birth and census records.

"What are you doing?" Smith asked.

"Just being thorough." He wasn't expecting to find anything and he got what he expected. "I was just seeing what I could find on the missing sister. It seems she had a child—a boy—at some point, but there's no details, not even a name...."

"That could mean a number of things, like the child died or he was put up for adoption," Smith said. "Most of those records are sealed, and it really doesn't matter because that isn't going to help us find a guardian for the boy."

"I know," Carter agreed softly—he didn't want the other officer to hear his voice crack. "I'm just holding out hope for Alex."

Smith sat down in the seat next to his desk. "Carter, I know what I'm about to say isn't going to be popular or probably welcome, but you need to step back and let this go. The department knows you spent the weekend with this kid and the social worker. Now, what you do in your private life is your business. But to be a good police officer you need to maintain a certain level of detachment. Just like doctors do with their patients. We can't get involved with every person we come in contact with." Smith's expression softened. "We all took this job because we like people and want to make a difference. That's what we do every day. But as soon as you start to get personally involved, it affects your ability to do your job."

"How can I not get involved? This is a little kid. His mother is dead and—"

"Emotionally involved," Smith said, interrupting him. "And you are emotionally involved with Alex. You care about him, and if you're not careful, you could end up heartbroken." Smith leaned a little closer. "I'm not saying this to hurt you, but to warn you. This youngster is the same age as my Carol, and I would kill before I let anything happen to her, so I have an idea of how you're beginning to feel. But you need to stop this and pull away."

"How can I?" Carter asked.

"What are you going to do with the next child case that comes your way? Are you going to love that kid too? And what about the one after that? There will be dozens, maybe hundreds throughout your career. We do what we can and then we have to let Family and Children's Services do what they do." Smith stood up. "I know how you feel because I felt the exact same way you do when I had my first child case." Smith bit his lower lip. "I found a small child, a baby, really, in a dumpster. The poor thing was crying and scared to death. I pulled her out and comforted her. Lorraine had just given birth to Carol, so I treated the little one just like I had Carol. I rocked her in my arms, and as soon as I could, I got her some food. When her belly was full, she went to sleep in my arms. She had to have been about six months old and as cute as a button."

"God…," Carter breathed.

"Yeah. I held her while the paramedics examined her, and then I rode with them to the hospital. She slept most of the time, and when she woke up, I made another bottle and fed her. When she was done, she smiled, and fuck if my heart didn't warm. Within a few hours I had formulated the arguments I was going to use on Lorraine to get her to adopt the baby." Smith shook his head. "I'm good at my job and figured out her mother had abandoned her. I tracked down her family, but when the grandparents came to take her the next day, I was still devastated." Smith looked around and lowered his voice. "I never told anyone because I didn't want them to think I was soft. But I still keep tabs on that little girl. She's in first grade, and I see her every now and then with her grandmother."

"That's nice," Carter said. He and Smith had never talked very much. Smith seemed to be a rather quiet guy around the station, and Carter felt a little honored that he was sharing this.

"It is. But I was a fool. I let my heart get nine steps ahead of my head and reality. Granted, I had a baby at home and I kept thinking how I would feel if this had been Carol. And I learned I can't do that. Because a year later there was another little girl… and then a little boy." Smith blinked. "Just for the record, I know where each and every one of them is. Some are doing well, and others not so much."

"You keep an eye on all of them?" Carter asked.

"I used to. But it got to be too much, and I was spending too much of myself on it. Time and love I should have given to Lorraine, Carol, and now Arthur."

"Did you adopt Arthur?"

"Yes. But he wasn't one of my cases. Arthur is Lorraine's sister's son and she wasn't able to care for him, so we gave him a home and eventually she signed over her parental rights so Lorraine and I could adopt him legally. She is still in his life to the best she's able with her continued mental illness."

"Okay. But I think you're confusing me a little."

"Probably. No one's life is ever simple. What I'm saying is that if I'd given myself to every child who crossed my path professionally, I wouldn't have had the energy or the resources to help Arthur when he really needed it."

Carter shook his head. "So what you're saying is to pick my battles carefully."

Smith paused. "Maybe a little. But I'm also saying make sure you're doing things for the right reason. I know this child got to you. Hell, his story got to just about everyone at the station, and if this is a battle you really want to take on, then make sure you don't go halfway."

"Smith, you're talking in circles." Carter's head was starting to spin.

"Probably. Lorraine says I do that all the time. My advice for now is to try to keep some professional distance. It will help you make better decisions, and if things don't turn out the way you hope, you'll be able to come out the other end with your heart in one piece."

Carter chuckled and then burst into laughter.

"You think I'm funny?" Smith asked.

"No," Carter gasped. "I just never expected you and me to be having a conversation about hearts, flowers, and feelings. You haven't seemed like that kind of guy."

Smith puffed out his chest and his smile evaporated.

"Now that's the Smith I know."

Smith stood up, expression hardening. "Okay, then. I said what I needed to, and I expect you'll keep this to yourself." His stare held an extra note of warning.

Carter glanced around as Aaron Cloud came into his office. "Of course. Your reputation is safe with me." He wanted to thank him for taking the time, but Smith was already gone. The last thing Carter saw was him stalking off and then the office door banging closed behind him.

"What's up with him?" Aaron asked, turning away from the now forcefully closed door. "Did you piss him off?"

"No." Carter turned back to his screen. Let Aaron think what he wanted; Carter was going to keep his promise.

Giving up on the search for Alex's relatives as fruitless, he decided to see if he could take a crack at the videos. He'd dreaded doing this, but he didn't have a choice. Carter logged on to the site using the hard-drive partition he'd made earlier and went through the process to change his password. He should have done that earlier, but now he had absolute control over the account, and short of its deletion, it was his. He carefully searched for the videos uploaded by Byron and began uploading them to a temporary drive and then over to a special secure partition that he could use. This whole thing made him feel dirty, but he did it and then began looking at them.

To say they were disgusting was an understatement, but he needed to see if he could catch a glimpse of anyone else in the videos or just off camera. After watching a few, he got to know the tone of Byron Harker's voice off camera and basically ignored the video and listened. He figured even if he didn't see anything, maybe he would hear it.

After an hour, he needed a break. He wanted a long shower with sandpaper instead of soap. His stomach had turned more than once. He read through the e-mails he'd received and picked up his phone.

"Smith."

"Which videos led you to believe someone else was involved?"

"The spanking videos."

Carter closed his eyes. Those were the exact ones he did not want to watch under any circumstances. "I was afraid of that."

"Look." Smith's voice got real soft. "This is what I was talking about earlier. You need to be able to do your job. Those videos were hell for all of us to watch, especially any of us with kids."

"But you got through them without any trouble?"

"We did what we had to do because that's how we keep our children safe. It may not be pretty or happy, but if it gets someone who does this kind of thing off the streets, it makes all kids safer."

Carter noticed that Smith didn't answer the question directly, and he didn't push. He imagined Smith pulling at his collar and wishing this conversation was over the same way he did. "Okay. I'll bite the bullet." He hung up and downloaded the videos he hadn't wanted to see.

Carter loaded the first one and let the video play. After about sixty seconds he began feeling sick. At the two-minute mark, he stopped the video, picked up the trash can, and lost his breakfast. Carter cleaned up the mess in the bathroom and splashed water on his face before returning to his desk. He had no idea how he was going to watch any more of this, but he forced himself to.

Alex was crying and begging for it to stop. Carter closed his eyes, and then he heard it.

"That's a good little piggy."

Carter gasped. That wasn't Byron's voice. He paused the video, listened again, and then worked to isolate the vocal tone. It took him a few minutes, but he was able to get a decent profile of the voice. Then he had the computer scan the rest of the video for the signature and isolated those portions. It was a painstaking process, but it meant he wouldn't have to actually watch them.

"Are you making any headway?" his captain asked just before lunchtime. Not that Carter was in the least bit hungry.

"I was able to isolate a second voice in a few places on the video. I was just about to see if I could use that to compare it to the others."

"Let me hear what you have," the captain said, and Carter played the compiled sections of the video that he'd enhanced to bring out the second voice. "Jesus," he said. "Is that enough to use for comparison?"

"I already did," Carter admitted.

"How long to go through the other videos?"

"An hour or so each, I'd guess," Carter answered. "I have to set them up and then scan them."

"All right. But I want you to play what you've already got for everyone in the office. If this guy is on the video, then he was in that house at some point and he may be local. It's a long shot, but what if someone recognizes him? I'll call everyone together, and you get the vocal track ready to play. Meet you upstairs in the squad room in ten." The captain left, and Carter began getting everything together.

Just before going upstairs, Carter called Donald.

"How's it going?" Donald asked.

"Not good on the family front, but I made some progress with the videos… after I got sick." Carter paused. "Do you think you can bring Alex down here in an hour or so?"

"An hour and a half works better," Donald countered, and Carter agreed.

"Be sure to bring some of his toys and his bunny. This is going to be hard enough. He should have familiar things around him."

"All right. I'm also going to ask one of our psychologists to come too. I know you'll look out for him, but…."

"I think it's a good idea," Carter said. "I need to go. But I'll see you and Alex in a little while. When you get here, be sure to ask for me, and I'll take you through. I can fill you in when I see you."

"All right."

Carter disconnected and hurried upstairs to the squad room. It wasn't very large and looked very little like what he saw on television. Mostly it was a meeting room that would fit the people in the department. A few white boards had been hung on the walls. They were clean now, but most of the time they were covered with theories and case details. The duty roster was posted on one of the bulletin boards, while another was covered with fliers and posters for events and things for sale.

"Let me have your attention," the captain said from the front of the room. "I know you're all busy, but we have a case that involves children and underage videos. Carter Schunk was able to isolate the voice of the man we're after. Our suspect in custody isn't talking about anything and we need to find this guy. He may be the financier behind this. So what I'd like you all to do is listen to the voice and see if he sounds familiar." The captain paused for a few seconds as murmurs rose in the room. "I know this seems like a long shot, but this is a small town, not New York. We meet and listen to people all day." He stepped back, and Carter got his player hooked into the sound system. Then he turned it on and the snippets from the video played. When it was done, he played it again.

"I was able to isolate that from one video, and it's possible he's on a few others. The thing is, the boy involved is five years old, and those things you heard were said to him." The room went quiet. "Yes—piggy, piece of shit—all those names were directed at a five-year-old who, when asked, actually thought P.O.S. was his name." Carter couldn't bring himself to say the words a second time. "We need to find this man and stop him." Carter backed away from the microphone and played the recording one last time to an otherwise silent room.

"Thank you, Carter," Captain Murphy said. "We need your help. Carter can send you the file if you need it. But think about what you just heard. Someone paid Harker for these videos. We've tried following the money, but the amounts are small enough to stay under the radar of most systems because he appears to have paid in cash. As you know, reports are required for larger cash deposits. So this is our first solid lead." He paused and a hand went up. "Yes, Cloud."

"Are there plans to release this to the media?"

"Not at this time. But we will consider it. The content isn't really broadcast material, but we may need to resort to that if we can't get anywhere. I'd prefer not to."

Carter stepped forward when there were no more questions, and Captain Murphy moved aside. "The little boy from the videos is coming here in little over an hour. He's five but looks younger, and sometimes gets scared, so if you see him, please say hello and smile. Alex needs all the people in his corner that he can get, and he knows who this man is. He's seen him. I'm hoping he can tell us something."

"But he's five," one of the officers said.

"I know what he tells us might not hold up in court, but locked in his head is a picture of the bad men who hurt him. He's scared to death of them. But he remembers. So if we approach it right, he might be able to help. All I'm asking is to try to make this as unthreatening a place for him as possible." Carter stepped away, and the captain dismissed everyone.

Smith hung behind and joined Carter as he was unhooking the audio feed. "I'd like to be there when you question him."

"He's going to be afraid of you," Carter said. "That isn't going to help."

"I know. But I'll be nearby if you need anything."

"Thanks," Carter said with a quick smile. "For everything." Carter finished and closed the audio cabinet. Then he went back downstairs to his desk and got to work on the videos. The second one he'd chosen didn't have anything that matched the audio signature, but the third one did. He checked the clock on the computer and saw he had ten minutes until Alex and Donald were set to arrive. He pulled up those particular sections of the video and viewed them. He hoped there was something for him to see, but the man stayed out of camera range and only his voice could be heard. He'd been hoping for something....

His desk phone rang. Carter answered it and then locked his system and went upstairs. Donald and Alex waited out in reception, along with a woman. Donald stood as he approached, and Alex hurried over when he saw him. "Mr. Carter," he said with a small smile, Bunny clutched in front of him. Carter lifted him into his arms, giving Alex a hug.

"This is Marie St. Clare," Donald said, and Carter shook her hand.

"I'm Officer Schunk. It's nice to meet you. Let me lead you back to where we're going to be." He set Alex down, then used his access card to unlock the door and walked them through and back to one of the breakrooms. "I thought this would be more comfortable." There was a sofa against one wall and a few chairs around a table.

"Very good," Marie said.

"This isn't an interrogation. But we all think Alex might be able to help us." Carter motioned for them to sit down.

"How do you want to do this?" Marie asked.

"I just want to talk to him," Carter explained as Alex climbed on the sofa next to Donald, his eyes wide as he looked all around. "Alex, I asked you and Mr. Donald to come here because I really need your help. See, I wanna catch the bad men and put them in jail where they can never get to you."

"No bad men. I good, not bad." Alex moved closer to Donald, his eyes widening even further, and he crushed his bunny to him.

"You were always good." Carter crouched down in front of Alex. "You are a good boy. Mr. Donald and I know that. The bad men were very naughty, and I need your help to find them. Do you think you can do that for me?" Carter kept his voice level and as kind as he could, despite the anger that welled up inside him. He understood in those few moments what Smith had been talking about. If he didn't maintain some sort of professional distance, he would never get the information he needed, and he was the only one from the department Alex would trust enough to speak with. He had to keep it together to help Alex.

Alex nodded really slowly.

"That's good. Now, is Mr. Donald a bad man?" Alex shook his head. "Am I a bad man?" Carter asked and got the same answer. "Is Mrs. St. Clare a bad man?"

Alex giggled. "She's a girl." Carter glanced at her and saw Marie nodding slightly.

"Okay. So girls can't be bad men. That's really good to know." He laughed too. "Do the bad men have names?"

Alex nodded. "Mr. Byron, he's a bad man." Alex shifted on the sofa like his little backside hurt. Carter knew the source of that and had expected that reaction.

"Mr. Byron is in jail, where all bad men go, and he's going to stay there." Carter lifted his gaze to Donald. "His bail was set sky high and no one will post it." He turned back to Alex. "I promise you. No more Mr. Byron." He smiled and Alex nodded. "Are there other bad men?"

Alex nodded and looked down at his feet. "I not piggy."

Carter shared a glance with the others. "Did the other bad man call you that?" Alex nodded without looking up. "That wasn't very nice."

Alex jumped down off the sofa, leaving his bunny behind. He raced around the room, pulling at the chairs. "I'm not piggy," he screamed. Carter wasn't sure what to do.

"Of course you aren't," Marie said in a gentle tone. "You're Alex, and that was mean of him to call you that."

"He's a… a… poopy head," Alex blurted, and Carter kept a grin off his face. He figured if Alex was fighting back in any way, it was a good sign.

"Did he have a name? Like you have the name Alex or like me and Mr. Donald. Did he have a name?" Carter tried not to get too excited.

Alex thought a few seconds and then nodded before walking around the table. He continued moving and Carter was getting impatient but didn't want to interrupt him.

"Mr. Boss," Alex said, and Carter suppressed a groan.

"Did Mr. Byron call him anything else?" Marie asked in a very gentle tone, but Alex shook his head and walked over to Carter.

"He called me piggy. I'm not a piggy!" he spat. Alex pulled on one of the chairs and it fell backward and crashed to the floor. Alex jumped and stared at it before turning to Carter. "No bad men. No spank. I be good." He placed his hands over his butt and ran toward the sofa. Carter caught him and hugged him tight.

"It's all right. The bad men are gone." He didn't give a crap about professional distance any longer.

"I'm sorry. I not bad."

"It's okay. The chair just fell." Carter held Alex for a few minutes and then shifted him onto Donald's lap. "You're a good boy." Carter crouched once again. "I'm really proud of you."

Then Carter picked up the chair and set it back in place.

Marie stood up and motioned him to the other side of the room. "You handled that very well. I'm surprised you got as much from him as you did. He's obviously still very traumatized."

"I know and I hate it."

"Give him a few minutes and then see if he knows anything else."

Carter nodded. He walked back to Alex and Donald and sat beside them on the couch. A few minutes later, he said softly, "Are there any other bad men?" Alex shook his head. "So just Mr. Byron and Mr. Boss? Those were the only bad men?" Alex nodded and buried his face on Donald's chest. At least Carter knew there were only the two of them, at least from Alex's perspective. But that still didn't get him any closer to who this "boss" actually was.

"Alex," Marie said softly. "Could you draw a picture for me?" She got up and pulled some paper and crayons out of her bag. Carter wasn't sure what this would get them, but Alex seemed to calm and went over to the table. "That's great. Just make a picture for me. Anything you want."

Alex turned to look at her and then back around and opened the crayons.

"We aren't going to get much more," Donald whispered.

"I'm afraid not. I think he's told us what he can," Carter agreed.

"He can tell us a little bit more. Just in a different way and with a little time," Marie said. "Sit down and give me a few minutes." Marie sat next to Alex at the table, and Carter sat down on the sofa with Donald. They shared a brief smile and then Carter returned his attention to Alex. "That's a very good picture," Marie said when Alex handed it to her. She set it aside and emptied the box of crayons onto the table. "I need you to be a really good, big boy for me. Can you do that?"

"Yes."

Carter picked up Alex's bunny and brought it to him. Alex took it and stared at Marie. "Very good. I want you to think of what Mr. Boss looked like. When I ask you a question, just pick up the crayon that answers the question, okay? That's all you need to do."

"Okay," Alex whispered.

"Now, what color was Mr. Boss's face?"

Carter wanted to interject to help him, but Marie shook her head. After a few seconds, Alex picked up the peach-colored crayon as well as the red one and handed them to Marie. Carter pulled his notebook from his pocket and began taking notes.

"That's very good. Where was he red? Show me on your face," Marie instructed. Alex touched his cheeks, and Carter noted it. "What color was Mr. Boss's hair?" Alex picked up the blue crayon and giggled. "Was it really?" Marie said as she chuckled. Alex set down the crayon and picked up first the black crayon and then a gray one. "His hair was both?"

Alex nodded and Marie took the crayons and placed them on the table.

"This is a hard one. Can you show me what color his eyes were?"

Alex grabbed the brown and handed it to her. "He's a poopy head," Alex declared. Carter turned to Donald.

"Should I be insulted?" Carter asked.

Donald shook his head. "He's associating that specifically with him. Unfortunately, he may not have brown eyes in reality. That could just be Alex's association."

Marie seemed to understand because she turned to them. "Does he have eyes like Mr. Donald's or Mr. Carter's?" Alex turned and pointed to Carter. That seemed to confirm it. "Thank you, sweetheart. You did really well. Do you want to go sit with Mr. Donald again?" He didn't move, and Marie leaned over and gave him a hug. "You're an amazing big boy and you did so good."

When she released him, Alex climbed down off the stool and walked over to where Carter and Donald sat waiting.

Carter put his pad back in his pocket and hugged Alex carefully. "You were a big help."

"No more bad men," Alex said softly, and Carter rocked him back and forth slightly. He knew this had been traumatic for him, and he was so proud of Alex. He'd done his best and he'd given them some information. A name would have been better, but they had the beginnings of a description. "Are you ready to go with Mr. Donald and Mrs. Marie?"

Alex nodded.

"Good. You have fun playing this afternoon. Okay?" Carter put Alex down, and Marie held out her hand. Alex took it, and she led him out of the room.

"What else do you have?" Donald asked after Marie and Alex had left.

"Not a great deal. His voice and what Alex could describe. We know he's a white guy with red cheeks, salt-and-pepper hair, and brown eyes. It isn't a whole lot, but it's more than I had. We know it was just the two of them as well." Carter was getting more and more frustrated. Every line of inquiry seemed to reach a dead end. "His mother's family is pretty much a dead end. There's a sister that we can't trace and a possible cousin, but the records are sealed." Carter sighed. "I've tried everything I can think of but I can't seem to help him."

"I think you already have," Donald whispered. "His primary abuser is behind bars and looks to remain there. The other guy has got to be scared shitless that Harker is going to talk or that you'll find a trail to him, so he isn't going to be doing anything."

"What did your supervisor say about Alex staying with you?" Carter asked.

"She's afraid I'm getting too close. The only reason she isn't ordering me to put him in a permanent foster home today is because of the police involvement. She thinks that would be too much to expect from a foster family." Donald swallowed and shifted his gaze across the room. "But I'm going to have to place him tomorrow."

Carter nodded. He'd known this was coming. "I know. I wish there was something else we could do."

"Do you really think there is some of his family out there?" Donald asked.

"Possibly somewhere. But it isn't likely that they're going to be willing to take him in."

"But can you try?" Donald asked. "Anything is reason for hope."

"I'll try. But I'm running out of things to do." They were alone in the room, and Carter reached for Donald's hand. When he didn't pull away, Carter squeezed it. "I'll do everything in my power to help."

"I know you will," Donald said.

"I got Alex's DNA profile, and I can see if I can run it against some known databases. Since his family is—or was—local, I might get a hit. It's going to take a while. But I could get a close match."

"Have you done that before?"

"A few times. Mostly to match a suspect, but there is a common data type used. I could see if we get lucky. Like I said, it could take a while, and it would only work if someone in his family happened to be on file. But it can't hurt." Carter wasn't particularly optimistic, but he had to give it a try. He stood and let go of Donald's hand. "I need to get back to work. Will you call me this evening?"

"Sure. You should spend some time with him." Donald sounded hopeless. The iceman was gone and in his place was a man full of fear and heartbreak. Carter felt it keenly because it echoed inside him.

"I'll see you later, then." Carter left the room and said good-bye to Marie and to Alex, hugging him before returning to his desk to write up what he'd found and get started on his next set of tasks.

AT THE end of the day, Carter was getting ready to go home when his cell phone rang. Carter answered it with a smile, recognizing Donald's number. "Hey."

"I just got home with Alex and he's asking for you. All he's done since we left the station was ask when he was going to see you."

Carter smiled and then it faded. He was thrilled that Alex wanted to see him, but it would have been nice if Donald had indicated that he wanted to see him as well. "I want to see him too." He almost added that he was equally excited about Donald, but held back. This was all so damned confusing. Donald had at least indicated he would think about what they'd talked about the night before, and he'd called, so that was a step forward. But....

"Look," Donald began, and Carter braced himself for what was to come. He'd heard that tone before from Donald, and it was the same one he'd used just before never returning his calls. "I think you and I need to talk. I'm making some dinner—nothing fancy—and then once Alex is asleep, we... I...." Donald paused and Carter held still with the phone pressing harder and harder to his ear. "I've been thinking about what you said last night... a lot."

"Okay...."

"We need to talk," Donald added just above a whisper.

"All right. I'm about to leave now. I'm going to go home to change first. I'll be there in an hour." Carter took a deep breath to still his racing heart. He dared not hope that what Donald had to say was going to be good news. He'd pulled away before, and it was likely this conversation was the precursor to him doing it again.

"I'll see you then," Donald said and hung up. Carter had been about to lock his computer, but he sat down at his desk and pulled up the search screens for the state criminal justice records. He knew Donald's information and entered it. Carter stared at the screen to make sure he had all the information and was about to press enter when he paused and backed out of the application. Sure, he could probably find out a great deal if he wanted to, but no. If he was going to find out about Donald, then it had to come from him.

Carter checked on the DNA searches he had running, then locked his system and left the building. It was raining hard when he stepped outside. He hurried through the parking lot, got in his car, and drove home as fast as he could.

Inside his apartment, he stripped out of his work clothes, secured his weapon, and then grabbed a shower. Usually he'd walk to Donald's, but because of the weather he drove instead. He found a parking space near Donald's house. Donald opened the door at his knock and let him in, saying a quick hello before hurrying back to the kitchen.

Alex raced over and grabbed his legs. Carter grinned from ear to ear. "Hey, buddy," he said and lifted Alex into his arms. He refused to dwell on the fact that he wouldn't be able to do this for long. "You were a big help today." He walked toward the kitchen, where he heard Donald working.

"Did you find anything?"

"Not yet. I have the search we talked about running, but it will take a while. There are lots of data points to match." He wanted to lean in for a kiss, but Donald didn't turn toward him. That right there told Carter a great deal about how the night was going to go.

"Dinner will be ready in just a few minutes." Donald drained the pasta and then began saucing it.

"Smells nummy, doesn't it?" Carter said to Alex, who nodded and licked his lips. He was adorable, and Carter did not relish telling him that tomorrow he was going to live someplace else.

"Alex, will you go in and pick up your toys for me?" Donald asked. Carter set him down, and Alex raced away. "This has been the day from hell," Donald said as soon as Alex left the room. "I asked my boss for a few more days, and she looked at me and then shook her head. I have to place Alex tomorrow... and I have to try to explain it to him tonight."

"You know there is an easy solution to all this," Carter began. Donald set down his pots. "Just take Alex and foster him yourself. It's obvious that you care for him, and you have child care while you're at work."

Donald shook his head. "I can't do that."

"Why not?" Carter asked, and immediately he ran up against Donald's brick wall of silence. Carter stepped closer. "I wish you'd trust me enough to tell me what has you so afraid." He wound his arms around Donald's waist.

"I can't."

"Why? What are you afraid of?"

Donald turned in his arms. "Honestly? That you'll realize just how broken and unrepairable I am." Donald looked away.

"Stop that," Carter said. "Look at me. I'm here and I've been here."

"You're only here because of Alex," Donald countered.

"Is that what you really think? He's an amazing little boy, and yes… I think I've come to love him and I'd hate not to see him any longer. The little guy worked his way into my heart some time ago, and I doubt I'll ever forget him, no matter what happens. But I'm here because of you." Carter tugged him closer. "Because of the smile I see every now and then when you don't think I'm watching. I'm here because in those few unguarded moments I see the real you, not the one that's hidden behind this block of ice you created." Carter turned toward the living room. "That little boy cares about you. If you're so unredeemable, do you think he'd trust you the way he does?"

"Alex trusts *you*," Donald countered.

"That's not entirely true. Did you see how he hurried to put his toys away? He's five. They never put toys away. But he's in there doing what you asked. It isn't just me and you know it. You're shutting yourself off again because you're afraid."

"You don't know anything," Donald protested.

"I know enough. I'm a good judge of character and I can tell when someone is hiding. That's what you're doing. I know it, and so do you." Carter started to question why he cared so much, but he knew: Donald was under his skin and in his heart. Donald just stared at him, and Carter stared right back. "I'm the one with two sisters and a brother. If you want a staring contest, I can do this all day and all night."

Donald turned his head away, but Carter felt no victory whatsoever.

"If things are as bad as you think and all you're going to do is push me away, then what do you have to lose by opening up? What does it matter if you freeze me out? Or if, as you say, I turn away because you're unfixable, or whatever the hell you said."

"Because it matters, okay?" Donald said, looking at him again.

"Because everybody leaves? Is that it? You think it will hurt less if you're the one doing the pushing? It doesn't. It hurts all the same, and you know what? You've guaranteed the outcome. So what if a miracle happens and I still think you're a hot guy who I happen to really like, and maybe more? What then?" Carter released Donald and backed away.

"You know, sometimes you talk way too damn much."

"And sometimes you're way too pigheaded for your own good." Carter flashed Donald a smile.

To Carter's surprise, Donald didn't turn away. "There's nothing sexy about finding out how big a mess someone is."

Carter shook his head. "You know what's sexy? Trust. Knowing someone is willing to trust you with their biggest secret. That's truly sexy."

"No, it's not," Donald said with a shake of his head.

"Yes, it is." Carter leaned against the counter. "Trust, affection, kindness—they're all components of something bigger with the potential to last. But if you don't take a chance, you'll never know. We'll never know."

"Okay." Donald returned to finishing dinner. "What's your biggest secret?"

"One my parents don't know? I once hacked into the computer system of a federal government agency to get information on a case that they refused to share with us. We couldn't use it in our case, but it put a dangerous man behind bars. One the feds were trying to protect under the guise of national security. I would have gone to prison if they had found out. I still could." Carter's heart rate spiked as he thought about it. "But I'd do it again to get a lowlife off the street."

"They never figured it out?"

"No. But I did make an anonymous call to tell them where their security hole was. I figured that was the right thing to do." Carter winked, and Donald shook his head in what Carter figured was disbelief.

"You actually did that."

"Sure. We're on the same side, and if I could get in, then so could someone malicious. I just needed specific information and took only what I needed. Someone else could take everything they could get their hands on and really do some damage. I haven't checked that they fixed the hole because I don't want to press my luck." Carter pushed away from the counter. "So you see, I'm an even bigger geek than you thought. And just so you know, I have never told anyone about that. Not even my captain. They asked how I got the info, and I told them they didn't want to know. I dropped the files on the captain's desk and walked out of his office. I'm a clean cop. I always stuck to the rules, and I felt as dirty after that as I did watching those videos from Harker's account."

"That's because you're a good, decent man," Donald said.

"Mr. Carter," Alex called from the other room.

"Go ahead and check on him. I'll call when dinner's ready."

Carter nodded and went into the other room. Alex had piled up all his toys in one corner. Carter wasn't convinced that's what Donald had meant when he'd asked Alex to pick up his toys, but at least they were no longer strewn around the room. Alex looked pleased with what he'd done. "Are you hungry?"

Alex nodded. Of course. This kid was always hungry.

"Let's wash our hands and then we can go see what Mr. Donald made for us."

Alex hurried to the kitchen, and Carter followed. Donald was still busy, so Carter held Alex up to the sink while Alex washed his hands. Carter sighed louder than he intended.

"Are you sad, Mr. Carter?" Alex asked.

"No. I'm fine." He forced a smile and put Alex down. "Go on to the table and get settled." Donald put some pasta in a bowl for Alex and then made plates for the two of them. Alex, of course, dug in like he hadn't eaten for days.

Carter kept watching Donald as they ate, fascinated by his incredible eyes. He figured it would be easier to figure out the mysteries of life than to try to understand what made Donald tick or why that was so interesting. Maybe Donald was just a challenge or Carter was a glutton for punishment. Maybe it was the fact that Donald had been the only guy he'd really connected with in so long that he was in sexual overdrive.

That was so true. Just looking at Donald made his heart race and his breath quicken. When those lips closed around his fork, Carter imagined them closing around something else. A soft moan formed in his throat, which, thank God, he could cover as being about the food rather than a completely different appetite.

"Is my food really that good?" Donald asked.

Carter colored and tried not to look too embarrassed. Then he figured what the hell. There was no use being shy. He grinned and continued eating, unconcerned and happy. After they were done, Carter helped Donald clean up, and then he spent some time with Alex, playing on the living room floor.

Eventually Donald sat down in one of the chairs, watching Alex as he continued playing. "You look like someone just said your mother died," Donald whispered, and Carter nodded.

"That's how I feel, I guess. Like something is ending."

"Everything ends," Donald said with little emotion. Carter turned toward him but said nothing, and they sat quietly for a while with Carter descending into unsettled thoughts.

"I think it's time for you to go to bed," Donald told Alex.

"A few more minutes?" Alex asked softly, but he stopped playing.

"Put your toys away, and then we'll go up so you can take a bath and then get into your pajamas. If you ask nicely, I'm sure Mr. Carter will read you a story before bed."

Alex hurried and put his toys into a crate Donald brought out from the closet. Once his things were put away, Donald and Alex went up the stairs. Carter stayed where he was and turned on the television, keeping the volume low. Not that he really paid much attention to it.

Eventually he heard rapid footsteps on the stairs and Alex raced over in airplane pajamas, carrying a book and Bunny. "Read to me." He climbed on the sofa and sat down next to him.

"You take Mr. Carter upstairs and get in bed. He'll read to you there." Donald stood on the stairs, and Carter got to his feet, lifting Alex into his arms.

"You're getting to be a really big boy. It won't be long before I won't be able to carry you." Carter pushed the thought aside that he might never be able to again after tonight. He carried Alex up the stairs and into his room.

Alex scrambled to get under the covers and held his bunny, looking up at him expectantly. Carter turned off the overhead light and switched on the one on the dresser. It was softer and much more conducive to Alex getting sleepy while Carter read him his story. Then Carter made sure Alex was comfortable and settled. "*Thomas the Tank Engine*," Carter read, and then he opened the book and began to read his last bedtime story to Alex.

CHAPTER

DONALD TURNED out the lights and locked the doors. The house was quiet as he climbed the stairs, except for the sound of Carter's voice from Alex's room. He stopped outside the open doorway as Carter read the last of the story. Donald peered in the room. Alex was still awake, listening to Carter, holding his bunny tightly with a smile on his cherubic face.

"The end," Carter read and then closed the book and set it aside. He settled Alex in bed and turned out the light. "Good night," Carter whispered.

"Good night, Mr. Carter. I love you."

Donald backed away and nearly ended up tumbling backward down the stairs. He caught himself, hurried to his bedroom, and closed the door. He tripped over the edge of the rug and fell forward, his upper body landing on the bed. He climbed onto the mattress and buried his head in a pillow.

Years of suppressed pain welled up from places inside him he no longer thought existed. He tried to stop it, to put it back in the boxes he'd held it in for years, but it wouldn't go back. All he could think was how much he'd have given to hear Alex say he loved him. Donald tried to remember the last time anyone had used the word love in reference to him but couldn't. His mind held no memory of his name and the word love ever being used together. No wonder he acted like his heart was made of ice.

"Donald." He heard footsteps and then the bed dipped next to him. "What happened?"

"Just go away," he croaked out. "Leave me alone."

"Oh for God's sake," Carter said. "Don't be so Jane Austen." Before Donald could ask what the hell Carter meant, Carter cradled him in his arms, holding him tight as he slowly rubbed his back. "What happened?"

"I heard you and Alex." Donald gasped. "Tomorrow I'll start the paperwork so you can be Alex's foster parent. He needs you. I'll help you get whatever support you need, and I'm sure the department has support programs for officers who are single parents." Donald wiped his eyes. "I should have been helping you all along rather than throwing up roadblocks. I heard him say he loved you."

"Yes. He said he loved me," Carter whispered as he lightly stroked Donald's hair. "He also said he loved you." Carter's voice broke.

"He did?" Donald wiped his eyes, finding that hard to believe.

"Of course he did. That little boy in there lost his mother and has nightmares about what bad men did to him, and yet he still loves you. Loves us." Carter held him tighter. Donald returned Carter's hug. "So I figure maybe between us, we can figure out a way to make sure Alex knows he's loved in return. You think I should be his foster parent. But I think he should stay here, with you, because it's already familiar to him."

Donald nodded, unable to speak.

"Go talk to him," Carter whispered. "He isn't asleep and he was asking for you."

Donald sat up and wiped his eyes. Then he got up and wiped his face, taking a deep breath to steady himself. "I don't know if I can." He was scared to death and had no idea why. Carter took his hand and opened the bedroom door. Donald took another deep breath and walked across the hall, clutching Carter's hand in his.

Alex lay on his side, but he rolled over as soon as they came in the room. "I wanted to say good night," Donald said softly. He released Carter's hand and walked over to the bed to sit on the edge. Alex scooted closer and then stood up on the bed and threw his arms around Donald's neck.

"Good night, Mr. Donald." Alex hugged him and then dropped back to the bed with a bounce before scooting under the covers. He turned onto his back, looking up at Donald with an adorable look on his face. How Alex could look as innocent and caring after all he'd been through was amazing to Donald. He'd always known children were resilient; he had been. Things had really started to go to hell as he'd gotten older. "I love you," Alex said. He sat up again, and Donald leaned closer, hugging Alex in return. How in the hell could anyone love him? But one look said that Alex really did love him. It was almost more than Donald could believe.

"I love you too," he whispered. "I was wondering if you'd like to stay here with me." Donald figured Alex didn't really know what Donald was asking him. "I want you to live here and this would be your room." Donald turned to Carter, who smiled and nodded. "Do you remember Mrs. Karla from my work? Well, I'll talk to her in the morning and arrange for you to live here if you want me to. No more bad men. We'll be a family. Is that okay?" He waited for Alex to nod and then hugged him again before settling him back into bed. "I love you," Donald said for the second time, leaning over the bed to kiss Alex's forehead. Then he stepped back and Alex rolled onto his side, holding his bunny. Donald lost track of how long he stood there. Carter eventually took his hand and gently led him across the hall to the bedroom.

"I'm so proud of you," Carter said.

"Is that okay? If Alex stays here? Earlier I said…."

"Hey. All I want is for Alex to be with someone who cares for him." Carter placed his hands on Donald's cheeks and gently guided him in for a kiss that deepened until Donald lightly patted Carter's chest. "What is it?"

"We can't do this," Donald said. "I can't do this. Not now."

Carter turned toward the door. "But I thought…."

"There are some things I need to tell you before anything else happens between us." Donald sat down on the edge of the bed. "My birth mother gave me up for adoption when I was a baby, and the parents I remember are my adoptive ones. I was four when my mom died. Dad said she had cancer and that he was going to take care of me. I remember that as clear as anything. He was a firefighter, and one day he didn't come home. A roof collapsed in a building while he was still inside trying to rescue some people who'd been trapped." Donald sighed. "At least that's what I was told, and I wanted to believe my dad was a hero. That's what kept me going."

"What happened after that? Did you live with your grandparents?"

Donald shook his head. "I ended up in foster care." He stared down at his shoes. "People kept saying that I would get adopted, but I didn't. I kept track after that, and from the time I was six until I was eighteen and graduated from high school, I lived in twelve foster homes. See, I know a lot of what Alex went through because I've been there. The longest I lived anywhere was two years, and I was happy there until my foster dad decided I should give him what his wife wouldn't." Donald lifted his head. "I guess I was a tough kid, because I lashed out at him. Threw a glass and hit him in the face. It cut him pretty bad. They tried to blame me for it, and I almost believed it until I got assigned to a new social worker. Her name was Clare, and she stayed with me longer than anyone. She stood up for me, and yeah, she moved me to different homes. But she was there for me."

"What happened?"

"I liked her and I thought she cared about me—"

"Did she hurt you?"

Carter's sharp tone startled him.

"No. She got pregnant and left to have a baby. I was reassigned and didn't see her anymore. I thought I was special, but I was just another case for her."

"I'm sure that isn't so. Are the kids you care for just cases for you?" Carter asked.

"No. I try my best for each one, and there have been kids I've followed. Even if I no longer have their case, I still go see them. They're some of the most in-need members of society. They don't have parents and rely on the kindness of others for their care and well-being. Most foster parents are caring, loving people."

"Is that why you became a social worker?"

"Yeah. I wanted to help kids so none of them would go through what I did." Donald met Carter's gaze. "I have the longest foster-care retention record of anyone in the department. That means that the kids in my care are less likely to move around the way I did. I help and I'm there for both the foster parents and the kids. But I can't let each story get to me."

"Ah. And after being with so many people and having others turn away, you found it easier to become detached, emotionally."

"It was how I survived. It's the only way I know how to keep going. That is, until I walked into that house last week. You and Alex entered my life and threw everything into chaos. What had been working for so long wasn't anymore. So I kept trying to pull away."

"Yeah, I figured that out." Carter took Donald's hand, stroking the back with his thumb. "What I don't understand is why you would be ashamed of any of this. You went through difficult years and survived. It shows you're a strong person, and none of it was your fault." Carter continued caressing his hand, and Donald closed his eyes. What he had to say next was the difficult part.

"After I left foster care I was on my own with pretty much no money and no job. My last social worker helped me get accepted to a college and I got some help with the tuition and things, but if I wanted to have anything to live on, I had to get a job." He turned toward Carter but wasn't able to look at him. "So I got one."

"What did you do?" Carter whispered, tension building in the room.

"I got a job at a club as a dancer. Basically I was a stripper. I danced and took off my clothes. That part wasn't so bad, I guess. But after a while I found out I could make more money after the shows were over. Guys would pay me a ton to go to a motel for a few hours, and I was tired of being hungry and going without... everything. The other kids got new clothes, video games, you name it, and I was struggling to eat on the days the dining hall was closed. If I worked a few days a month, I could make more than what I needed. So, yeah, I went with guys and did what they wanted."

"If that's how you really feel, then why were you so ashamed of it?" Carter asked with an innocent expression that Donald knew held a lot more than Carter was giving away.

"I did what I had to do then. I'm not proud of it now. But I got through school and was able to get a real job after I graduated."

"And you didn't catch anything? You aren't ill, are you?" Carter peppered him with questions, just not the ones Donald had been expecting.

"I'm fine. I was always careful and had rules I wouldn't violate. I played it safe and I stayed that way." Donald dared a glance at Carter, who was staring at his own shoes. He should have known. Carter couldn't bear to even look at him. "That's what I had to do to make it through college."

"What? Give blowjobs to old men who paid you?" Carter snapped, and Donald moved away. "No one should have to do that." Carter stood up and walked toward the bedroom door. He was leaving, exactly as Donald had feared he would. "You didn't have to do that. You could have found a different way."

"How? Working at McDonald's? I would have had to work full time there to make what I could get a few weekends a month. This way I had time to study and I was actually able to get an education." Donald shook his head. "I should have known better than to expect you to understand. You have a family that cares for you. I had nothing at all. No one. You say your dad doesn't talk to you, but mine is dead. After that I had foster parents who were paid by the state to take me in. You can bitch and complain all you want, but you don't know shit." Donald cradled his head in his hands. "I should have kept quiet and left things as they were."

Carter whirled around. "Hey," he snapped in what had to be his policeman voice. "I'm mad as hell, but I'm not angry with you." Carter strode over toward him. "Yeah, you probably shouldn't have been doing some of the things you were doing, but that's in the past."

"It's what? You're what?" Donald rubbed his ears to make sure he'd heard right.

"If you think for a minute that I'm happy about what you did, I'm not. No one should ever feel as though they have to do that." Carter knelt in front of him. "I hate that you danced on stage, and I'm shaking with rage when I think of guys using you like that. It pisses me off, okay? But I'm not mad at *you*. Just like, in general, I guess."

"Bad shit happens…."

"Maybe. But it hurts when bad shit happens to someone you love. You want only good and happy things for them. Not stuff like that. Never things like that." Carter's voice broke. "I just have one question."

"Only one?" Donald asked.

"Well, maybe two. You don't do that anymore, right?"

"No. Not since I graduated from college."

"Okay." Carter moved in closer, and Donald stilled. This was too much to hope for, too good to be true, so he had a hard time believing it.

"You said there was a second question," Donald prompted, but Carter's lips met his and questions were forgotten for the moment. Donald closed his eyes and soaked in the gentle caress of Carter's lips on his. He gasped and his throat ached from disbelief and unbelievable relief.

"Have you told anyone about that before?" Carter whispered, his lips so close his breath ghosted over Donald's face as an ethereal touch that quickly faded, but had still been there.

"No," Donald said barely above a whisper. "This isn't a part of myself I share with anyone." He lifted his gaze from the floor. "If I had it to do over... I don't know. It wasn't like there were lots of opportunities for a kid like me."

"Where did you go to school?"

"Shippensburg, because they gave me the best overall deal." Donald could already see Carter's mind going. "One of the others guys I knew danced as well, and he'd give me a ride. We danced together on stage. Mostly it was for women, and they're wild. But the men paid better. At the time it didn't really matter. I had long hair, and everyone liked the way I looked. I was hot, or at least that's what people told me." Donald shrugged.

"Do you miss the attention?"

"Not really. I'm a private person. I think you know that. Being on stage was something I felt I had to do, but it wasn't something I really wanted to do." Donald swallowed hard. "They hired me because of the way I looked. My friend Forrest danced as Danny Dreamboat or something equally tacky, and he took me in with him one night. I'd told him how hard up I was. Anyway, I was scared crapless. This room full of women who were screaming and yelling. I could dance and wasn't a total doofus, but they dressed me as a policeman and sent me on stage.

"The yelling and screaming were almost deafening, and here I was, a kid from Mifflintown who had never been anywhere with anyone, up on stage in front of a hundred screaming, drunk women, and I was supposed to take my clothes off. I thought I was going to be sick right there on stage, but then the music started and I ignored them and just started to dance. Before I knew it, I was being felt up and pawed, and I hated it." Donald shivered as he remembered customers touching him like he was a prize cow. "I remember having to keep from pulling away as they grabbed at everything. But at the end of the night I had enough money to eat for two weeks. They hired me and got me some special costumes... and...."

"At first they didn't do shows for men, but after a while the offers got too good, so they booked some shows at gay clubs and we made even more those nights. Instead of three hundred, I'd take home five or six, and if I was willing to do some after-hours work, sometimes a thousand on a weekend. I had nothing and it was too tempting to pass up."

"I'm not judging you. The decisions you made are done. That's in the past, and God knows we all make decisions we might regret later. It's the ones now that count." Carter hugged him tighter. "All of that went into making you the person you are now." Carter kissed the top of his head as Donald rested against his chest, inhaling the light herbal scent of Carter's soap mixed with the heady musk that was just him. "Without the adventures in foster care, college, dancing, and everything else, you wouldn't be the Donald Ickle that I love."

"Huh...?" Donald lifted his head so he could see if Carter was kidding him. "You're so full of shit."

"No, I'm not. I'm being honest. If you hadn't been to hell and lived through it, you wouldn't be the strong, capable social worker who goes the extra mile for each of the kids in his charge."

Donald shook his head. "That's bull."

Carter released him. "No, it's not. If you hadn't been through all that, you'd have sent Alex to the county home and you would have gone back to your life. That's what anyone else would have done."

Donald tilted his head slightly.

"Yeah, I know I goaded you into it, but you still agreed, and that little boy loves you. Not because of what you did for him, because he doesn't even understand that. He loves you for you." Carter pointed toward the door. "So while you might think I'm full of it, you're the one who's wrong. We're all the sum of our experience—good, bad, and ugly."

"Has anyone ever told you that you can be preachy as hell?"

"It comes with the territory," Carter explained with a wry grin. "So are you going to cut yourself some slack? Or do I need to keep preaching. Because I might be my father's son, but unlike him, I will talk your ear off. God knows I love the sound of my own voice, and I can talk and talk and—"

Donald pulled Carter to him and kissed him just to shut him up. Of course, that had been Carter's aim all along. And who was he to deny him?

"Mr. Donald."

They pulled apart. "Stay right here. I'll see what he needs." There was a frantic edge in Alex's cry, so Donald hurried out of the room. Alex was sitting up in his bed, eyes wide, shivering, when Donald came in. "What is it?"

"The bad men were back," Alex said, and Donald sat on the edge of his bed, holding Alex in his arms.

"It's all right. It was just a bad dream." Donald knew Alex was going to have them for a while and he made a mental note to call Camp Koala in the morning. They were a nonprofit group in town that worked with grieving children, and Donald knew they would be able to help Alex deal with the loss of his mother. He figured a lot of these dreams about bad men were wrapped up in his mother's death as well.

"I want Mommy," Alex whimpered.

"I can't give you Mommy. She's with the angels, but I'm here and I'll stay as long as you like." Donald rocked Alex and whispered softnesses of comfort. They weren't really words, but that didn't matter. Being held and comforted was what mattered now. Alex needed to know he wasn't alone and that someone cared about him. "I promise I'll be here." He held Alex a little tighter, enjoying his warmth next to him. After a few seconds, Donald wondered who was comforting whom. Maybe they were comforting each other, because holding Alex and having him cling back, like Donald was his life preserver, warmed his heart and gave him purpose.

"Can I sleep wif you?" Alex asked.

That wasn't a good idea. He wanted to say yes, but couldn't until things were more permanent.

"Why don't you hold Bunny?" Carter said softly as he came in the room. "He'll keep you company." Carter began making exaggerated hand motions over the stuffed toy. "See? Bunny is now magic. He'll keep the bad men and nightmares away as long as you're holding him. If they happen again, all you need to do is tell Bunny to keep them away and he will."

"Really?" Alex asked, wiping his eyes and sniffing.

"Yes. Bunny will protect you, and so will Mr. Donald and me. Remember, I'm a policeman, so I know how to protect people." Carter smiled, and Alex settled back in Donald's arms.

Donald shifted him until Alex rested his head on his shoulder. Then he simply held him until Carter motioned that Alex was nearly asleep. He carefully maneuvered Alex into bed and covered him up. Alex turned on his side, holding Bunny the way he always did. Donald didn't get up right away, and Carter turned before quietly leaving the room. Donald sat where he was, watching Alex to make sure he didn't wake up. How a little boy could enter his life and in a few days turn everything on its ear, in the most wonderful way humanly possible, was a complete mystery to him. His life had been in a holding pattern for years, like he'd been waiting for something to happen. He hadn't even realized it until Alex brought Carter and a bucketful of change to his life. He hadn't been living—he'd been existing.

He carefully stood and walked away from the bed. At the doorway he checked one more time and then closed the door most of the way before walking to his own room. Inside he found Carter in bed, waiting for him. "I'll be right back." Donald went into the bathroom, took care of business, and then undressed before joining Carter in the other room. He climbed into bed, and Carter spooned to his back, holding him tight.

After a few minutes, Donald rolled over to face Carter. "Earlier, did you say what I think you said?"

"What did I say?" Carter asked sheepishly, and Donald squeezed his shoulder.

"You know what you said. Or God I hope you said what I thought you said." His ears might have been playing tricks on him. Had Carter really said he loved him? Carter moved forward, rolling Donald onto his back before kissing him hard.

"Instead of telling you… again, how about if I show you?" Before Donald could answer or really think too much about what Carter had said, he was on his back and being possessively, deeply, kissed breathless.

He arched his back, pushing his chest to Carter's, sliding their cocks along each other. Donald gasped, loving every inch of the man pressing to him.

"I stopped at the drugstore on my lunch break," Donald whispered.

"Me too," Carter whispered between panting breaths. "I think we're going to have enough supplies for a while."

Donald chuckled. "I wouldn't count on it."

"So you're saying you think we're going to have cause to use them all?" Carter nuzzled his neck, lightly licking right at the spot near the base that sent shivers zinging along his spine.

"We'd better," Donald retorted. Instead of a comeback, Carter licked down his chest and sucked on a nipple, and then reached for Donald's hands, holding them over his head while he explored. "God," Donald whimpered when Carter located a spot just above his hip that sent shivers through him. He tried to pull away. "What the hell?"

"You have little spots all over you that will turn you into Jell-O. It's my job to find them, and the search is half the fun." Carter went right back to it, not touching his dick, but licking and kissing him all over. If Donald's breath caught, Carter sucked until Donald was gasping. When his form had been fully explored, Carter rolled him onto his belly and explored his sides and down to the small of his back.

Donald's legs twitched as Carter got closer to his ass. He massaged Donald's cheeks and then kissed, and scraped his teeth over the skin. Donald gripped the headboard, holding still when Carter parted his cheeks and ran his tongue lower and lower, until….

"Jesus!" Donald cried louder than he intended. He gripped the wood as tight as he could, thrusting back and spreading his legs as wide as possible. "Damn…."

"Yeah," Carter whispered. "I knew this would drive you out of your mind. I'm going to tongue-fuck you and then fill you so full." The words stopped as Carter did just that, thrusting his tongue inside him. Donald had never thought being rimmed would be so mind-blowing. But, damn, nothing compared. He felt so open, so trusted and trusting. He was completely exposed, and yet as he pushed back, he felt in command as well. It was hot and sexy, and….

137

Donald wondered what happened when Carter stopped. He looked over his shoulder, waiting for what was to come next. "Fuck me."

"I intend to." A snick reached his ears, and then after a few seconds, Carter teased his skin. A long finger slowly sank into him, spreading, filling. Donald groaned as Carter continued stretching him. "Is this what you want?"

"Yes," Donald whimpered and pressed back into the sensation. Then Donald pulled away and held his breath, waiting for what he was certain to be the main event. Carter lay down next to him, guided Donald onto his side, and slowly pressed inside him.

Carter wrapped his arms around Donald's chest, hands splayed on his skin, bringing them closer until Carter pressed against him, cock buried, joining them together. Donald had never felt so full or fulfilled.

Carter's movements were slow and languid, thrusting deep in rhythm with Donald's breathing. "I do love you, Donald." Carter filled him and stilled, holding him even tighter. "You're a dear special man. And yes, you did hear me earlier. I did tell you that I loved you and I do. You have a kind heart that you try to hide, but I see you for who you are. You're as hot deep down as you look right now." Carter moved slowly, deeply, withdrawing almost the entire way before sinking back inside. Donald had been with men before, God knew, but never like this. Carter touched his heart just as he touched his body. "Do you know what love is?" Carter whispered into his ear.

"This?" Donald asked, hoping like hell he was right. He'd asked himself that question a few times and had never come up with an answer because he had no frame of reference.

"No. This is *making* love." Carter moved slightly, breathing into his ear. "Love is what you did earlier. Love is letting someone know who you are, the good and the bad, letting them in and taking the chance that no matter what, they will want us and care about us. That's love. I see you for who you are." Carter tightened his hold. "Love is never wanting to let go, touching your heart and holding it delicately in your hand. It's sex, caresses, words, and everything in between, soothing away nightmares and holding you in the dark. It's everything, all of that, and what I want to do with you for the rest of my life."

Carter started thrusting faster, sliding a firm hand down Donald's belly and then to his hip before slipping around him, holding his cock and stroking to the same pace as their movements together. Donald closed his eyes, giving himself over to Carter. He'd never allowed that to happen before. Every time he trusted someone they seemed to disappoint him, but Donald was beginning to believe that Carter wouldn't do that.

He shivered and moved his hips. When he moved forward, Carter gripped him, and when he shifted back, Carter filled him even more. It amazed him, how he could have everything he'd dreamed about, and have it come true in a matter of a few days. Now he was on fire, making love for the first time in his life.

"Donald," Carter whispered. "Stop thinking so much and just let yourself go. You're incredible when you just feel." He pulled out and rolled Donald onto his back. They locked their gazes together, and Carter lifted Donald's legs, positioning his feet on his shoulders. Then he slowly entered him once again, sliding into him inch by glorious inch.

Donald breathed deep and long, trying to control the desire that swept through him. "Oh my God," he whispered and held Carter's shoulders as he snapped his hips faster and faster. The bed shook and the force rippled through him with each snap of Carter's hips. Donald gripped his cock, fisting himself wildly in an uncontrollable urge to come.

"That's it. You can come apart all you want. I'll be here to catch you."

"Good, because I'm falling."

Everything around him narrowed until there was only Carter and him. Nothing else seemed to exist. Carter's deep brown eyes shone in the light that came through the window from the streetlight. He could bask in his gaze forever. That was what Donald wanted more than anything, and now he actually dared to hope that would come to pass.

Donald grabbed the bedding with one hand, pounding his cock with the other as Carter filled him like no one else ever had. The man was big, but not too big. In other words, perfect for him, and while Donald wanted him to never stop, Carter's rhythm became ragged. Donald knew exactly how he felt. All the sensation threatened to overwhelm him. He shook with barely controlled ecstasy, tightened his muscles around Carter, and began slipping into the daze of release.

Within seconds, his breath caught, muscles clenched, and he gasped as he reached the peak and held there, balancing on the edge for what seemed like a blessed eternity. Then he tumbled into the blinding blaze of release, with Carter following right behind him.

Donald sank into near oblivion, mind floating, Carter's weight gloriously anchoring him to the here and now. He held on and kept his eyes closed, willing the endorphin high to last as long as possible. When conscious thought returned he found Carter kissing him gently and caressing his cheeks as he soothed him. "I told you, you're amazing when you let go."

"I try."

Carter shook his head. "That's the beauty of it. You don't need to try. All you have to do is be yourself and trust."

That was the hardest part for him. Donald didn't give trust easily, but he was willing to try with Carter.

"I know it's hard, but you have to," Carter said. "A relationship that lasts is built on trust, among other things."

"Like what?"

Carter kissed him. "Passion, love—God, don't make me try to list them. I can hardly think right now. Just accept it."

"Okay," Donald agreed. He was too tired to argue and he felt too amazing not to want to think Carter was right. He closed his eyes and lay still, luxuriating in the afterglow. Eventually Carter slipped from under the covers. Donald knew he was cleaning up a little, and when Carter returned, Donald smiled as Carter wiped and dried his belly. When he came back from the bathroom, they curled together under the covers.

A ding broke the quiet of the room. Donald started slightly as Carter moved away. Carter fiddled in his pants and pulled out his phone. He looked at it, the light from the screen illuminating his face. He smiled at first and then looked up at Donald before returning to the screen. Carter spent a second scrolling through something and then put the phone back in his pocket.

"What is it?"

"One of the searches I was running came up with a positive match."

Donald stiffened. "Which searches?"

Carter rolled on his side toward him. "I was running the searches we talked about. The ones for Alex's family."

"And you found someone." Donald closed his eyes and wished he could stop up his ears as well. He didn't want to know the answer. Then the fantasy he'd allowed himself to believe was real could last more than an hour.

"Possibly. I don't know how close a match it is, just that there is a result that met the parameters I set. It might be nothing. I'll need to look into it further when I get into the office."

"But these parameters you set, they were the right ones?" Donald persisted. He had to know.

"They were the ones I thought would get me close. It doesn't mean that it will actually provide a relative, or beyond that, someone who would be willing to raise Alex." Carter tugged him closer, and Donald tried to get away, but Carter wouldn't let him. "Don't get upset."

"I'm not."

"Yes, you are," Carter countered. "I can tell and I understand."

"No, you don't."

"Yes, I do. You opened yourself up. You decided to let Alex and me into your life." Carter shifted and then sat up. "Within hours of doing that, of getting the family you've always wanted, but never had, it's immediately threatened." Carter paused. "How close am I?"

Donald blinked. "Don't be a shit, Freud."

"I might be right, but you know it will be okay. You're strong, and the result is only a possibility." Carter leaned over him and then lowered his lips to his without quite meeting them. "I'm not going anywhere." The slight hitch in Carter's voice told him that he felt the same way. Somehow that made Donald feel a little better. But his heart ached. Why, he wasn't sure. He'd been fighting to push Alex, and Carter, for that matter, out of his heart ever since he'd met them. Now he'd capitulated, surprisingly happily, and it could be taken away.

"Dammit," Donald whispered.

141

"Hey," Carter said, wiping his cheeks.

"It's just that Alex is the first person to say he loved me, and…." Dammit. He was not going to cry. That was just stupid and was so not happening.

"Actually, if you remember, *I* was the first person to tell you I loved you." Carter met his gaze, and Donald threw his arms around him and held him close. That was true and Donald had nearly missed it. "Not that it matters. All that really counts is that you are loved, and no matter what this search result tells us, Alex isn't going to stop loving you. And you love him, right?"

Donald nodded. This whole situation was getting to him a lot more than it should.

"Then that never goes away. The people who love you and whom you love in return stay with you."

"How do you know that?"

"I had another brother. His name was Chip." Carter got out of bed and pulled his wallet out of his pants. "No one really talks about him much." He opened the wallet and pulled out the picture of a child not much older than Alex. "He died twenty years ago. I was eight and he was five, almost six. He woke up one night screaming at the top of his lungs about how it hurt, everything hurt. Mom and Dad rushed him to the hospital, but they weren't in time. His appendix had burst and spread infection everywhere. He only lasted a few days after that." Carter carefully put the picture back in his wallet. "But I know he loved me." Carter's voice broke. "He was my pesky little brother who worshipped the ground I walked on and wanted to do everything I could do. Chip was a happy kid—energetic, fun, and the apple of my dad's eye. He was also the best little brother ever. At home I have a picture he drew me for my eighth birthday. My mom kept it and gave it to me when she was cleaning out some things in the house a few years ago."

"You still miss him," Donald whispered into the near darkness.

"Yeah, but he's been gone a long time. Now it's like he's with me when I need him. You know. The grief is long spent, but sure, I miss him and wonder what kind of person he'd have been when he grew up. I'd like to think that he and I would be friends and maybe even brother officers. Chip always said he wanted to be a policeman and that we would be partners someday." Carter chuckled lightly. "See, Chip is always with me." Carter took Donald's hand and placed in on his chest. "I keep him here, along with you and Alex and the rest of my family." Carter kissed him and then they settled on the bed.

Donald lay down and wished he could let go of the worry. If Alex had family out there, he deserved to be with them. No matter how much it might hurt… and saying good-bye to Alex was going to hurt, no doubt about that. Donald just hoped it didn't rip his heart completely from his chest.

CHAPTER
Nine

CARTER ROLLED over when Donald shifted for the millionth time, his agitation and nervousness increasing throughout the night. Carter wondered what he could do to help him, wishing he'd kept the message to himself. He tried to explain that many things could result in a false reading, but there was no stopping Donald from growing quiet and jittery. "Is it time to get up?" he asked.

"I don't know," Donald answered groggily.

Carter checked the clock and lay back down. It was the middle of the night. He slid closer to Donald, wrapping an arm around his chest. "Go back to sleep if you can. We don't need to be up for a few hours yet."

Donald sighed and seemed to relax a little. "I'm concerned."

"I know. But try not to be. It's just a possibility. It will take me some time when I get in to check things out, so please just don't worry about it." He tried to soothe Donald as much as possible. "There are still a lot of things about DNA profiling that we need to learn and perfect. What I did was basic at best, and it will only get me to the first step. It may not really mean anything." Carter stroked Donald's cheek. "Why don't you get up and check on him. Make sure Alex is okay."

"He's asleep," Donald protested.

"Probably." Carter didn't want to push, but his mom had told him once that she spent the last two nights with Chip watching him sleep. She'd known he was slipping away, but spending all the time she could with him helped. It meant she'd done everything she could for him for as long as she had him. What Donald was feeling for Alex wasn't

144

exactly the same, but Carter figured it was along the same lines. His mother had known her time with Chip was limited, and Donald thought the same with Alex.

From the beginning, their time with Alex had always had the potential to be limited. Alex could have been sent to foster care immediately, or there could have been close relatives to take him. But Carter knew that for Donald all that had changed when he'd told that little boy he loved him. Donald had opened his heart, and the thought that he could get it stomped on made Carter ache for him. He knew Donald was hurting and he wanted to make it stop.

Donald pushed back the covers and got out of bed, then slipped on his robe before leaving the room. Carter wanted to follow, but didn't. Donald needed some time alone with Alex, and even if it was the middle of the night and Alex was asleep, it still allowed Donald to be alone with him. Carter didn't want to intrude on that.

Carter turned over, and after a few minutes his eyelids drifted closed. He tried to stay awake until Donald came back to bed, but fatigue won the battle. He woke alone a few hours later. He lifted his head off the pillow to check the time and groaned. He pushed off the covers and got out of the bed, gathering his clothes from the floor along with Donald's and draping them over the end of the bed. He dressed quickly and went to find Donald.

He was in Alex's room, sitting in the chair next to his bed, head back, mouth open, sound asleep. Carter woke him gently and helped Donald back to his room. "I need to go in so I can figure out what's truly happening. I should know something in a few hours. So if you want, bring Alex by and we can go to lunch. By then I should have better information, good or bad."

Donald nodded. "I feel like such a fool. I should be happy that there's a chance that Alex could go live with someone who's related to him. Instead all I can think about is that if he does, then I won't…."

"Hey. You opened your heart, and when you do, this can sometimes happen. But let's deal in facts and what we know rather than what we feel. I have to get ready to go, and you need to get Alex up and start your day. I promise I'll call you if I find anything at all." Carter kissed him, savoring the taste of Donald's sweet lips before stepping away. "Tell Alex that I'll see him later."

Donald nodded, and Carter kissed him again before leaving the room and descending the stairs. Outside, he got in his car and drove right home, where he showered and dressed in his uniform before heading to the station. When he arrived, he checked his duty schedule and then hurried down to his desk. He checked on the results of his searches and found that he had three potential results. Two of them he could eliminate after just a few minutes. They had met the overall parameters he'd set, but on close inspection they were easily discarded. But the third was much closer.

"Have you had any further luck with the voice?" Captain Murphy asked as he paused at Carter's desk.

"Unfortunately not. Voices aren't things we keep databases on."

"I was afraid of that. A few of the officers thought the voice sounded familiar to them, but it's difficult when it's just a voice. And the words are so... unusual." The captain shuddered and did his best to cover it. "Where do we go from here?"

"We have a basic description from Alex, but it isn't much. I've gathered everything I have and added it to the case file. I'm afraid short of more information, we're at a standstill." His captain inhaled, and Carter knew he wasn't happy. "We might be able to get something from Alex if we were to show him the video, but there's no way Social Services will allow it. Hell, I won't allow it. He's been through enough already."

"So what do you suggest? Let this scum continue abusing children?"

"No, sir. We'll need to continue to follow up any leads. But I suspect our suspect is crapping in his boots, afraid that Harker is going to rat him out."

"Harker isn't talking at all. I tried again late yesterday, and all the guy did was cross his arms over his chest and stare at me. He's a piece of work."

"Some people won't work with the police no matter what, and he isn't going to do anything because when he gets out, he'll go right back to what he was doing and he'll need his contacts. So he stays quiet and gets rewarded in the end." It was just an observation on Carter's part, but his captain nodded. They seemed to be of the same opinion.

"That's why we need to nail this guy. Keep on it."

"I will." Carter wasn't sure where else he was supposed to look.

"What were you working on?" Captain Murphy peered over his shoulder.

"We got DNA from Alex, and Donald from Social Services suggested I run a DNA search to see if we could find a relative. It was a long shot, but I got three hits. Two were false, but the third seems to be a close match. I'm doing some double-checking now, and then I'll bring up the identity of the individual. Because of the databases I was using, I need to protect individual privacy." He was following the rules with this one to the letter. "I want to be sure." He needed to be certain before he disappointed Donald and had to give him the bad news. Even if they found a relative, they might not be willing or able to take Alex in.

"All right. But don't let that interfere with your primary tasks."

"I won't." Carter wasn't making headway with finding a match for the voice on the video, and at this point, it didn't look as though he was going to anytime soon. It pissed him off no end and he kept thinking there had to be something he could do. But child pornographers and abusers came from all walks of life and weren't necessarily creepy-looking, like they were in the movies. "I'll be done here soon." One of his systems beeped, and the captain shifted his gaze.

"I'm also working on a search for Smith. It's unrelated to this case."

"You obviously have things in hand. Carry on." Captain Murphy turned and left the area. Carter got back to work, sending Smith the information he'd requested and looking deeper into the genetic match he'd gotten. It looked really good, but he wanted a second opinion, so he packaged the information and picked up the phone to call his friend Roddy. He and Roddy had gone to college together. Carter had gone into criminal justice while Roddy went into genetics. They had been close friends in school, but Roddy's work had taken him to Philadelphia, so Carter didn't get to see him very often.

"Roddy," Carter said happily when his good friend and colleague of a sort answered. After they graduated, Roddy had decided to teach and was considered an expert in genetics. "How are you?"

"Good. Have you got something interesting for me?"

"A kid and a possible relative. I'm sending you their DNA profiles. They look pretty close and I need a confirmation as soon as you can."

"What's the rush?"

"This might be the kid's only living relative." The thought crossed his mind that if he buried all this, then Donald would be happy. But Carter would never be able to look at himself in the mirror again. He couldn't steal Alex's family away from him… again. He'd already had his mother ripped away, and Harker had stolen some of his childhood; Carter wasn't going to be another person to take from him. "I just need confirmation."

"I can do that. I have some time this morning, so send it over and I'll take a look as soon as I can."

"I really appreciate it. I need to be 100 percent sure before I try to locate this individual."

"Of course," Roddy said. "On a more personal note, are you going to be coming out to Philly soon?"

"I don't know." Carter smiled. "I've been seeing someone and…."

"You dog," Roddy teased. "It's about time you met someone."

"Is there any chance you'll be settling down anytime soon?"

"Me?" Roddy giggled. "You've got to be kidding. I love the gayborhood and the clubs. I don't think I'll ever stop the party life, and this city is perfect."

"Okay. Why don't you come here for a visit? You can meet Donald and possibly Alex. He's the little boy we're trying to find family for." The entire story was too much to explain over the phone. "I'll tell you the whole story when you come for a visit."

"Okay. It'll be good to see you. I'll call later in the week and we'll arrange a visit." Voices sounded from behind Roddy. "I need to go, but I'll call as soon as I have an answer for you." Roddy disconnected, and Carter hung up, sent the information off to Roddy, and went back to work.

Carter's phone rang a number of times, and each time he snatched it up, hoping it was Roddy, but it wasn't. He called Donald and explained what he'd found and what he was waiting for, knowing he'd be nervous.

"Do you still want to go to lunch?" Donald asked.

"Yes. Why don't you bring Alex over and we can walk to the Back Door Café for lunch. They have things Alex will like, and hopefully I'll have an answer by then and this whole issue can be put to bed." He tried to reassure Donald that there was nothing to worry about, but he didn't seem to be buying it, and Carter couldn't blame him. "I'll see you in an hour or so." Carter hung up and continued working.

He hadn't heard anything back from Roddy by the time he got the call that Donald and Alex were waiting for him in the lobby. He took a few minutes to set up some searches other officers had requested and locked his systems before heading out for lunch.

Alex raced over to him as soon as Carter came through the door. He nearly leaped into his arms. Carter hugged him and carried Alex to where Donald waited nervously. Carter shook his head so Donald would know he didn't have any answers yet. "Are you ready for lunch?"

"Yes!" Alex said happily. "I made this for you." Donald handed him a sheet of paper and Alex gave it to Carter. "I drawed it for you."

Carter set Alex down and looked at the drawing. "Is that Bunny?"

"It's Roger," Alex answered as though Carter was supposed to know who Roger was.

"Louise in my office brought her dog, Roger, into the day-care center this morning. Apparently Alex was particularly taken with him, and he and Roger are now really good friends," Donald explained. "He's talked about Roger almost nonstop on our way over."

"Thank you," Carter said with a smile, hugging Alex in appreciation of his gift. "I love it." He looked toward the desk. "Is it okay if I leave it here with the policeman until I come back?" Alex nodded, and Carter handed it to one of the officers, who winked and made a show of placing it in a very important spot. Alex preened and stood up straighter. Then Carter took him by the hand and led him out of the station and out to the sidewalk.

"Do you want to walk?" Donald asked. It seemed Alex did, so they each took a hand and headed toward the restaurant a few blocks away. Alex was tired by the time they reached High Street, the main east-west road in town. Carter lifted him into his arms, and they turned in the direction of the restaurant.

"No!" Alex cried and turned in Carter's arms, hiding his face, grasping Carter's neck tight enough he could hardly breathe. "Bad men. No bad men." Alex shook and Carter glanced at Donald and then around the street. A man who had just stepped out of one of the shops matched the information they'd gotten from Alex. He glanced toward them and then turned away. Carter handed Alex to Donald.

"Go inside the restaurant and stay there," he snapped. Carter quietly radioed in and began walking down the sidewalk behind the man. He wasn't sure if this was the individual on the video. All he knew was that he needed to try to speak to him. He pulled out his phone and snapped a picture as the man stopped at the crosswalk. Using an old trick, Carter pulled out his wallet, took out a five, and put the wallet back. "Sir, did you drop this?" he asked.

The man turned around. "I don't believe so," the man answered. Carter instantly recognized the voice.

"I'm sorry to have bothered you." Carter wasn't sure what else he could say. He didn't have enough evidence to arrest him simply because of his voice. He also couldn't follow him without any sort of backup. The man seemed relieved and turned, walking away a little faster than necessary, like he wanted to hurry, but didn't want to look like he was hurrying.

A squad car pulled up and Smith got out.

"What's going on? I got a call from your friend."

"Alex went nuts. He calls the men who hurt him 'bad men,' and I think he saw one of them. I spoke to him briefly and recognized his voice. He seemed a little familiar and I was able to snap a picture of him." He showed Smith the image.

"That's him?" Smith asked, pointing. "I know him. That's Gordon March. He's on the borough council. I've known him for years." Smith's mouth hung open. "My God. Now that you mention it, I recognize his voice too. Jesus Christ, this is going to open a world of hurt, and we'll need to be careful, but it gives us a definite line of inquiry." Smith smiled. "Good work, and you were right to let him go. We don't have enough to charge him, and when we do it has to be airtight. I'll see what we can get from financial records. Where is Alex?"

"He and Donald are at the restaurant. I wanted them off the street and in a public place."

"Go join them and return to the station at your usual time. He was most likely heading to the borough hall next to the station, and if he sees a lot of immediate activity, especially if it involves you, since you approached him, he might get suspicious." Smith rubbed his hands together. "We're going to nail this bastard."

"I hope so." Carter hated letting him just walk away. He'd wanted to press him to the ground and take him into custody immediately.

"We will." They walked toward the restaurant, and Smith went inside with him. Donald and Alex sat at a table in the back, Alex clinging to Donald like a lifeline.

"It's all right, buddy. He's gone."

"Was that the man?" Donald whispered.

"Alex thinks so, and it sounded like him," Carter answered very quietly. "I think we need to get both of you to the station. I got a picture of the guy. Did you order?"

"No, but Alex is really hungry," Donald said.

"You all stay here and have your lunch. I'm going to head back to the station and get things started. Once you're done, come back as though nothing has happened," Smith instructed.

"What's going on?" Donald whispered.

"Not here. We'll explain when we get to the station. For now, focus on getting Alex fed and calmed down." Smith was a smart man. He knew they needed time for Alex to settle, and the station wasn't particularly conducive for that. Smith left the restaurant, and Carter watched him get into his car and drive away.

Carter sat down. "Is everything okay, Officer?" a server asked.

"Yes. I think we're ready for lunch. Sorry if we were a disturbance." Carter picked up the menu and opened it for Donald. He ordered their drinks, and when the college-age server returned, they placed their orders.

"He's still shaking," Donald said softly.

"I know. But we're getting closer and it's almost over." It had better be.

"What about… the other?" Donald asked.

"I have a friend checking over the results."

"So there is a possibility?" Donald asked and then glanced away.

"Yes. I don't know who it is yet because I stripped out all personal information from the search. I'll match it up once I have confirmation." Carter didn't want to upset Alex any further, or Donald, for that matter. He'd hoped for a quick answer from Roddy, but these things sometimes took time. "I know this is hard." It was hard for him too.

"We'll do what's right. No matter if it hurts or not," Donald said firmly as he tightened his hold on Alex. "Are you getting hungry?" he asked Alex. "I have some milk for you and lunch should be here soon."

Alex turned around slowly and sat next to Donald. "You promised no bad men."

"I know and he's gone."

"You scared him." Alex seemed to brighten after he said that, as if the bad men being afraid of Carter buoyed him. They should be afraid, because Carter and the rest of the department were coming for him. He couldn't hide now. Carter knew who he was, and if there was any sort of trail that led to him, they would find it.

"I know." He shared a grin with Alex as they waited for their food.

"Do you know who that was?" Donald asked. Obviously from his tone, he recognized him.

"Yes. And that's half the battle. Now that we know his identity, we'll build a link and get him." Part of that was bravado, but it was what he felt deep down. The evidence was out there; they just had to find it. Enough evidence for a search warrant could return evidence on computers. They had a path forward now, and Smith was hunting those down like a bulldog as they spoke. The server returned with the food. Alex ate the way he usually did, while Donald picked at his sandwich and helped Alex. Carter ate a few bites, then took Donald's hand under the table while they waited for the check.

"Please don't tell me it will be all right." Donald wiped Alex's hands with a napkin. "Things I want have a tendency to fall flat."

"What do you want, Mr. Donald?" Alex asked.

"It isn't important."

Carter knew that was a lie. What happened next was very important to Donald… and to him. Alex deserved to be happy, but so did Donald. Carter wanted them both to be happy, and he had a feeling that was becoming an impossibility.

The server brought the check, and Carter paid at the register. Then the three of them walked back to the station, with Donald carrying Alex and Carter hyperaware of everything and everyone around them. When they arrived, Carter led Donald and Alex to the same room they had used before and said, "I'll be right back." Carter found Smith at his desk. He was on the phone, speaking very animatedly, and then he hung up.

"Captain Murphy called in the FBI. They're on their way and should be here soon. And based on Alex's ID, you recognizing the man's voice, and me knowing who he was, the captain is working on getting a warrant issued for March's home and computer, as well as his office. The FBI wants to take part so they can help wrap up anything that goes outside our jurisdiction. Do you want to be included?"

"God, yes. Donald and Alex are in the breakroom."

Smith stood right away. "Let's go." Smith strode off and Carter followed, stopping just outside the breakroom. "I want to see if we can get Alex to confirm that this is our man before we go any further," Smith said. "Can you show him the picture?"

Carter didn't want to do it, but he had little choice. "Alex," Carter said as he walked in. "This is Officer Smith. He's a really good man and he needs your help. Can you do that for us? We want to put the bad man in jail."

Alex nodded and Carter pulled out his phone. "Do you remember when Mr. Byron used to spank you?" Alex nodded and rubbed his little butt. Carter was getting used to seeing the more animated Alex, but instantly he looked exactly like the terrified boy he'd found behind that bed in the attic. "Mr. Byron is in jail, and he is never going to hurt you again. Both Mr. Donald and I promise you that." Carter sat down and tugged Alex onto his lap. "You know both Mr. Donald and I love you, and that means that we'll never hurt you."

"Yes."

"Okay. When Mr. Byron spanked you, sometimes there was another man there."

"Mr. Boss," Alex said.

"Yes." Carter brought up the picture he'd taken. "Is this Mr. Boss?"

Alex began to shake as soon as Carter showed him the picture. Alex stared at it and then slapped Carter's hand hard, nearly knocking the phone away.

"Is that him?" Carter asked.

Alex nodded and hid his face against Carter's shirt. "No bad men," he whimpered.

"Get the warrant, and I damned well want to be there," Carter told Smith. Then he hugged Alex and let him cry it out. "It's okay. That was just a picture. He isn't here and you're safe."

"Mommy, Bunny, Mommy," Alex chanted, going back and forth.

"I'll go get Bunny," Donald said and stood up to leave.

"Give me your keys," Smith said. "I'll send someone out to get it. We don't want either of you leaving the station while all this is going on. Your safety is paramount, and we don't know if he saw or recognized Alex outside the restaurant. Call who you need to to let them know you're okay, but he must be safe." Smith left the room, muttering about their case hanging by a thread.

Donald looked at him with concern in his eyes. Carter waited until he was out of earshot. "Smith is an excellent officer, and he's in our corner." Carter moved closer. "He has a reputation as a hard... you know."

A few minutes later, White, a rookie, came in carrying Bunny and looking amazingly uncomfortable. Alex jumped down and raced over, grabbed the bunny, and held it close. Every time he did that, it tore at Carter's heart. Alex deserved to feel secure.

"Schunk, we're getting ready to serve the warrant," Smith said.

"I'm on my way." Carter turned back to Donald. "Please stay here. Call your office and tell them what's happening and where you are. Have the desk sergeant verify it if you need to, but don't leave. Both of you will be safe here, and I need to know that." Carter leaned close and gave Donald a quick kiss. "Please."

"We'll be here," Donald said, and Carter left the room.

"Please see they get anything they need," Carter told White before hurrying to catch up with Smith. As they walked outside the station. Smith gave a subtle signal to two other uniformed cops, who got in a squad car parked behind Smith's, and two men in suits standing next to a Crown Vic. Those had to be the FBI agents, Carter realized. He was amazed they'd arrived on the scene so quickly.

"Have you done this before?" Smith asked. "I don't mean that as an insult. You do a hell of a job with those computers and you've helped everyone make a case at one point or another."

"Yes, I can watch out for myself."

"Good, because you have my back and I'll watch yours." Smith drove into one of the nicer neighborhoods in town and pulled to a stop in front of a modified ranch-style house. It was large and had been added onto and upgraded over the years. It had a perfectly manicured lawn and shrubs trimmed so not a single branch was out of place. Carter let Smith go first, and the group approached the house. Smith knocked, announced their presence, and added that they had a warrant.

A woman in a designer outfit answered, carrying a tumbler of what looked like Scotch.

"We have a warrant to search the house and any computers found on the premises," Smith said firmly.

"Is this about my husband? Or should I say soon-to-be ex-husband?" she asked dryly.

"Yes, ma'am," Smith answered.

"Then you go right ahead. Look anywhere you want. His office is off to the right and his bedroom is down the hall on the left." The vehemence and the reference to *his* bedroom was telling. "I'll be out on the sunporch." She motioned, and Smith asked her to sign the warrant. She did and then glided away, ice tinkling in her nearly empty glass.

They spread out through the house. "Schunk, take the computers while we search the rest," Smith said. He motioned the team into the office. Carter sat at the desk and proceeded to see what he could find while the others searched the room. The computer was clean, but a secondary drive found locked in a desk drawer contained everything they needed and more. Videos, pictures—disgusting stuff, but it was all there.

He even found individual pictures of Alex, the boy leaning over the arm of the sofa. It looked like they had been taken with a camera. Carter would know more once he examined the files. "I got plenty in here," Carter called. "Pack up the computer, the drive, everything. We need to take it all." One of the uniformed officers jumped to do as he asked, and Carter went in search of Smith.

"Any luck?" Smith asked when Carter found him in the dining room.

"All we could hope for and more. Production, possession, and distribution. The trifecta." Carter smiled as the FBI agents grinned.

"We'll need the computers," one of them said, but Carter shook his head.

"I'll get you copies of all the evidence we find, but the computers are mine and they've already been tagged." He stepped closer. "I'm the one who started this, and I'll end it. You can help by getting that website shut down and putting the people behind it out of business."

"We're already on it," the agent said with a slight sneer. "Are you sure you can handle what's on those computers properly? We have—"

"Don't you dare," Smith interrupted. "This is the man who did your work for you. Show him some respect or you'll get nothing from this but grief." Smith puffed out his chest and stared the FBI agents down until they backed off.

"You'll see to it we get copied on everything," the agent said, still showing some attitude.

Smith looked at Carter. "You'll get what he decides you'll get. So I suggest you put a lid on the crap." Smith walked away, and Carter left as well to make sure the computers were packed properly.

They were still working when someone spotted March's vehicle pull up the street and then speed past. Carter wasn't involved in the pursuit, but March's capture made the news, as did the details about what he was running from. March's wife left, and the house itself was sealed as they gathered evidence. Carter knew he and the FBI were going to be very busy for a long time attempting to locate and contact various victims and their families.

"Head back to the station and get to work," Smith said a couple of hours later. "March is in custody, and we'll finish up here. Make sure Alex and Donald know that they're safe and neither of them has to worry about this guy ever again. He'll spend the rest of his life in prison." Smith seemed to take a particular delight in that. "I'll fill you in on anything you miss."

"Okay." Carter left the house, pulled off his gloves, and caught a ride with the uniformed cops taking the computers. At the station, he directed them to take the computers to his work area and swore death to anyone who touched them or let anyone near them. "Especially the FBI."

"I thought you wanted them in on this," Captain Murphy reproached lightly as he came closer. "You're in charge of that evidence, so pull off everything you can. March has already lawyered up, but it won't do him any good if we can build an airtight case." The captain went on his way, and Carter found Donald sitting on the breakroom sofa with Alex curled up asleep beside him.

"What happened?" Donald asked in a whisper. "Alex just went to sleep a few minutes ago. He's exhausted and so scared. He keeps expecting bad men to walk in the room."

"Well, we got the bad man this time. He's been arrested, and I need to spend some time with his computers so we can charge him with everything humanly possible." Carter sat down carefully next to Donald. "You didn't get in trouble for not working today, did you?"

"No. My boss understands these things, and when I tell her you got the slime behind all this, she's going to be thrilled. If it makes children safer, we're all for it." Donald began gathering Alex's things.

"Hey, buddy," Carter said gently, stroking Alex's arm. "It's okay. Mr. Donald is going to take you home. We got the bad man, and he's in jail." Carter stroked Alex's back lightly, and after a few minutes, Alex climbed onto his lap. "I promised you no more bad men, and I meant it. He'll be in jail for a long time."

"We should go now," Donald said and held out his hand. Carter set Alex down, and he took Donald's hand. "Let me know if you hear anything about the other...."

Carter had been so engrossed in the search for evidence and catching March that he hadn't really thought too much about the DNA search. He checked his phone, but there were no messages. Once Donald and Alex had left the station, he went right down to his lair and got started. He checked his e-mail, but had nothing from Roddy. He'd been hoping to hear by now.

"Do you mind if I help?" one of the FBI agents asked. "I was told you were down here, and I have a lot of expertise in computer forensics."

"All right. I'll create a partition and then we can segregate the data before examining the files for source. The hardest charge to prove is going to be creating the material, so that's where we need to start. If we can do that, then we should be able to prove distribution if those files were uploaded to the website."

"Sounds right. Let's get to work. I'm Brad Phillips."

Carter introduced himself, and they divided up the tasks and got to work. Carter preferred to work alone, but Brad obviously knew what he was doing, and the discovery went much quicker than Carter expected. As the hours passed, the mountain of evidence grew higher and higher. When afternoon turned to evening, Carter suggested food. "Is Chinese okay?"

"Great," Brad said with a smile that Carter found difficult to read.

"It's just Chinese," Carter said. He wondered what was going on with that goofy smile.

"I wanted the chance to work with you," Brad said. "I was curious about you and thought it would be cool to get to know you." He continued working on the computer, but looked up at him every few minutes. "I overheard one of the guys say that you were gay, and I thought…."

Now Carter understood. "I have a boyfriend." God, he hoped he did. He and Donald hadn't really talked about relationship stuff. They'd declared their feelings for one another but they hadn't talked about things like dating. Heck, he didn't even have a picture of Donald to show Brad.

"Was he the guy you were talking with earlier? The one with the kid?"

"Yeah, and just so you know, Donald is a social worker and that little boy started this entire investigation. He's a very sweet kid who's been through hell. He lost his mother, he's featured in a few of these videos, and he's having a hard time adjusting to all the changes in his life. Donald is helping him get his feet under him and hopes to provide a home for Alex." Carter huffed. "They're both pretty special."

"Dang." Brad turned back to the screen. "It figures I'd be too late."

"Sorry," Carter said with a smile. Brad was handsome with nice eyes and highlights in his hair. It was attractive in a rather made-up way. Like he was really trying, but would look better if he were just himself. "Are you almost done?"

"Yeah." Brad yawned. "You know, we could finish this up in the morning. I'm getting tired, and you have to be too. We have the core evidence we need."

"True," Carter agreed. He checked his e-mail one last time for something from Roddy. The note was there but Carter was scared to open it. He screwed up his courage and double-clicked on it. Carter scanned the note and stopped on the words he'd been dreading. He'd been right—the results had indeed turned up a cousin.

"What are you staring at?" Brad asked.

"It's a good news/bad news sort of thing." Carter was tempted to let it go and say nothing to Donald, but instead he matched the result with the other information and reluctantly pulled up the results.

CARTER PULLED up to Donald's house, exhausted. He knocked on the door, and when it opened Alex raced up to him for a hug. Carter picked him up and swung him around before setting him down again.

"You're in a good mood," Donald said.

"It was a good day," Carter said.

"Did you hear anything?" Donald said, and Carter nodded. "I did, and I think you and I need to talk. We can do that after we put Alex to bed."

"Okay," Donald agreed.

"On second thought, he should hear this too." Making Donald wait wasn't fair. "I did find one of Alex's relatives. See, his mother had a sister, and she had a child that I couldn't trace. And I figured that boy had been adopted. It appears that he was, but since those records are sealed, I couldn't get to them. But the DNA test cut through all that." Carter turned to Donald. "Did you have a DNA test done in order to find your biological parents?"

"Yeah, about three years ago. It didn't come to anything."

"Actually, it did." Carter reached into his bag, pulled out the results, and handed them to Donald. "You are Alex's cousin. You were born in the Mifflintown area, or at least at the hospital there. I can tell you that your mother and grandparents are gone. I don't know who your father is, but your mother was Alex's mother's older sister, Dorothy. Apparently Alex's mother was a late-in-life baby."

"You've got to be kidding," Donald whispered.

"No. All your life you've been looking for family. Well, he's right there." Carter was finding it hard to talk. "All you have to do is accept it."

Donald looked overwhelmed and totally disbelieving of the news he'd just been given. "It seems impossible."

"It isn't. I had the results checked. The conventional records didn't show me any more than you got when you looked for your family, but DNA can't hide anything and it cut through to the truth. You had an aunt who will need to be interred once the body is released. And you have a cousin who needs you." Carter stopped short of saying that he had him as well.

Donald gently tugged Alex to him. "Do you understand what Mr. Carter said?" Alex shook his head exaggeratedly. "It means that your mother and my mother were sisters, and that makes you my cousin." Alex still looked confused. "Well, it means that you're my family and that I'll be yours if you want me to be. You can live here with me."

Alex looked up toward the stairs and then back to Donald. "I can stay here?"

"Yes. You and Bunny will live here because I love you."

Alex threw his arms around Donald's neck. "I love you too, Mr. Donald."

Donald stood and held Alex close, swinging him around in a display of proud parental joy. Carter's heart skipped a beat and then warmed considerably when Donald stopped and extended his hand and tugged Carter close to join them.

"What about Mr. Carter?" Alex asked.

"He's going to be my boyfriend, if that's okay," Donald explained to Alex.

"Is he going to stay with us too?" Alex asked.

"He can if he wants," Donald whispered. Carter wasn't sure he'd heard the answer correctly the first time. Donald held him tighter, and Alex shifted until he was in Carter's arms. He stepped back and lifted the giggling little boy toward the ceiling. Carter could see the day when he'd be a parent, one of Alex's parents, and there was nothing he wanted more.

"Did you have dinner?" Carter asked and gave Alex a tickle. Alex had been with him and Donald for less than a week, but the change in him was remarkable. His eyes were clear and his smile huge. He was still small and thin, but that would change. Carter knew that over time Alex's nightmares would diminish as well. The men who had hurt Alex and had most likely brought about his mother's death were in jail and set to be charged with enough to keep them that way for years to come.

"Yes," Alex answered, pulling Carter from his thoughts.

"Come on," Donald said to Alex. "You can help me make something for Mr. Carter." Alex practically skipped along as they went into the kitchen. Carter followed and sat at the table, watching Donald as he helped Alex.

Donald was something else. That cold heart of his had been melted by a five-year-old boy. Carter wanted to take some credit for it, but truly, the cause of the change in Donald was Alex. His smile and energy in the face of everything that had happened to him were amazing, and Carter swore that little boy could charm the bees out of their honey.

"Can Mr. Carter have ice cream for dinner?" Alex asked.

Donald laughed. "Oh, *you* want ice cream, and yes, once Mr. Carter has finished eating, we can go get ice cream." He lifted Alex into his arms. "You're my ice cream monster." They laughed. "But I'm the tickle monster." Donald lightly poked Alex's belly until he laughed and squealed with delight while trying to get away at the same time. It was the happiest sound Carter could recall hearing recently.

Eventually Donald released him, and Alex hurried over to Carter. He scooped Alex off his feet and into the air once again. Carter kept Alex occupied while Donald heated up some dinner and then set a plate on the table. Alex settled on Carter's lap and, to no one's surprise, "helped" Carter eat his dinner.

"You're a bottomless pit," Carter teased as Alex took another bite of the creamy macaroni and cheese Donald had made for dinner.

"I'm Alex." He turned to look at Carter and then stole another bite from his plate.

"You're the food stealer," Carter accused with a grin. He managed to get a few bites before Alex snitched another one for himself.

"There's more," Donald said as Carter ate the last bite from his plate.

"I'm great, thanks. We were going to order dinner, but then we decided to take a break for the night. I would have been home a while ago except the results came in and I knew you were anxious." Carter grinned. "I was expecting"—Carter swallowed hard—"a very different outcome."

"So was I," Donald admitted.

Carter turned to Alex. "Let's help clear the table so we can go get that ice cream." He lightly patted Alex's belly. "That is, if you still have room for it."

Alex jumped down and lifted his shirt, pointing to his side. "I have room right here." Carter reached out to tickle his belly, and Alex giggled as he thrust down his shirt and ran into the living room. After a few seconds, the sound of wooden blocks crashing to the floor reached Carter's ears.

"He's something else," Carter said.

"Yes, he is." Donald sat in the chair next to Carter's. "I enrolled him in Camp Koala this afternoon. They have room for him starting next week, and he'll go there for a few hours each day. They'll help him deal with the loss of his mother."

"I thought he was taking it very well," Carter said.

"He hasn't dealt with it. Not yet. He's cried a few times and said he wanted her, but in a few weeks or months, the enormity of what happened will sink in. Alex is still expecting his mom to come through the front door at any time. Watch the next time someone knocks at the door. You can see hope blink behind his eyes, and then when it isn't his mother, it slowly goes out. Sometimes he says something and other times he returns to what he's doing, but he almost always has his eye on the door."

"I see," Carter said, even though he didn't.

"Kids react to the loss of a parent in a lot of ways. Some get really quiet for a long time, while others act out. Some, like Alex, keep putting it away so they don't have to deal with it. But he will eventually, and the staff at Camp Koala will be able to help us when that time comes. It will also give Alex an outlet so he knows he isn't alone."

"It sounds complicated," Carter said.

"It isn't, really. We need to keep doing what we're doing and be there for him. He'll deal with his loss when he's ready and able."

Carter jumped when another tower bit the dust, one of the blocks sliding all the way into the kitchen. Alex appeared a few seconds later, snatched up the block, and hurried back into the living room. "I guess I have a lot to learn."

"I know. We're adults, we tend to deal with things in a more straightforward way. Children don't always. If he asks questions, be honest and prepared for an outpouring of emotion or grief."

Carter reached for Donald's hand, took it in his, and made little circles on the back of it with his thumb. "I think Alex is very lucky to have you."

Donald leaned closer. "I think we're both very lucky to have you." He moved closer, and Carter met him halfway.

"Kissing," Alex said in a singsong way before laughing. "Boys are supposed to kiss girls, not boys."

"Who said that?" Carter asked with a smile. He held Donald close and didn't let him pull away.

"Chucky," Alex said.

Carter looked quizzical as Donald shook his head.

"Well, you tell Chucky that boys can kiss boys." Carter leaned in and kissed Donald again. "If he asks why, tell him boys taste better than girls." Carter kissed Donald again, aware that they had an audience who giggled and then hurried away. "I guess we weren't that interesting."

"I can't believe you said that. Now he's going to be telling everyone about us and that boys taste better than girls. He might even want to prove it."

"Oh God," Carter said, pulling back. "Me and my big mouth."

"Yeah, well. We should put it to better use." Donald kissed him once more. "Let's get all this put away and we can walk over with Alex for ice cream."

They got to work putting the food away and doing the dishes. Every few minutes Carter checked on Alex to make sure he was okay. Once they were done, Alex put his toys away and the three of them left the house. They decided to walk the few blocks to Brewster's. Alex held Donald's left hand, and after a few minutes, Carter took Donald's right. Eventually Alex shifted around until he was between them, jumping for a swing every now and then.

"Is he your son?" an older woman asked Carter while they waited in line holding Alex's hand.

Carter shook his head and was instantly overcome with a sense of loss. He realized he wanted to say yes, but couldn't. Alex wasn't his son, nor was he Donald's.

"He's my cousin," Donald answered. "But due to circumstances, I'm going to adopt him." He smiled, but Carter saw the worry lines around Donald's mouth.

"My son and his partner just adopted their first child. They're thrilled, and from what I understand are thinking of trying for a second." She smiled at them. "I never thought I'd be a grandmother after Phil came out, but so much has changed now." She turned away as the line moved.

They continued holding Alex's hands as they got closer and closer to the window. Alex kept changing his mind. First he wanted rainbow, then strawberry, and by the time they reached the front, it was bubblegum. Thankfully he returned to strawberry just in time, and they placed his order along with butter pecan for Donald and dark chocolate for Carter. Once they got their cones, Carter found them a table.

"Sit down and eat," Donald instructed, and Alex sat before half inhaling his small serving.

"What's bothering you?" Carter whispered to Donald.

"I keep wondering if I'm good enough. What if I do something wrong?" The worry was clearly real to Donald.

"What would you tell a father who asked you that same question when you were at work?" Carter asked and then licked his cone. "You'd tell him children don't come with a manual and parents figure things out as they go. And you'll do the same."

Donald reached over and took Carter's hand. "We'll do the same." Carter lifted his right eyebrow. "I don't think I can do this without you. Heck, I don't *want* to do it without you."

"Then it's a good thing you won't have to." Carter squeezed Donald's hand and then turned to Alex, who was crunching on the last bite of his cone. Man, that kid could eat fast. "Alex, buddy, you need to slow down. Donald and I aren't going to take your food, and you can always have more if you want it."

His lower lip quivered. "I'm sorry."

"I'm not mad." Carter realized he'd sounded like he was scolding when he hadn't meant to. He set his bowl aside and gently tugged Alex onto his lap. "You aren't in trouble. I just want you to eat slower so you don't get sick." He kept his voice soft and as soothing as he could.

164

"I'm not bad." Alex shook in Carter's arms.

"No, you're not bad." He needed to accept that everything in Alex's life wasn't going to change overnight. Alex might be insecure about food for a while. He certainly was going to be scared of upsetting people. "I'm sorry I made you feel that way. Do you want some more ice cream?"

"No. I'm full now." Alex settled on his lap, resting his head on Carter's chest.

"I think he's had a long day," Donald commented. "We all have. There's been plenty of excitement, and Alex got to talk to a lot of the policemen." Donald lifted his gaze. "They were really kind to both of us while we waited. All the guys stopped in to say hello to Alex whenever they had a few minutes. He drew a ton of pictures and handed them out to everyone."

"I work with good people. I was nervous about coming out, but Red had already paved the way, so it wasn't a big deal." Carter finished the last of his ice cream, and then Donald took care of the trash. Carter shifted Alex into his arms and stood. Alex got comfortable and then dozed off as they started the walk home.

"You know, you were right. I've been looking for a family for a while. I tried to find my birth mother but gave up." Carter stopped, and Donald walked around in front of him and gently rubbed Alex's back. "I can't believe I found him... that we found him. I have a family now."

"Yes, you do. And you have as big a one as you could want. My family loved you. Well, I can't speak for my father, but the rest of them loved you. And I think they'd be happy if you became a permanent addition to my life.'

"Is that what you want?" Donald asked just above a whisper.

"Of course it is," Carter said, extending his hand. "Why would you think otherwise?"

"I don't know. I guess I have a hard time believing you would want to be with me. I can understand you wanting Alex—who wouldn't?— but me...." Donald faltered.

"You need to get this foster-child mentality out of your head. You aren't a child any longer, but a man who can make his own decisions and is worth getting to know. You are one of the strongest, most caring people I know, but you've spent so much time hiding behind your own walls…." Carter stopped walking. "You've walled yourself in as much as you kept everyone else out. It's time you let yourself care and be cared for."

Donald nodded slightly. "You're very insightful. Maybe you should have been the social worker."

"What we do are just two sides of the same coin, and they require a lot of the same skills. You have to understand people and what they need as well as the government system in order to help them. I have to read people so I know when they're lying or trying to hide the truth, or if they represent a danger to me or themselves. I also have to understand government procedures and the system so I can help, just like you. We have similar skills but use them differently. Besides, I seem to have made a study of a certain handsome, dark-haired man over the past few days."

"I guess you have." Donald started walking again, and Carter caught up and fell in stride with him.

"Let's go home so I can make another of those studies, extra close and very personal," Carter whispered, and if it hadn't been for Alex, he might have gone a little further right there. Damn, he wanted to. But he contented himself with walking a little faster.

By the time they got to Donald's, Carter's heart was racing. Of course as soon as they got inside, Alex woke and Donald bundled Alex off to bed. Once he was settled under the covers, he called Carter in to read him a story.

"Why can't Mr. Donald read the story?" Carter asked as Alex handed him a book.

"You make better cow sounds," Alex answered, looking at Carter expectantly as Carter saw the book title, *Click, Clack, Moo*. Carter wasn't sure if he should be insulted. Donald tried covering his mouth but then laughed out loud.

"Okay. I'll read the story with the cow and chicken sounds, and then you need to go to sleep." Carter got comfortable and began reading the story of Farmer Brown and his animals. He wanted to ask where Donald got this one, but forgot about it as he got down to the task of reading.

By the time all the animals and Farmer Brown were tucked in bed for the night, Alex was nearly asleep. Carter closed the book and kissed Alex good night before turning out the light and leaving the room as quietly as he could.

"You do make better cow sounds than me," Donald teased once Carter had nearly shut Alex's door.

"Thanks," Carter said drolly.

Donald grinned. "He loves when you read to him, and you know it has nothing to do with cow sounds." Donald pushed open the door to his bedroom and stepped inside. Carter followed, and Donald closed the door. As soon as the latch clicked home, Carter tugged Donald to him.

"I do love you," he whispered. "You make me very happy."

"I don't know how. I've never been a happy kind of person." Donald smiled. "Well, at least not until lately." He moved closer. "I have you to thank for that."

"No. You have *you* to thank for that. You were the one who let yourself open up, and when you did that, then both Alex and I could love you," Carter whispered.

"I think you have things turned around a little," Donald protested.

"Nope," Carter countered with self-satisfaction, kissing away any further argument Donald might have, deepening the kiss as he pressed Donald back toward the bed.

They pulled at each other's clothes. For Carter, it was as if he couldn't get to Donald fast enough. He needed to feel the other man's body press against his, and once their underwear joined the growing pile, their desire turned to frantic kissing and exploration. Carter was already familiar with every contour of Donald's body, but he took time to relearn it again and again. The little moans and cries that denoted Donald's pleasure grew and built on each other like the components of a symphony. When their bodies joined and Carter locked his gaze onto Donald's, it was like the moon and stars were reflected back at him. "I love you," Carter whispered into the darkness.

"I love you too," Donald gritted between clenched teeth and then tumbled over the edge of sweet oblivion, carrying Carter along with him.

CARTER RETURNED from the bathroom a while later and joined Donald in bed after a quick cleanup. He rolled onto his side and slowly stroked Donald's chest, his warm skin with its dusting of hair sliding beneath his palm.

"You always knew how to touch me," Donald whispered. "If I hadn't been a fool, we could have had months together."

"No. You weren't ready." Carter smiled. "I like to think that we met too soon. Luckily it didn't take years for our paths to cross again."

Donald remained quiet for a few minutes. "So you believe in fate, then?"

"I don't know. Maybe fate has a hand in it. If it does, then I'm thankful for the intervention." Carter moved closer and found Donald's lips, kissing him softly. "I think that people meant to be together will find each other… that fate, luck, or maybe Cupid will have a hand in seeing it through." He chuckled. "Because Lord knows if it was up to you and me, we'd founder in the dark."

"Cupid?" Donald asked teasingly.

A knock sounded on the bedroom door and then it opened. Alex stood in the doorway, silhouetted against the light from the hall. Donald took his robe from the chair near the bed and pulled it on. "I had a bad dream," Alex said, holding his bunny in front of him. Donald stood and lifted Alex into his arms. Carter took a few seconds to pull on his underwear and robe. Then he followed Donald's whispers to Alex's room.

"It's okay. It was just a dream." Donald soothed Alex back into his bed. "No one is going to hurt you because Mr. Carter is here and he's a policeman."

"You mean he'll shoot the bad men?" Alex said.

"Mr. Carter will protect you, you can count on that," Donald said. "So go to sleep and dream about puppies and bunnies."

"I want a puppy like Roger," Alex said.

"Let's start with dream puppies first." Donald leaned over Alex, gave him a kiss, and then stood. "Sleep tight," Donald whispered and left the room. Carter stayed in the hallway, wrapped an arm around Donald's waist, and peered into Alex's room.

"What are you thinking?"

"Nothing. Just that you were making fun of my analogy a few minutes ago."

"What do you mean?" Donald whispered.

Carter tilted his head toward Alex. "Cupid."

Epilogue

"ALEX, YOU need to finish getting dressed so we can go to Grandma's," Carter said as he tried to hurry him up a little. Alex raced down the stairs and flopped on the sofa. "You don't want to be late or Uncle William will eat all the turkey."

Alex pulled on his shoes and then put on his coat when Carter handed it to him. Donald came down the stairs, and against all the odds they were in the car and on their way within ten minutes. "Just lie back and rest," Donald said as he drove. Carter had worked most of the night so he could have the bulk of their first Thanksgiving together off. Carter sighed and put his seat back, closing his eyes. That was the last he remembered until Alex tapped him on the shoulder.

"We're almost there," Alex told him excitedly. Carter imagined him bouncing in his booster seat as he put his seat upright. Alex loved visiting Carter's family. Things still weren't great between Carter and his dad, though they seemed to have lapsed into a silent truce. Carter had given up trying to figure out why they struggled to get along and just did his best not to pick a fight that would ruin the occasion.

"Thanks, buddy," Carter said, wiping his eyes and trying to find some energy. He'd probably fall asleep in one of the chairs, but that was okay. He'd worked out this schedule for Alex and Donald and he wasn't going to disappoint either of them, especially once he learned that neither of them had ever had a real family Thanksgiving. His mother had been appalled and insisted they come down.

Donald pulled up and parked on the street in front of the house. Alex was out of his seat and had the door open almost before the car had pulled to a stop. "Put on your coat," Donald instructed, and Alex paused to shove his arms in the coat before continuing across the yard. Blaine and Robert met him at the front door and ushered him inside.

"It seems he's all set," Carter observed and then yawned before he could stop it. He always felt stress when he visited, and Donald took his hand without a word and gently squeezed his fingers.

"It's going to be fine," Donald whispered reassuringly as they walked to the front door. "I know you worry about your father, but just stay away from him if you want. You're tired, and if you get into things, you'll say something you regret."

Carter nodded. He was too tired to argue about anything. "I'll try."

Donald held the door for him, and Carter stepped into the house, which was filled with overlapping conversations. The boys had already settled on the living room floor to play. The men were in front of the television, and female conversation and laughter drifted in from the kitchen. For Carter, a very typical Thanksgiving, but when he glanced at Donald, all he saw was a smile of contentment. Carter's loud, boisterous family members had opened themselves to Donald. There were few things that made him happier than being able to give Donald what he truly wanted.

"Donny," Carter's mother called as she hugged him tightly, the way she greeted all her children. Once she released Donald, she hugged Carter as well. "You look terrible," she observed, and Carter rolled his eyes.

"He worked last night so we could be here," Donald explained.

"Dinner will be about an hour. Do you want to lie down?" Carter's mother had already taken him by the arm and was leading him toward the hall.

"I'm fine, Mom. I napped in the car and I'll probably doze after dinner." Carter patted her hand, and she stepped away. After hugging each of his sisters, Carter went into the living room and settled in one of the chairs. It was comfortable, and despite the game and other conversation, Carter closed his eyes. The next thing he knew Donald whispered to him that it was time to eat. Carter was comfortable and didn't want to get up, but he did it anyway. He sat next to Donald and Alex while the food was put on the table. His father sat at the end and carved the turkey, like he always did. Plates were filled and passed around the same way they had been when Carter was a child.

There was something calming about the familiar ritual. Of course, Alex began eating as soon as he got his plate, and Donald reminded him to wait until everyone got theirs.

"It's all right. The young ones can eat," his mother said, and Alex tucked in.

"Thank you, Grandma," Alex said between bites, and Carter was about to scold him for talking with his mouth full, but decided against it. Alex had improved and no longer wolfed down his food, but he always ate fast and plenty. Over the past five months he'd gained some weight and had come alive. He had also matured a lot. He still carried his bunny with him sometimes, but he had caught up to the other children in many ways. Carter and Donald had enrolled him in prekindergarten. He was going to start after the holidays and would go on to kindergarten in the fall.

"He seems to be doing so well," Karen said from across the table. Her boyfriend, Steven, took that moment to clink his glass.

"Karen and I have a small announcement," Steven began.

"We're going to get married next September," Karen cut in excitedly and looked to Carter and Donald. "We want Alex to act as ring bearer."

Donald nodded but Carter noticed he didn't say anything at first. "That would be very nice," he finally said. "But don't you want one of your nephews?"

Karen leaned across the table. "I picked one of my nephews." She sat back, and Carter took Donald's hand under the table. "When do the two of you plan to make it official, now that marriage equality came to Pennsylvania?"

"They aren't going to do that," his father said distastefully.

"Of course they can, Dad. Don't be an old prude," Karen countered, then turned back to Donald and Carter. "So have you given it any thought?"

Donald shifted nervously as Carter answered. "This past week I finished moving in with Donald and Alex. I gave up the apartment. Donald is still going through the legal process of adopting Alex, and once that's done he and I will discuss setting a date."

"So you are getting married?" Karen was like a dog with a bone sometimes.

"Carter asked me last week, and I agreed." Donald shifted in his chair. "We haven't set a date, but we want to make it official. We want the three of us, our family, to be real." The others around the table looked perplexed, but Donald continued. "I didn't have a real family for much of my life, and Carter, as well as all of you, have helped show me that's what I want. We have to complete the adoption of Alex because that is already in the works, but then Carter and I will get married. But I promise it won't be next September," Donald added, and everyone chuckled.

"That calls for another toast," William said, standing up. "To all the new members of our family." Everyone raised their glass and drank. "We have so much to be thankful for."

Carter knew he certainly did.

"There's one more thing, and we've waited as long as we can," Carter's mother said. "The children have finished eating, so I have a surprise for them." His mother stood and walked to the back door. She opened it, and two black puppies raced into the kitchen. The kids were off their seats and on the floor within seconds. "A close friend's dog had puppies, and they need a home. One is for Blaine and Robert and the other one is for Alex."

"Me?" Alex asked loudly as he sat on the floor. One of the puppies crawled onto his lap, standing up to lick his face, tail wagging a mile a minute.

"Yes, sweetheart. It looks like this little guy is yours." Carter stood and walked to where his mother was watching her grandsons on the floor with the puppies.

"He's been asking for one," Carter told her.

"What little boy doesn't want a puppy?" she said quietly and rubbed her eyes. "It's a wonderful thing, what the two of you are doing." She hugged him, and Carter thought she might be crying. "When you told me you were gay I didn't think you could have a family of your own." She released him and stepped back carefully. "Boys, you carefully take the puppies out to the garage to play while we finish eating."

Alex picked up his puppy and carried him out into the garage, with Blaine and Robert following behind.

"I'll go watch them," Liz volunteered and left the table.

"Did you know about this?" Donald asked him, and Carter shook his head.

"Is it okay?" Carter asked. He loved the idea of Alex having a dog.

"Yeah," Donald said with a smile before returning to his chair. The others did the same, and dinner resumed.

"I got all the supplies to send home with you," Karen said happily.

The back door opened and Alex raced in and up to the table. "He peed on the papers."

Donald laughed and Carter tugged Alex to him. "Part of your job is going to be to help me teach him to do that outside." Alex hugged him and then turned and hugged his grandma before racing back out to the garage.

The adults finished dinner, and then Carter and Donald went out to the garage. All three boys sat with the puppies crawling all over them.

"He's a very happy little boy," Liz said as she walked over. "I know he's been through a lot, and his happiness is a testament to the both of you."

Carter wasn't sure what to say to that. He liked to think she was right. "Alex, have you thought of a name for him?" he asked.

Alex shook his head. "Puppy?"

"I don't think that's going to work. What about when he gets big?" Alex smiled and petted the wriggling, happy puppy.

"Oh."

"Let's think of a name."

"Wiggles," Alex piped up with a grin. Carter could just imagine him and Donald calling for Wiggles to come inside.

Carter knelt down. "How about Cupid?"

Alex thought for a few seconds and nodded.

"Cupid," Donald said softly, testing the name.

"The Roman god of love."

"It's perfect," Donald whispered into his ear before putting his arms around Carter's neck, holding him close. Alex shifted closer, holding the puppy, and the two of them melded him into their hug. None of them realized Liz had snapped their first family picture until later.

Don't miss how the story began!

Fire and Water

Carlisle Cops

By Andrew Grey

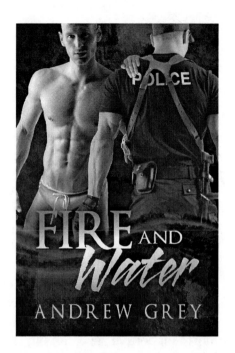

Officer Red Markham knows about the ugly side of life after a car accident left him scarred and his parents dead. His job policing the streets of Carlisle, PA, only adds to the ugliness, and lately, drug overdoses have been on the rise. One afternoon, Red is dispatched to the local Y for a drowning accident involving a child. Arriving on site, he finds the boy rescued by lifeguard Terry Baumgartner. Of course, Red isn't surprised when gorgeous Terry won't give him and his ugly mug the time of day.

Overhearing one of the officers comment about him being shallow opens Terry's eyes. Maybe he isn't as kindhearted as he always thought. His friend Julie suggests he help those less fortunate by delivering food to the elderly. On his route he meets outspoken Margie, a woman who says what's on her mind. Turns out, she's Officer Red's aunt.

Red and Terry's worlds collide as Red tries to track the source of the drugs and protect Terry from an ex-boyfriend who won't take no for an answer. Together they might discover a chance for more than they expected—if they can see beyond what's on the surface.

http://www.dreamspinnerpress.com

ANDREW GREY grew up in western Michigan with a father who loved to tell stories and a mother who loved to read them. Since then he has lived all over the country and traveled throughout the world. He has a master's degree from the University of Wisconsin-Milwaukee and now works full-time on his writing. Andrew's hobbies include collecting antiques, gardening, and leaving his dirty dishes anywhere but in the sink (particularly when writing). He considers himself blessed with an accepting family, fantastic friends, and the world's most supportive and loving husband. Andrew currently lives in beautiful historic Carlisle, Pennsylvania.

E-mail: andrewgrey@comcast.net
Website: http://www.andrewgreybooks.com

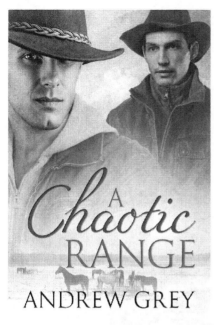

http://www.dreamspinnerpress.com

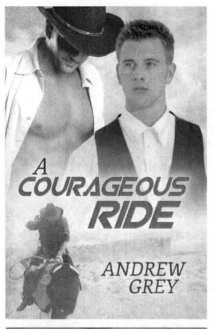

A COURAGEOUS RIDE

ANDREW GREY

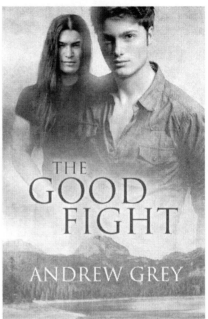

THE GOOD FIGHT

ANDREW GREY

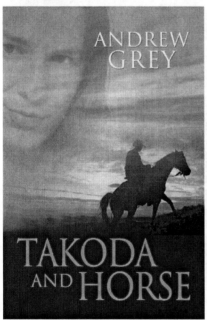

ANDREW GREY

TAKODA AND HORSE

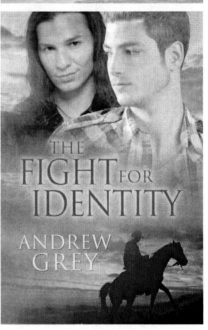

THE FIGHT FOR IDENTITY

ANDREW GREY

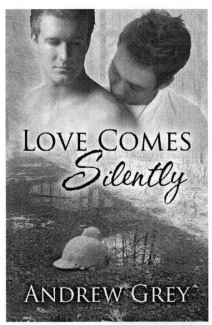

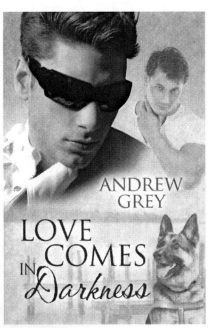

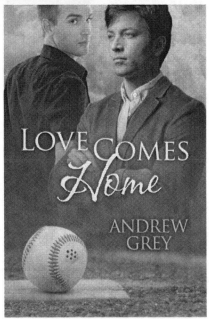

http://www.dreamspinnerpress.com

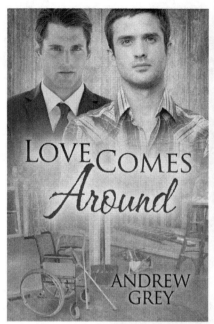

http://www.dreamspinnerpress.com

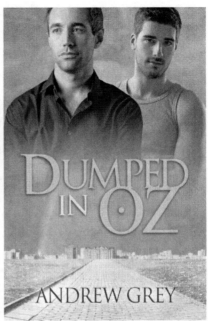

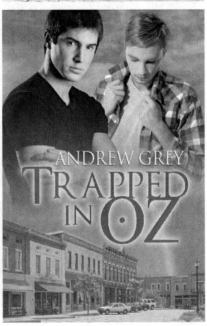

http://www.dreamspinnerpress.com

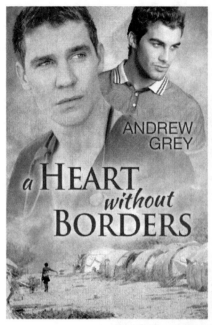
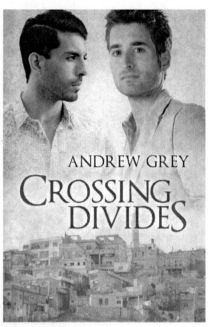

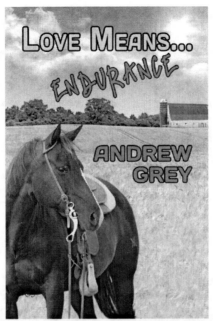

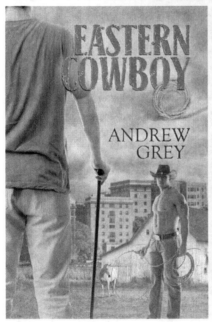

http://www.dreamspinnerpress.com

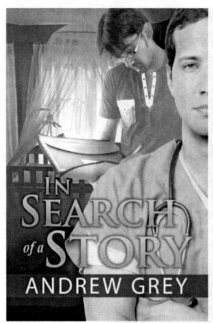

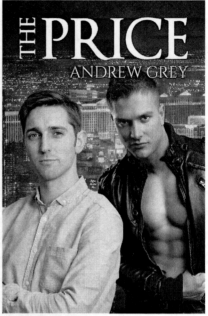

http://www.dreamspinnerpress.com

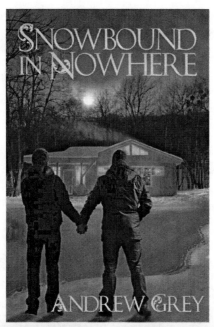

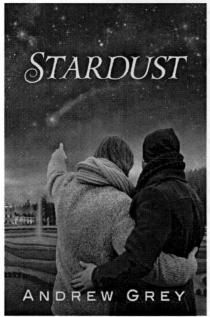

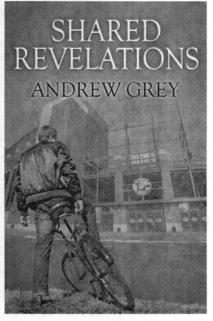

http://www.dreamspinnerpress.com

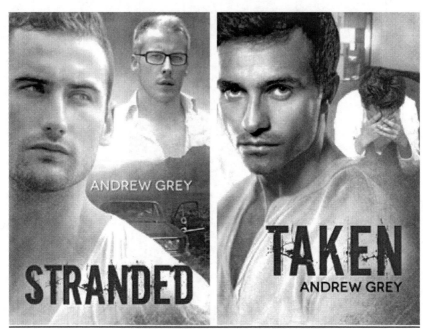

http://www.dreamspinnerpress.com

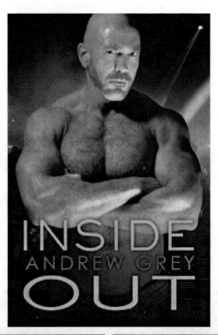

INSIDE
ANDREW GREY
OUT

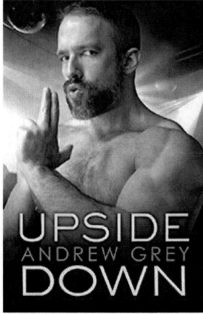

UPSIDE
ANDREW GREY
DOWN

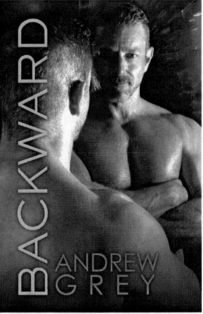

BACKWARD
ANDREW
GREY

http://www.dreamspinnerpress.com

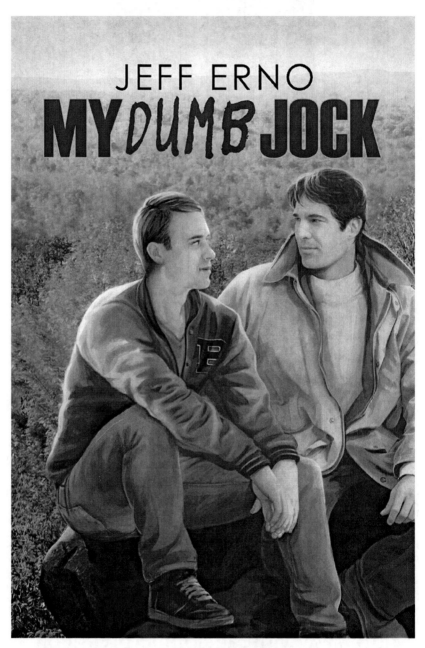

JEFF ERNO

MY DUMB JOCK

http://www.dreamspinnerpress.com

Just the Way You Are

E E MONTGOMERY

http://www.dreamspinnerpress.com

CPSIA information can be obtained at www.ICGtesting.com
Printed in the USA
LVOW08s0743010715

444450LV00020B/345/P